THE WEIRD
OF THE WANDERER

BEING THE PAPYRUS RECORDS
OF SOME INCIDENTS IN ONE OF THE PREVIOUS LIVES
OF MR. NICHOLAS CRABBE

HERE PRODUCED BY
PROSPERO & CALIBAN

THE WEIRD
OF THE WANDERER

BEING THE PAPYRUS RECORDS
OF SOME INCIDENTS IN ONE OF THE PREVIOUS LIVES
OF MR. NICHOLAS CRABBE

HERE PRODUCED BY
PROSPERO & CALIBAN

FREDERICK
ROLFE

WILDSIDE PRESS
Doylestown, Pennsylvania

First published in 1912.

The Weird of the Wanderer
A publication of
Wildside Press
P.O. Box 301
Holicong, PA 18928–0301

www.wildsidepress.com

ROMAN of Rome, Senator of the Kingdom, Knight of the Order of Civil Merit of Savoy, Officer of the Order of St. Maurice and St. Lazarus, Commander of the Order of the Crown of Italy, D.C.L. (*honoris causá*) in the Universities of Oxford, Athens, Krakow; Professor Emeritus in the University of Pisa and the Royal Higher Institute of Florence; National-Member of the Royal Academy of the Lincei, and of the Royal Academies of Sciences of Naples and Turin; Academic-Correspondent of the Royal Academy della Crusca; Correspondent-Member of the Royal Institute of Lombardy and the Veneto, of the Royal Academy of Sciences of Bologna, of the Royal Academies of Munich and Copenhagen, of the Imperial Academies of Vienna and Petersburgh; Foreign Member of the Institute of France; Ordinary Member of the German Archeological Institute of Rome, of the Archeological Society of Athens, of the Syllogos Filol. of Constantinople, of the Ugro-Finn Society of Helsingfors, of the Estone Society of Dorpat, etc. etc. etc.

Misce stultitiam conciliis brevem
Dulce est desipere in loco.

Horace to Vergil, *Od.* 13, *Lib.* iv.

PROSPERO loq. . . . . . I pitied thee,
    Took pains to make thee speak, taught thee each hour
    One thing or other: when thou didst not (savage)
    Know thine own meaning, but wouldst gabble like
    A thing most brutish, I informed thy purposes
    With words.

CALIBAN loq. . . . . . Remember,
    First, to possess his books: for, without them,
    He's but a sot, as I am.

Shakespeare's *Tempest*

Prologue

A Letter from the Splendor of Arry, Grandmaster of the Order of Sanctissima Sophia, Plas Hoel, Hoel, South Wales, to the Reverend Adam Howley, Professor of Hivite Literature in Saint George's College, Oxford, and Honorary Consultor to Cardinal Bensington's Institute of Archives and Inscriptions.

"My dear M.W.S.

"Congratulations on achieving the Chair. You thoroughly deserve it.

"I am sending with this the key of a largish deed-box, which my man Anderledy (P.M. of the 'Isaak Newton,' by all the gods!) will bring you in the course of the day. The box contains the papyri about which I wired to you from Smyrna last New Year's Day; and you are to consider yourself at liberty to deal with them in any way which you may deem suitable. If you should think them worthy of being submitted to His Eminency, I should not feel able to resist your judgment.

"The box also contains other matters, which (in my humble opinion) ought to be considered along with the papyri: but you will know best about that. Meanwhile, it will perhaps be as well if I set down here (for your guidance) more detailed particulars of the circumstances of the find.

"You know that Luke and Lombard and I went out to Armenia, in the spring of last year, on a little private expedition of our own, to hunt Assyrian and Persian antiquities; and I need not go into that now, as R.H.B. says. Nor need I trouble you with a description of our early successes and failures in digging. But it will be better for me to come straight to the point at issue, namely, our chance-discovery of a rock-tomb concealed behind a ruined chapel, which rewarded our exertions at precisely 15 o'clock on the third of last December.

"As soon as I had had cleared away some of the rubbish and broken stonework of the chapel, I became aware (from the apparition of brilliant mural paintings on what seemed to be a doorway in the natural rock) that a really important discovery was in my hand. Lombard was trying to take a siesta in his tent, and Luke was with him singing something about filling a cup with golden wine: but I at once summoned them; and together we proceeded to investigate.

"Of course we were soon surrounded by a mob of Scottish-looking fanulloni, who annoyed us with screams and gestures as we uncovered the painted doorway; and it was not long before one of them proclaimed himself to be the owner of the site and demanded compensation. Lombard promptly tried him for the 'Apprentice,' and got the 'Fellow-Craft,' but not the 'Master': whereupon I at once staggered him by offering to purchase the place outright; and, after half-an-hour's fierce haggling, I obtained it for about a couple of sovereigns' worth of the silver money current in the district. Then, I arranged for half-a-dozen of the less anointed-looking ruffians to work for me; and soon cleared the rest off my new property. It was getting too dark to do more that afternoon: so, for safety's sake, we had our tents moved on to the scene of our find, and camped there for the night.

"The next morning, Luke took several photographs illustrating the rock-tomb from the outside and every single step of our subsequent investigations. You will find platinotypes of all these (duly numbered) in the deed-box with the papyri; and here you must let me say that it is entirely due to you that we were able to make so complete and so permanent and so irrefutable a record of our work. Both Luke and I agree that, had it not been for the peculiar cameras which you had made for us and the singular instructions which you gave us, such a record could not have existed. I know you say that you received these secrets of photography from a dying man, who himself had them from our late Lord Hadrian and only to be used for great and singular enterprises: but, my dear

Howley, do let me affectionately ask you whether you have ever considered the loss to humanity which is involved in the keeping of such amazing powers in the hands of the few. However, all this rambles away from my mark. I merely mention the point, and leave it to your discretion, which I do not doubt for one moment.

"I regret to say that, in cutting-out the outer door of the rock-tomb — it was a marble monolith, painted all over on the hither side with a design of palm-branches and the emblems of *Cancer* and *Luna* — we slightly damaged an inner door of cedar-wood, magnificently carved and inlaid with silver arabesques containing the same zodiacal symbols in mother-of-pearl. I ought to add that after we had examined and photographed the whole tomb *in situ,* I had it all carefully removed in numbered lots, which (at the moment of writing) are being put together again on the south side of the narthex of my chapel here at Plas Hoel.

"To describe the interior of the tomb. It was twelve feet long by six feet wide by seven feet high inside measurement, and completely lined with silver and mother-of-pearl worked in designs similar to those of the above-named door: excepting the far end, which has a singular Tau-shaped cross-potent, four feet long by one-and-a-half feet wide, in a vesica-shaped oval of Egyptian ankhs. The center of the floor-space was occupied by a huge chest of black basalt, eight inches in thickness, on which was no carving of any kind: excepting an uncial inscription on the lid (which had never been sealed up), as follows:

ΗΝ ΕΝ ΕΠΙΧΘΟΝΙΟΙΣ ΧΑΡΙΕΣΤΑΤΕ ΞΕΙΝΕ ΔΙΥΛΛΟΣ
ΟΝ ΠΟΤ ΑΡΜΕΝΙΗΙ ΠΟΛΥΜΗΤΙΣ ΕΦΥΕΣΝ ΟΔΥΣΣΕΥΣ
ΤΟΝ ΔΑΠΑ ΩΣ ΗΚΟΥΣ ΕΚΑΛΟΥΝ ΝΙΚΟΛΑΟΝ ΕΤΑΙΠΟΙ
ΑΛΛΟΤΕ ΔΑΥΘ ΩΣ ΜΑΝΤΙΣ ΕΩΝ ΒΑΔΘΑΖΑΠ ΕΚΛΗΘΗ

I suppose we may as well translate: *'I was Diyllos among men on earth, O most kindly stranger, whom, once, ever-ready Odysseys begat in Armenia. Surely, as I hear, his comrades called him Nicholas: but, at other times again, he (as being a Mage) was styled Balthazar.'* I shall be curious to know what you make of that.

"The basalt chest contained two small silver urns hermeti-

cally sealed, one on each side of the head of a mummy done
in a positively amazing manner, which I will describe presently. At the feet was a largish oblong silver box: this held the
papyri which I am sending to you.

"You will be able to follow our proceedings from the
photographs. Luke and Lombard and I are all agreed that
such splendid photographs as these, of a dark interior, would
never have been done but for the six oxygen lamps for
burning powdered aluminum which you provided. If you
decide to lay our discoveries before His Eminency I must
insist that you shew him this letter in order that he may know
to whom any credit (which may be awarded) is actually due.

"The following were the contents of the two small urns.
Both contained a limpid viscid substance, which (of course)
at one time had been preserving oil. In the first urn, we found
a Smith & Wesson's Hammerless Safety revolver and a denar-
ius of Augustus, wrapped first in linen and then in canvas.
In the second, was a gold watch with a badly cracked dial and
no glass, number 7634291, made by Dent of Trafalgar Square
– and, also, a coin of Ptolemy the Piper (the value of which
I do not know), both similarly wrapped in linen and canvas.

"From the masons' marks on the ruined chapel which had
concealed our rock-tomb, Lombard declares it to be a work
of the ninth century after Christ. (Lombard, I may remind
you, is P.G.D. of England and in the thirty-third degree.) And,
from the fact that, between the hill-end of the chapel and the
outer slab which closed the tomb, there were quite six feet of
soil beside the wall which masked the said marble slab, it is
evident that the builders of the chapel (whoever they may
have been) were quite ignorant of the existence of the tomb
behind it. The Vali of Van also, whom I questioned, asever-
ated that he had never even heard of any kind of tradition,
connected either with the chapel or with the tomb, during
all his twenty-four years in the valiwick.

"Now I come to something even queerer. Luke solemnly
swears that the revolver which we found was not made before
the year 1898; and Dent (to whom I submitted the watch)
tells me that (according to his books) it was made in 1899
and sold to a Mr. Nicholas Crabbe of Crabs Herborough in
Kent. And yet, please note that both these things have been

discovered in an Armenian rock-tomb dating from something
B.C. and only just now brought to light.

"But I must get on.

"We did not examine the mummy, or even unswathe it,
until we got it safe home to Plas Hoel; and, in fact, we only
finished with it yesterday. Here are the particulars.

"The body is that of a very handsome lad indeed, of about
nineteen years of age, and most magnificently made: indeed
I only know of one specimen of physique at all comparable
with it in splendor of symmetry; and that is the statue of the
Athlete with the Strigil, by Lysippos, in the Vatican collection.
There is absolutely no trace of decay about it; and it looks as
fresh and feels as soft (though of course it's cold) as the body
of a young sleeper. Another curious thing about it is that it
does not appear to have been eviscerated, or treated internally
in any way. Luke and Lombard and I have been over every
inch of the skin with magnifiers; and have quite failed to find
anything like a likely incision. Nor are there any indications
of the actual cause of death. The lad evidently had been in
the wars, for his body has twenty-one frightful scars: but,
though four of them at least ought to have been mortal
wounds, they are perfectly cicatrized and healthily healed.
The four scars, to which I specially allude, are as follows: a
thrust through the inside of the right thigh from front to
back which might very well have tapped the femoral artery:
another through the left armpit upward, with emergence
inside the collar-bone: two clean round punctures through
the neck from front to back, one on each side of the throat.
There are also seventeen cuts, none less than four inches long
and all deepish, on the face and the muscles of the arms and
the front of the thighs. But they are not at all disfiguring: for,
as I have said, the skin is supple, very fine and smooth and
young in texture, and also exquisitely sunburned throughout.
Whoever he was, any man might be proud of being his father.
As for the skull, it is small and of a very perfect facial angle
of the best Greek type. The eyes are closed; and I frankly say
that we've none of us had the heart to open them. As for that
dear soft-hearted Luke, he declared that he'd never speak to
me again if I attempted it. The mouth is a bold firm one —
a little large perhaps: but splendidly shaped. I don't as a rule

care for a Cupid's bow in one of my own sex: but this one is that, and as noble as one could wish, as well. The lips are as red as beef; and the teeth are perfect, quite white and rather large. The hair is short, and of a pale flaxen color, almost white: though the man was obviously under twenty years of age. Now for measurements. The height is sixty-eight inches: leg inside fork, thirty-five inches (singularly long, according to modern proportions): chest, thirty-six-and-a-quarter inches: weight, hundred-and-thirty-seven pounds ten ounces. All the above are taken naked. On the third finger of the right hand is a silver signet, very massive indeed, the device being a crucified Love (the cross is the peculiar tau-shaped cross-potent noted above) with the legend ΨΥΞΗΣ ΑΚΟΝΗ which Luke poetically renders *The Whetstone of the Soul.* On the shoulders of this ring are two eye-chalcedonyxes set in the sign of the Crab; and on front and back there is the sign of the Moon in blue-moonstone and rock-crystal respectively. Under the linen shroud, which (mark you) was a large sheet and nothing at all like the ordinary mummy-bandage, the body was clothed in a short linen tunic under a shirt of silver mail reaching to the middle.

"Among the usual spices which formed a bed at the bottom of the basalt chest, we found four English sovereigns, dated 1884, 1889, 1890, 1897. The two first are much worn: the 1890 piece is in fair condition: while the 1897 one has been pierced and has a small ring through it of very red gold.

"Professor Monteagle of Cambridge, who has been staying here, gives it as his opinion that the mummy is not more than two thousand and certainly not less than nineteen hundred years old. He was, however, frightfully disturbed about the sovereigns: while the revolver and the watch, which we discovered without his help, appear to have disconcerted him most seriously. I am, indeed, convinced that he will go back to Cambridge and tell everybody that we have been trying to pull his leg: which in fact is not the case.

"However, the whole affair bristles with incomprehensibilities, to my mind; and I only hope that you, my dear Howley, may be able to find some solution of them when you decipher the papyri. Of course I will gladly furnish any further information which you may require and I may be able to offer.

And I hope you won't mind my saying that it will perhaps be better for both of us if you will kindly have your translation of the papyri type-written at my charges. There is a most satisfactory little person at 7 Broad.

"Believe me,
"Very sincerely yours,
"ARRICUS: *Magnus Magister*"

A Letter from the Reverend Adam Howley, Professor of Hivite Literature in Saint George's College, Oxford, and Honorary Consultor to Cardinal Bensington's Institute of Archives and Inscriptions, to The Splendor of Arry, Grandmaster of the Order of Sanctissima Sophia, Plas Hoel, Hoel, South Wales.

"Dear Arry:

"These papyri are written on in Greek of the first century Ante Christum, by several different hands (three at least). A few words in late Victorian English are by another hand. I am sending type-written translations herewith. Don't you remember what a fuss there was about Nicholas Crabbe's mysterious disappearance from Cyprus just after the Dilimile's hysterical howls for ten thousand flying machines? The Eminency of Cardinal Bensington desires me to thank you for your offer; and proposes, if agreeable, to pay you a visit at Plas Hoel, after Pentecost, for the purpose of restoring the papyri to their proper place, and of closing up the rock-tomb with all its contents in your chapel with Christian Rites. Now then! His Eminency, however, intends to name you to our Most Holy Lord the Pontiff for the gold research-medal called the 'Lesser Wisdom' for this year. I hope that this will suit your plans.

"Personally I must beg you not to take me as expressing any opinion on this, or on any other, matter.

"They say that dear old Parke wants to give up his living and come back here as archivist.

"Billy Buffell's got a baby.

"The weather is fine, but cold.

"Yours truly,
"A.H.

"*P.S.* — The following chronology is the best I can compile:

"1. Mr. Crabbe seems to have disappeared from civilization *circa* A.D. 1899.

"2. He then, apparently, engaged in experiments in Egypt. The result was that he took an unintentional toss backward through Time to the reign of Ptolemaios Ayletes, *i.e. circa* B.C. 80-51. (*Cf.* Papyri IIII.-XII.)

"3. We now learn for a fact (what must have struck a good many earnest thinkers who had the privilege of knowing him here and elsewhere), that he actually is Odysseys reincarnate; and of course Odysseys originally flourished *circa* B.C. 1180. (*Cf.* Papyrus XII.)

"4. However, Mr. Crabbe (as Odysseys reincarnate) enjoys infernal and olympian experiences (*cf.* Papyri XIII.-XXIII.), obviously *circa* B.C. 51-44. This date can be fixed, with comparative conclusiveness, from the allusion to Caesar's murder (*cf.* Papyrus XXXI.), which, we know, took place in the latter year.

"5. I fancy that a fair case might be made out for the theory that the Papyri themselves could very well have been written between *circa* B.C. 44 and the Christian Era. There can be little mistake about the 'Star' (*cf.* its prediction, Papyrus VII.; and its occurrence, Papyrus XXXIIII.).

"6. I am almost inclined to permit myself the use of the epithet 'annoying' in reference to the twenty-one additional papyri (giving an account of the very imperfectly known state of Moxoene *circa* B.C. 44 and A.D. projected in Papyrus XXXIII.), which are, I might almost say, as it were inaccessible, at least for the present.

"A.H.

"*P.P.S.* — I fear that my translation is perhaps a little loose: but then the style of the original by no means errs in the direction of concise regularity — as one, considering all the circumstances, might reasonably expect.

"A.H.

"*P.P.P.S.* — His Eminency says that you may publish these naïve and almost Dantesque and sometimes quite Homer-esque fragments, if you care to and have nothing more serious to occupy yourself with. If you do, it will be positively fascinating to observe which, of the apparent inconsistencies, will be selected for execration by smart sciolists of our own hysterical age.

"A.H.

"*P.P.P.P.S.* — Before you do publish, if you determine on that course, I think you ought to peruse Mr. Rider Haggard's brilliant treatise on Helen of Troy. I believe it is called The World's Desire: and of course you can get it from the T.B.C.

"A.H.

"*P.P.P.P.P.S.* — On the whole, I really think I would, you know, if I were you. Upon more mature consideration, I am inclined to fancy that it might turn out to be (what we used to call) rather a 'Lark.'

"A.H.

"*P.P.P.P.P.P.S.* — Publish, I mean.

"A.H."

The First Papyrus

I, WHO have been, or will be, Nicholas Crabbe of Crabs Herborough in the duchy of Kent — and who am Odysseys son of Laertes, an immortal and sometime inhabitant of olympian palaces — but now known as King Balthazar of Moxoene which will be called (or which was once called) in the time whence I came (or in the time to which I yet shall come) Van in Armenia — I swear, by my honor and by my faith as a king who never has built altars to Roma and Julius (like the Ephesians and Nikaians) or to Rome and Augustus (like Bithynia and Asia), that the things which I here cause to be written, and write, are true.

May Osiris, and Zeys, and Mithra, and all great gods of the past and the present and the future, masters of wisdom, blast me — and may The One Signified scorn me, if these written words do not agree with the facts which befell me, who am fallen backward through the rolling wheels of time. Thus, I, an immortal and a king, swear. And may he who belies me rot and wither and evanesce in the uttermost depths of Tartaros whither I have been thrice, or of Amentet, whither I have been once, or of that Hell to which I will not go. I have sworn.*

---

* So far the papyrus is written in late-Victorian English, in what I take to be Mr. Crabbe's own hand. I may say that I am not inclined to discredit any of the statements, abnormal or otherwise, made by the King of Moxoene (that is to say, by Mr. Nicholas Crabbe). The Oath Compelling Truth, which he here uses, is a recognized and quite respectable formula, and I am not aware of any instance on record of its ever having been belied in any particular,

Now I, King Balthazar of Moxoene in Nairi or Armenia, the Viceroy of Victory queen of the stalwart stately Anglicans, say thus to Empedokles my scribe, in my royal palace on the shore of my Thospitian Sea, within my kingdom, which I do not hold from Rome, having taken it myself by favor of Great Zeys.

Let it be known that I, King Balthazar, was called, in an age which is to come, Nicholas Crabbe the Impossible. I lived peacefully as might be. I have nothing to say of my origin in that life, or of my early years: for, in good sooth, most of the things which then happened to me were so incredibly cruel and so unspeakably hideous that I wish to forget most of them, and the rest have been smudged (mercifully) on the tablets of my memory. It shall be enough to tell that, as a scope for my energy, I forced myself (in default of all other interests) to become a seeker after wisdom, a client of the Muses and of far-darting Phoibos Apollon, an ardent student of all branches of music and gymnastic,* and chiefly of those branches which taught my subtle adept mind to do what all other men never even dreamed of doing, and my strong nimble body to do what all other men dare not do. For I penetrated into the occult arcana.

Under pretext of studying the surgery of ancient Egypt, I learned to read hieroglyphics; and, in time, my exertions and my energies culminated in a single desire to get to the root of white magic as contained on papyri in tombs of archpriests of temples of Isis. For a whole year I pondered the difficulties and the dangers, delaying to gratify my desire, expecting a sign or a companion from the blessed gods. None came.

Arrived at the end of my patience, I acted very suddenly. For, having provided myself with gold money and circular notes,† I went my own way to Alexandria, departing from my

---

however minute. Indeed, in so far as Truth is the Agreement of Words with Facts, all history seems to shew that the solemn swearing of this Oath Compelling Truth is perhaps the most irrefragable warranty of Truth, as such, which our present state of information can supply. — A.H.

* I take it that Mr. C. uses these words in a Platonic sense, as signifying mental and physical activities respectively. — A.H.

native land which now is the barbarian Britannia. And, at Alexandria, I hired a boat with boatmen and servants: for it was in my noble mind to sail up River Nile, staying when and where I listed, exploring ruins above Assiut, specially small ruins, in the hope of finding mummy-chests ripe for rifling or hieroglyphics crying to be read on pillars or walls of unknown temples. During eight months, thus I did: but I found no more than three unopened mummy-chests, and (beside them) little of worth. Nevertheless, one of the said chests contained certain superior matters: to wit, a magic staff of silver and ebony, and a silver divination-cup chased with sacred creatures, which things I did not examine closely till I came to Philai. But, there, my labors were rewarded: for a small temple at Philai yielded no less than three-and-forty mummy-chests, carven and painted, containing the remains of persons who (in their time) had been most mighty. And, of these, I will name one, having many matters to narrate concerning him. But he was the priest Amenemhat, sometime hierarch of the temple of Isis at Tanis by the mouth of Nile. Moreover, I found a manual entitled *For the Use of Priests;* and it contained the rules by which mortal men may communicate with the immortals, whom the Egyptians call Osirians. And this was by far the most noble thing which I discovered. But I must not omit to mention also a divination-ball, of rock-crystal of the bigness of a baby's head, which I found in a mummy-chest: it was banded with silver set with large blue moonstones, and a silver chain was attached to it. Now I took this for a favorable omen, very apt indeed to me: for, having been born under the moon and the sign of the crab, and being therefore crab by nature as well as Crabbe by name, the heart in my dear breast rejoiced greatly to possess so beautiful a jewel, formed (indeed) of the very stones and of the very metal which (as is well known) are proper to a native of that sign and of that planet. But I hanged it by its chain to the magic staff already named.

When, at length, I had leisure to study the papyrus manual, I became aware of the vast power which it put into my hands. It contained a very long and useless introduction, including

† These two words are written in English in what I take to be Mr. C.'s own hand. — A.H.

oft-reiterated laments because Okhos (the Persian successor of the deposed Nebk-Neft) had degraded the hierarchy of Khem, striking a blow at the prestige of all hierarchs. But, this being ended, the gist of the work was clearly set down: nor could anything more be added necessary to enable one (possessed of the magic implements, as I was), to commune with long-dead sages, mages who had relinquished the use of their bodies and dwelt no more in the sweet sunlight, obtaining from them the wisdom of the past, and the power which such wisdom gives, both unpossessed by men alive.

But it appeared that I still lacked certain spices and sacred combustibles, both essential in magic operations. Wherefore, being always young and headstrong and (therefore) of a spasmodic habit, I turned about instantly to those places where I could purchase myrrh and cassia and gum-olibanon and gum-tragacanth and spikenard and red-sanders and saffron and cinnamon and sulfur and powdered ivory and pepper and pepperwort and mastic and certain other substances the names of which may not be written on account of a religious reason. And four months passed before I had finished this quest in Cairo and Alexandria and Arabia and Byzantium and Massilia, filling a cabinet with potent essences and very virtuose quintessences.

In this manner I reascended the sacred river, until I came to Korte.

The Second Papyrus

BUT I had determined to do my magic in an inner court of the temple at Korte, unknown to persons liable to disturb my peace. And, with incredible toil, I cleared the said court of sand, having left my servants in charge of my boat a mile away. Furthermore, in the hard red-granite pavement of the court, I cut a circular channel of sufficient depth to contain a certain very holy liquid; and this I did with nineteen days' incessant labor, using a hammer and a well-tempered chisel. But the trench was three paces and nine in circumference, and half-a-span in width, and a quarter of a span in depth.

In the midst of the circle and on the base of a fallen column, I set my silver divination-cup; and, by it, I placed my cabinet of essences and quintessences: but I hanged my divination-orb to my left arm by its silver chain, holding the magic staff in my hand. The fullness of the moon agreed with what was described in my papyrus manual; and, when all was ready, I filled the circular furrow with a bright-green essence, pungent, mysteriously potent, continuing to pour till the trench was lip-deep with the emerald fluid. Next, I filled the divination-cup with water from the sacred river, lowering the orb of divination therein with my left hand, and sprinkling the circle with gum-tragacanth while I intoned the incantation called *Of the Buckle of Red Jasper Dipped in Water of Ankham Flowers and Inlaid in Sycamore Wood and Placed on the Neck of the Shining One*, which is the Power of Isis.

The moon grew brighter and more fierce, till she well-nigh rivaled the sun in brightness; and her hot rays made me sweat profusely. Wherefore, at the proper time, I was glad to strip me naked; but I began to stir the water in the cup with the magic staff, saying: *"The Blood of Isis, the Charms of Isis, the Power of Isis, be a protection unto Me, the Master, crushing that which I abhor, making all Ways passable or flyable or swimable unto Me: and I stretch out one Hand to Heaven and the Other to Earth."*

In the glare of almost unbearable moonlight, I saw that my crystal orb was becoming red-hot notwithstanding that it was immersed in Nile-water. But I poured the proper unguent of aloes into my cup, with nine tears of gum-olibanon; and the green liquid in the trench blushed with ruddily gleaming access of fury. But I, looking again on my papyrus manual, read these words: *"See that thou grasp thy staff firmly, not letting it fall from thee through any pang, be thy pangs never so keen; likewise, when the clear sphere gleameth redly, hold thy staff as though it were thy life, for so it is, and if thou lose it thou shalt die."* And hardly had I read this rule (which I had never seen before: although I had collated the whole manual with some care during my four-months' quest for spices), hardly, I say, had I read these awful words, when I felt the magic staff growing hot in my hands.

I gripped it more closely: but its heat increased. I felt it searing my flesh. I saw the smoke rise. I heard the flesh frizzle like the hissing collops of an acceptable sacrifice farced with select fats. And, all the while, lurid lightnings leaped from the liquid in the trench.

At last, so poignant was my anguish, that I determined rather to risk death than to see and hear and smell my living hand burned off while I stood. But, at the very moment, piercing through the sputtering of the white-hot lambent rod in my defenseless hand, there came a divine voice from I know not where, saying in the Argive tongue: *"Be of good heart, my child, and endure for all my pain: for many of us who inhabit olympian palaces have suffered."**

Whereon I nerved myself, dismissing base thoughts of surrender. And all grew black before my eyes; and my soul was shrouded in obscurity. So I stood, enduring unmentioned and unthought-of anguish with all my might; and I indeed was on the very verge of swooning: when suddenly the

---

* *Cf.* a similar divine voice, *Iliad,* v. 380–410. – A.H.

admirable voice came again, ringing triumphantly, saying:
"*Hail, Conquistator of Self! Hail, Nicholas, the Victor over many
Peoples!*"

And immediately the staff became cool; and my reeking
wounds vanished, and only the memory of my ordeal remained.

I turned to inspect the divination-cup. Pale flames leaped
silently therein from the crystal orb, of such intense heat as
comes from an open furnace to the well-reddened watcher at
its door: but the Nile-water lay limpid and cold above and
about the raging globe of the seven-times heated fire. But I,
mindful of the rules in the papyrus manual, cast in myrrh
and powdered ivory; and I intoned the incantation called
Demands on the gods, which old Menes had composed many
centuries before.

The verdant flame in the trench gave forth volumes of
suffocating green vapor, filling the whole court, and beating
me brow to pavement. But I ceased not from my chanting;
and, when I came to the famous verse, "*Nor shall ye slay us by
choking: thus we adjure you,*" the green steam suddenly arose,
till it seemed that I was enclosed in a dome-shaped cell of
malachite, so solid did the vapor appear. Whereupon, with
the mightiest voice of me I uttered the summons, "*O souls, be
seen!*"

Instantly there was a crash of thunder and the inmarcesible
glow of uranian fires. The earth beneath me quivered like a
woman; and the temple rocked as ships are rocked (in his
spasms) by the azure-haired earth-shaker, lord of the stormy
sea. But, above me, the green dome expanded, stretching to
unfathomable abysses of space; and I perceived that its place
was becoming filled with fiery faces of base grotesque and
adipose dignitaries, archbishops of malevolent allure having
pleats about their eyes disdainful of obscure persons. Nor
were any of them alike for any moment of time: but they
waved and flickered like the myriad leaves of a forest blazing
with autumnal glory. But out of this maze of bodiless faces
came a tired moaning, demanding why they had been summoned.

Now I indeed was serene; and my heart and lordly mind
exulted greatly: for I knew that I had the Power. And, holding

out the magic staff with my right hand, and placing my left on the cool crystal orb, I cried: "I summon none but Amenemhat, the priest of Tanis."

Eight flamelike shapes flickered downward, individuals glabrous and mouthing, the torsions of whose pulpy lips avowed their invirility; and they stood before me, but on the further edge of the redly-glaring moat; and each one wailed: "I am Amenemhat, the priest of Tanis."

Then for the moment I was nonplussed: but I remembered that eight men, all named Amenemhat, had been (in their turns) priests of Tanis. Wherefore I cried again: "I summon none but him who was Amenemhat, the priest of Tanis, at the time when Ptolemais Ayletes reigned as Pharaoh in Khem."

And now but one flamelike shape flickered outside the circle; and it simply sighed, saying: "I am that Amenemhat; and I am here."

So I commanded him to lie quietly down and lap the emerald liquid in the trench as a test of his good faith. But I conjured the others to return to their own places in Amentet, using the *Name Ineffable* to compel them, the *Spell* which may not be spoken save in direst need, nor written save on virgin papyrus by a priest who knows himself to be without blemish. And they bowed thrice when I named the *Name*, wailing wearily. And there was thunder and lightning and a heaving of all things at their going; and they seemed to melt together into one vast fiery arrow, which sped (like a bolt shot by the lord of the silver bow) upward and away into the arcane of the outer immensity.

But Amenemhat, the priest of Tanis, lay prostrate before me, meekly lapping. And he no longer had the shape of a flame: for, now, the chariot of Helios Hyperion had emerged from the crocus-hued gate of dawn. Ashen-grey was Amenembat, and hard indeed to see: for, being but an Osirian, he cast no shadow, nor did he obstruct my view of the columns of the court behind him. And I was in the mind to laugh at the thought that, after all, so high a priest as he was should have no more solid shape than a jellyfish, tinted like a rainbow where the rising sun's radiance touched him. But I remembered that Death comes to all, and that rain-born Iris (a divine one of goddesses) is also thus primarily tinctured; and I hastened to intone the *Spell of Embodiment*, touching what there was of Amenembat with the magic staff, and saying: *"Advance, thou Dweller in the Outer Space, and be a thing of earth again till I release thee."*

Thus I spoke: but he rose like a brilliant mist, ever thickening into opacity and taking the form which my lordly mind hurriedly made for him. Mother-naked, even as I was, he crossed into the mystic circle which my staff opened to him. I touched his brow with the crystal orb, and placed his hands in the sacred water of Sihor in the divination-cup. And vital fluids came back into his veins, so that he became a thing of earth and fit for reasonable conversation. But I also gave him the *Heart-touch*, saying: "Receive thy mortal life in lease from me for a season."

But he stood at his full height, looking into my eyes; and he said: "O thou, unknown, who has called me from Amentet, and hast given me again a mortal body with blood and lifelike juices, be ware lest I shall overcome thee. Thus I warn thee, in accordance with the immutable law of Osiris where it is written, *He who is summoned shall warn his summoner."*

But I was not afraid. And I laid the *Spell of Obedience* on Amenemhat. But, when I had thus secured my own safety and also a trusty friend and familiar who was to instruct me in unmentioned and unthought-of magic, then, indeed, I took liberty to give way to a human weakness, having already tolerated enough to slay nineteen ordinary men — to wit, the agony of the scorching staff, and the long labors under the fiery moon, and the stifling green vapor, and the horrid vision of the flickering faces; and I took liberty, I say without shame, to swoon away into oblivion.

When, at length, the mind in my dear breast awakened, I found my new familiar faithfully ministering to me, gently holding the thread of life which bid fair to fray out in my enfeebled grasp. But we two, having clothed ourselves, returned to my boat, there to live in tranquility while I recollected myself.

But there remained much to be done yet by me. I felt that I would have been quite content to spend the rest of that life as Amenemhat's pupil, learning from him the occult and affascinating arts of the hierarchs of ancient Khem. For we read together in the many rolls of papyrus which I had collected; and it was easy to know that, whereas I was like a clever child who early has learned to read, he was a perfect adept who (by long experience) was able to understand what was read. But, by chance, the precise method of working a certain enchantment, which opens the Hall of Double Truth and Right, baffled us both. And it was of the very gravest import that I should know how to practice this enchantment: for thereby I could learn the whole secret of a man using himself Bai and Ka and Khou as might seem good to him: which, for a miserable mortal, is much to be desired, as being uncommon.

But the rede of Amenemhat was that I should repeat the *Spell of Summons,* summoning a Great One of the Greater Ones, from whom I should require an instruction. But, for some time, I withstood the priest: I know not why, unless it be that habit and temper make me prompt to resist direction that I may steer my course in accordance only with the mind in my lordly breast.

But there came a night, when we by chance were sitting together on the deck of my Nile-boat in the clear of a full moon; and great peace came upon me, so that my soul swelled sweetly within me, letting me know that I was full of wiles and furnished with inexhaustible reserves of power. And I said: "At dawn we will go southward; and, at the temple of Korte, at a moon-birth, I will use my power for summoning a Great One of The Greater Ones."

Thus I spoke. But Amenemhat answered me, saying: "Nay, O Summoner, why toil so far, seeing that there are places nearer where this enchantment may be worked with equal ease?"

"I know," quoth I, "of no place as free from the risk of disturbance as the temple of Korte."

"Thou hast but to command," he responded "and I, O Summoner, must reveal to thee the secret fanes of Khem."

"Reveal them, thou," I promptly said.

"There is one at Heliopolis —"

"Too near to noisy Cairo."

"There is another at Ptolemais, now called Thomis —"

"I saw there a galosh-factory, when last I descended Sihor's sacred flood."

"There are those vast secret halls of Thebes —"

"Ruined."

"Thebes above ground indeed is ruined, O wise Summoner, but not the Thebes which lies below."

"How know'st thou this?" I said.

"From the gods who revealed the fact to me in my former life: for when I was a priest in Khem, I learned many things which in time would be. And it was given to me to know how that the temples of Khem should be desolated and the peoples of Khem destroyed. And it was shewn to me for how many centuries the secret halls of the three priestly colleges at Thebes would remain forgotten. But I, also, am ware of an entrance, well-concealed, very hard to find, which I can shew to thee if thou desirest to make use of those dim halls as they were wont to be used."

Thus he spoke. And the mind in my breast exulted. But I said: "Surely the adits will be blocked with shrubs and fallen masonry?"

"That may not be, O Summoner," he answered, "for the adit of which I speak is in the open plain."

"Then we will go to Thebes; and the thing which has to be done shall be well done, there."

But when, at length, we were come to the ruined capital of the Upper Land and the Lower, having left some of our baggage at the paltry village of Luxor, concealing the rest, anon we pursued our way across the sandy plain thereby, until we reached a certain pebbly strip of land which was unencumbered, excepting by a low pillar of granite. And the pillar, being no more than a span in height, would have been quite unnoticeable had any ruins approximated: as it was, I almost trod upon it before I perceived its weather-worn surface, deeply graven with the dead tongues of tombs, and undecipherable for all who have not (but I have) a knowledge of those tongues from the tongue of one who himself had used them. Time-worn was that little pillar, as well it might be: for Amenemhat said that, in his own day, it had been more venerable than the oldest fanes. Also, he narrated a tradition, which said that a remote ancestor of Menes found it there, marking the site where Divine Osiris first placed his foot on the hallowed soil of Khem: but Amenemhat said (as well) that this tradition rested on no sure warranty, for that Menes himself had taken the pillar from a temple builded many ages before Khem was a country, and had it set there to mark the entrance of the secret halls which he himself was building.

But I instantly put this saying to the proof. For we strove to move the pillar in its socket, where during nineteen centuries at least it had been undisturbed. And, when we turned it round, the slab supporting it sank slowly on a hinge: but sand with many pebbles slid downward on to the stair which was revealed.

Thus then was manifest the entrance to the Secret Halls of Thebes.

The Third Papyrus

*H*AVING lighted lanthorns, I began to descend the stair with my familiar: but a very noxious vapor drove us back. And, while I chafed at this delay, Amenemhat reproved me, saying: "Why wait hours for nature to effect that which thou (with magic art) couldst do in a moment?"

And this having been the second time when I myself had forgotten the power which I possessed, till reminded of the same by my familiar, I, indeed, held a sort of council with myself; and I determined that, in the future, I no longer would live as men of my own race are wont to live, in helpless abject obedience to so-called natural laws, seeing that (for me) such laws did not exist, but that I would be limited solely by the mind in my lordly breast, willing what I pleased, and causing its performance by forces amenable to my magic art. And, having thus determined, I instantly invoked certain airy sprites, yellow as sunflowers, who, with millions of legs alternately coming and going, purified the staircase and the edifices to which it led.

The passage having thus been rendered favorable to earth-walking men, we again descended: but, when we came to certain gates beyond the forty-ninth antechamber, some mysterious energy barred our progress. That is to say, when we reached the said gates, my head would have gone through, but my feet refused to budge — though Amenemhat went forward without difficulty, whom I, seeing that he was my familiar and his place behind his lord, recalled. For, if I could not proceed (on account of some inexplicable impotence on the part of my blameless feet), neither might he, for a servant may not go before his master in a case of this kind.

Wherefore, I used my magic art again; and I uttered several spells one by one, excepting the *Spell of the Name Ineffable* which I do not deem fit to say in any need but that which seems extreme. And none of my spells availed me anything.

But my mind mentioned that Amenemhat's ability to go forward, and my inability, might perchance indicate some difference of character between us two; and I used my wiles for pondering possible differences. In this manner I perceived that whereas he was a priest according to the highly respectable rite of Khem, I was no more than a Tonsured Clerk of the Latin Obedience. For it may as well be known by all men living that, in my early (or later) life in the kingdom of Victory queen of the stalwart stately Anglicans, one of the many incredibly cruel and unspeakably hideous happenings which marred me and soured me was as follows. The Divine Ones of the Latin Obedience called me to serve them as flamen sacrificing for the Blessed Dead; and I willingly responded to the call. In token whereof I was admitted to the first grade of the flaminian estate, being marked apart from other men by the five-pointed tonsure.* And immediately, by the blundering of blind guides (the most righteous of men), confirmed by hierarchical timidity or stupidity or malignity, I was denied my heart's desire, and bile was mingled with my blood. I, then, endured my torments disdainfully, as my habit is, saying all those invectives which my mind gave me to say as rudely and as loudly as possible. And there appeared unto me processions of heresiarchs and schismatarchs (all blameless), wearing altogether prestigious habiliments, and using gestures (almost salacious) which ran along their bodies and suggested things not said, who proffered to me priesthoods (and in one case) a pontificate. But none of their pretty things pleased me, not being of valid or desirable origin. And I

---

* The tonsure is, of course, not pentagonal but circular. The bishop who confers it does, however, ceremonially dip the clerk's hair in five places, *e.g.* front, back, right, left, and crown, while teaching the tonsured to twitter: *"Dominus pars – haereditatis meae – et calicis meis – Tu es Qui restitues – haereditatem meam mihi."* Hence, perhaps, the epithet "five-pointed." – A.H.

remained where I was, ready to go forward, ruthlessly refusing to go back.

But now the blessed gods inhabiting olympian palaces were permitting me to find in Thebes the representative of a religion prior in time to, and by no means a dissent from, my own — a religion, furthermore, which was to mine what the flower is to the fruit. Wherefore, being denied the fruit, I made no more ado: but I clutched the flower.

For this cause, I retraced my steps, returning to Luxor, where I commanded my faithful Amenemhat, the priest of Tanis, to give me the order of priesthood according to the rite of Khem. And this he did when I had sworn the great oath of an Egyptian priest, which oath bound me, till Mother Isis herself released me, as I shall narrate hereafter. But Amenemhat gave me the unction of sacred nard, with the white linen robe and the silver ankh, breathing on my head, and laying hands on me, saying: *"May all the gods bless thee: may Heru-p-Khart love thee: may Isis nurture thee: may Osiris guide and prosper thee, so that thou never look back but alway forward on the illimitable field of wisdom hereby opened to thee. And, by the power committed to me, I Amenemhat, make thee, Nicholas, a priest of Khem, in the name of Apis Osiris the great god who sitteth in Amentet, ever-living lord, ever-lasting ruler, deliverer, sustainer, who is Osiris, who is Nu, who is Ra, who is Tum, all whose feathers are upon him, and who giveth life forever and forever."*

These matters, then, being accomplished, we returned to Thebes; and nothing impeded my entrance to the subterranean palaces.

But we transported my magic apparatus, on a truck, into the forty-ninth antechamber of those secret halls, to be convenient for our operations at a fitting time. But, because the fidelity of the servants whom we left with the rest of our baggage by the river-side (excepting that which I myself had concealed) was not above suspicion, I, indeed, took with me all my money, to wit, five-and-fifty gold quarter-ounces of Victory queen of the stalwart stately Anglicans,* and some Egyptian silver. Also I armed myself with my death-spitter,†

---

* I surmise that these "gold quarter-ounces" were sovereigns. — A.H.

† The words "death-spitter," "death parcels," and "time-

and with a belt containing four-and-sixty death parcels, for there was always a chance of an encounter with barbarian tomb-riflers in Egypt of the nineteenth century to come. Also, I took my gold time-teller: for that was the last thing which I bought before I left the land of my future birth.

But we stood before the hitherto-resisting portal. A touch from my magic staff caused the massive gates to creak and to yawn with much groaning before us. Having crossed certain vast secret halls, walking at a slow but even pace for an hour or more, we came to the verge of a subterranean lake. I flashed my lanthorn over the watery expanse: but we saw no distant shore. A narrow causeway, only a few spans higher than the dark flood, was all that met our eyes; and that lost itself, twenty cubits away, in impenetrable gloom. I stooped and dipped my hand into the water: by which act I perceived that what I had taken for a lake was actually a strong stream; and I opined that it was some subterranean collateral of sacred Sihor.

But I boldly stepped out on to the causeway, bidding Amenemhat to follow me and to push before him the small wheeled truck, light to lift, easily propelled, which contained my cabinet of essences and quintessences, with my divination-cup and my crystal orb of divination banded with silver with adornments of rose-crystals and blue moonstones, together with a skinful of Nile water and certain alimentaries. And, as my eyes became accustomed to the murky blackness, I perceived the outlines of colossal columns on both sides of the stream: these supported a carven roof strangely painted with cats and weasels.

But, after a journey which seemed to be interminable owing to the darkness and the silence, though it was not actually more than a thousand paces, the causeway widened suddenly; and, on peering for the edge, I was ware that I had crossed the dark river as by a bridge. That dark river of running water divided my life as a liegeman of Victory queen of the stalwart stately Anglicans from a life which lay before.

New wonders arrested the melancholy dejection of my mind. In front of me, there appeared a wall painted with

teller" are written in late-Victorian English by what I take to be Mr. Crabbe's own hand. — A.H.

figures representing the initiation of priests in the divine Isidian mysteries; and this wall was pierced by three doors. Not for me was it to hesitate. Not for me was it even to ask guidance of my familiar. But these opinions did not prevent me from contriving a wile, observing with the corner of my eye that Amenemhat's glance instinctively went to the door on the right hand. Which door I instantly laid open with a touch of my magic staff; and, having passed along a corridor, richly adorned, very fair to see, we emerged in a vast circular hall, columned, and surrounded by a cloister having a series of apsidal chapels in its outer boundary. And the place was indeed marvelous. For, in the middle of the hall, four-and-twenty circular stairs soared to a circular platform, whereon sat a lonely altar; and the whole place was made of some clear white stone like polished marble, dazzling snow-white marble without veins or mottling, and without any of the joints which are formed when slabs of stone are laid in order one upon another: so that I could not determine whether the wall had been builded with hands, or cut with incalculable toil from the virgin quarry, or merely called into being by art magic. But, though the hall was of most candid whiteness, the altar on the summit of the circular foot-pace was of blood-red porphyry. And, being (as it was) deep in the bosom of the grain-giving earth, the place was lighted by a radiance, perennial, most agreeable to the eyes, the source of which I am not at liberty to tell. Such was the secret hall beneath Thebes.*

But I placed my magic apparatus on the altar, and on the foot-pace pertinent thereto, all in proper order; and I sat down, with Amenemhat, on the lowest step, to refresh our bodies with a meal in preparation for the work before us. And, when we had dismissed the desire of eating and drinking, so sitting we conversed as follows.

"I do not remember this white hall as it now is," said Amenemhat.

---

* Mr. C.'s statement would almost seem to indicate that Messrs. Currelly, Dennis, Dalison, and Naville, the learned and assiduous excavators of the subterranean sanctuary at Thebes (*cf. The Times,* Tuesday, viiij Apr.) are only at the beginning of their labors. — A.H.

"Hast thou then seen it before?" I inquired.

"When I was priest of Tanis, I oft-times celebrated the mysteries here."

"And to what was it like then?"

"It was draped with white carpets of silk embroidered in silver with images of the assessors of Amentet. And a carpet was hanged between every pair of pillars, veiling the cloister from the hall."

"Yet the hall will serve our purpose as well without its hangings?"

"Doubtless. But still it seems that some malignant sprite might lurk in the shadow of those columns, watching, with intent to interrupt our sacred rites."

And hardly had the Tanitic priest uttered the last word, when a blameless shape (very loathsome and ferocious, shewing nothing but the accentuation of a tattered pendulous head and the thick rictus of parts of a face), emerged from those very shadows, and rushed upon us with mouth-foamings and hiccoughs and eye-rollings, hideously screeching.

Amenemhat withered away with terror; and his mind wilted as he fell swooning on the steps. But I, strongly bounding, leaped to the altar; and, having seized my magic staff, and having made the terrible *Sign of the Godlike Rulers,* then indeed I proclaimed the *Spell Which Binds.*

The Shape stood, held by the mighty enchantment, a ridiculous and cruel personage, gross and ceruminous, with an incomplete head dandling on a tendinous neck. But I descended to recover my familiar. And, having further bound the Shape with the *Word of Fear,* I drew back the mind of Amenemhat to his body, fattening it with comfortable words. And anon I required the Shape to decline to me his generalities, telling who and what he was.

But he responded very obediently, saying: "I am Sanes, priest of Osiris, warden of yonder purple altar, and long it is since I have formed mortal speech with these remnants of my tongue."

I then demanded, "Why, O hideous and excessive prelate, didst thou rush out so menacingly upon us?"

"Because," he said, "having seen no man since I know not when, I was fearful that ye had evil designs. But, seeing that thou hast the *Sign* and the *Spell* and the *Word,* I must believe thee to be present with the sanction of the gods. Yet, seeing that I (in my lifetime) was the warden of this place, seeing that no man hath deposed me, seeing also that (after my accidental but lamentable death) I was not properly embalmed but did myself fulfill the cavities of the holy crocodiles who ate me, I still must deem myself its warden."

Thus having spoken, he wept fragmentarily. And I will say that I rarely have seen anything more frightful than the tears of a shape which (some centuries before) had been an eaten clergyman. Wherefore, having required him to make his Mark with his finger (as it were) on the stainless floor, and having counted the angles of the same, I said: "Poor faithful Senior, thou shalt be relieved of thy wardenship and speeded whither thou shouldst have gone ages ago."

And I removed *Spell* and *Word.* But, intoning the *Speeding Hymn,* I bade the Shape to begone in peace to the dull region of Amentet, giving him the *Word of Entrance,* and praying the Assessors to deal leniently with him. For surely so dreary and so patient a watch and ward as his should suffice to smooth many wrinkles from his sphere of gold.

And, with a joyful cry, the Shape collected his parts; and, leaping, he evanesced. But we turned to the matter which engrossed us, having dismissed the long-delayed ghost to his rest.

In this manner, I began to use my magic art in the secret hall of Thebes.

The Fourth Papyrus

*T*OUCHING the ordeal of the scorching staff, I consulted Amenemhat. He had grave doubts as to whether it was lawful to protect the hand with a magic unguent, or to hold the staff with tongs; and he stood by the injunctions of the well-written papyrus which ordained that the staff must be held in the hand. But, as for me, my dear mind foamed with blood, and my stomach shifted inch by inch, and the gorge of me swang to and fro, at the anticipation of the grievous anguish which I was to undergo: although I knew that, by enduring the ordeal the first time, I had summoned from the dead a master of magic, from whom I was learning ineffable wisdom, and, that, by enduring the same a second time, I should call from the dead a master of masters of magic, from whom I might learn wisdom absolutely illimitable. But, notwithstanding this, the heart in my bosom would take no cheer, but remained dull and spiritless and weighted with premonitions of disaster.

Furthermore, while my mind was thus obliquing brusquely in the manner of a crab, I needs must add to my perturbations by certain thoughts about the gods of my own motherland. And I pondered the question again, asking myself whether what I was meditating actually amounted to apostasy. And I went over much old ground: for the point was a very nice and subtle one. I told myself how that bad hierarchs and far-from-immaculate anointed ones, all the most righteous of men, of my race and age and tongue, had refused to let me serve my gods and theirs in the manner which those divine ones inhabiting heavenly palaces had themselves designed.

And I enumerated, one by one, all the occasions when the same blameless persons, out of spite or out of pique or out of merely natural and ungracious cruelty, had chased me from temple after temple with secret anathemas, denied me my rites, and withdrawn from me the very hem of the skirt of fellowship. And I postulated that a well-minded man must have a religion. Therefore, without disloyalty to the gods of my own land, from whose worship my fellow-worshippers cut me off, I pronounced that it was permissible for me, in default of fullness, to use a moiety. Thus, then, I argued with myself, until I was satisfied, that is to say satisfied as nearly as might be.

And anon I addressed myself to my task, placing the crystal orb in the silver cup, and filling the last with Nile water, while my familiar poured into the thirsty trench below the steps that magic emerald-colored liquid, whose exact ingredients may not be told at large. Which having been well-done, we prepared to summon a Great One of the Greater Ones out of the Outer Immensity. And, for this cause, that the one whom I was about to summon was coming from so vast a distance of time, I knew that the heat of my magic staff would be immeasurably greater at this second summons than at the first. For movement is heat and heat is movement; and, the faster and longer the movement, the fiercer the heat of the burning.

But, while the priest Amenemhat sprinkled beautiful-smelling gum-tragacanth, I intoned the hymn *I am the One among the Forms which the Eye the Only One hath created,* and the incantation called *Of the Buckle of Red Jasper;* and then we both prayed to Ptah the Pain-lessener to make my ordeal as endurable as might be. It is true that I was not to have an additional burning from the fierce clear of the moon, since I was (this time) far beneath the earth: but I ceased not from my pure-minded prayers to Ptah, even when the crystal orb began to glow. For I was convinced that some catastrophe was at hand.

Wherefore, fearing lest the sudden death of his summoner (and I expected no less) should leave Amenemhat to drag out a weary existence forever on man-breeding earth — for a spirit reincarnated by means of Nile water must remain incarnate until his own incarnator shall permit him to depart his body

— then, indeed, I hastily gave to my familiar the *Word of Freedom*, saying: "O Amenemhat, it seems that the time of our separation is at hand. But I am loath to part, for thou hast taught and served me well: but I will not help myself at another man's serious cost. Therefore I free thee from my bond of rule, that thou mayst return to thy place when it shall seem good to thee. And, for thine own sake setting thee free, O Amenemhat, I bid thee farewell."

But his response came to me very thinly, very reedlike: for his body instantly began to fade away from him; and he was fast becoming an Osirian and a spider's-web-colored mist in my sight. And he said: "O Nicholas, Conquistator of Peoples, I indeed thank thee for the respite from the gnawing weariness of Amentet which thou hast granted to me, by summoning me to tread the kindly earth for a space; and, in return, I will unfold to thee some pages of the book of thy destiny. For, having been and being now about to be an Osirian, I can read plainly in that book: yet I may not tell thee all, for the gods have forbidden it. And, ere thou hast lived another moon's age, thou shalt see me as I used to be: for I and thou are linked together in an unbreakable cycle of nigh two thousand years. And I and thou will meet again in this land of Khem, I the priest of Tanis, and thou: for that awful round of years is ——"

Thus he departed, leaving the unfinished phrase lapping against my mind. But I was very grievously perturbed: for, unless I read his prediction awry, I was doomed to die within the month. And I was not ready, having an infinity (an inconceivable infinity) of things to do, of souls to save, of sufferers to soothe, of oppression to remove, of wrongs to put right, of liars and thieves and slanderers to confute and to despoil and to shame, of cruelties to avenge with head-diggings and eye-gougings and revenges and slaughters and maimings and stonings and spine-impalings with much moaning, and many other mind-grieving evils. For which causes I was not ready to die then.

Wherefore, arising with shoutings from my lethargy, I adjured the mind in my dear breast to be very strong, very valiant indeed, very alert to withstand Death's insidious onsets. For, though I had seen many things, I never yet had met personally beautiful Death the soother of men. And first, I set myself to endure the ordeal in which I was engaged. For lurid gleams were leaping from the emerald liquid in the trench, wafting hot breaths in my direction.

Instantly, stripping off my linen robe and casting it outside the circle, I again ascended to the porphyry altar; and grasped the magic staff with my bare hand. Now that my mind was blazing with firm courage, the staff at first seemed cold. Anon, a gentle wave of warmth flushed through it; and a dart of anguish shot into my flesh. Pang followed pang: stab pierced stab. More swiftly came fiercer thrusts of pain as the heat increased. But I kept my mind fixed and my lips addressed to Ptah the Pain-lessener. Great scorching flames flowed from the staff over my hand and arm. I seemed to be holding a nineteen-times-heated fire; and, yet, amid all the intolerable agony, I was ware that this was but the beginning of my torment.

The heat of the flame was so intense, that I looked for my arm to vanish away in impalpable ashes. Irresistible desire of dropping the staff assailed me; and my fingers loosened a little against my will. Like as the helmsman of a ship, whose rudder is shattered by wintry storms, and who (knowing the right course) is unable to steer his vessel, even so was I then. The staff fell out of my grasp: but the silver chain, which looped it round my wrist, prevented it from rolling away.

Instantly, the flames expired; and the lambent streamers in the divination-cup died down. But I stood, alone, in darkness.

After a space of gloom and silence, I saw tiny golden sparks floating in the vast circumferent void. But I watched them: for there seemed naught else for me to do, nor was my will any longer inclined to force leadlike unwilling limbs to act. And the sparks became spots. And the spots became swiftly-rolling globes of light. I tried to utter a *Spell:* but voice and hearing had deserted me.

I lay, crouched against the blood-red altar of porphyry. The globes of light changed, taking wonderful forms. All my members were enfeebled; and, indeed, only the mind in my breast was me. For my body had renounced its allegiance to my sway, and had gone apart from me in shocking rebellion, leaving me to die having nothing but my mind and my mind's eye, which saw and thought the very queerest things, the most terrible, the most unheard-of.

All round me, I saw the spirits of my senses standing. On the left, was my hearing: on his right, was my smell: on his right again, was my sight: on the right of that one was my taste: on his right was my touch. Above these, hovered my life, in the form of a small white bird like a beautifully-crowned hoopoe. Behind them, were my powers of speech and movement, very large, and sudden, and frightful. And the mind in my breast told me that these things were so.

But all these shapes mopped and mowed and sighed at me; and my voice made as though he would have derided me, his fallen master: but the bird of life forbade him. And the shapes wagged and wavered horribly, gesticulating among themselves; and some seemed friendly: but others were undoubtedly hostile. And, suddenly, with a pitiful gesture, my hearing put up his hands and dived cleanly into me; and I heard faint voices, as one hears the whimpering of miners coming up a pit-shaft. For my powers and my senses were arguing against me: but the bird of life argued for me.

"Ye shall not leave him thus:" cried the bird.

"And who can prevent us?" shrieked the rebels.

"I," said my life, "for I will not leave him; and how can ye wander lifeless through the wide-bosomed earth when I am here refusing to die?"

Then, indeed, the mind in my noble breast spoke unwinged words, saying the *Spell of Not Letting the Powers and Senses of a Man be Taken from Him in the Netherworld;* and, afterward, I intoned aloud: "How now, rebellious creatures, why dally in idleness when work remains to be done? Know ye your master; and obey."

And, with shambling gait and visages rueful and ashamed, my senses and my powers obliqued each to his separate task.

But I staggered to my feet; and, seizing the divination-cup, I drained its cool contents, looping my arm through the chain of the crystal orb. And, at the moment, flames began to rise from the summit of the purple altar. Whitish-green they were, ever-increasing in volume, as though some mountain (a forge of the Kyklops) were vomiting from a new vent. And the flames rose higher and higher, till they licked the very apex of the hall ninety men's heights above me; and there was neither smoke nor vapor: but only fervent flames, humming and buzzing and bounding upward with irresistible leapings. But, changing to violet, they vanished, leaving the place in a violet glare wherein was the whirring of wheels.

But I dismissed inertia; and, having my faculties under order, I began to look upon these happenings with a wholesome curiosity.

In the midst of the wheels were faces and figures and events, faint indeed at first, but growing clearer and firmer and more violent in movement till they displaced the wheels. But I watched very intently; and I saw the histories of mortal men of many different races being enacted before my eyes. For, things (which then were past, and since have been) were done in my sight in that secret subterranean hall of Thebes. Kings and queens and emperors and princes and republicans and patricians and plebeians swept in reverse order across my view, all doing their deeds. Time rushed enormously backward in tremendous panoramas. Great men died before they won their fame. Kings were deposed before they had been crowned. Nero and the Borgias and Cromwell and Asquith and the Jesuits* enjoyed eternal infamy and then began to earn it. My motherland, the kingdom of Victory queen of the stalwart stately Anglicans, melted into barbaric Britain: Byzantium melted into Rome; Venice into Henetian Altino; Hellas into innumerable migrations. Blows fell; and then were struck. Bearded men became smooth-skinned boys. Death came first; and birth came last. All things changed save one: silver Sihor's living waters rolled down through the green streak of Egypt and the sacred Delta to the innumerably smiling sea.

Thus, was I whirled back through the rolling wheels of Time.

At length events were still. The medley of scenes vanished. And I was ware that I was alone with Another, Unknown, in a void of blackness, impenetrable, save where the blood-red altar glimmered obscurely; and, on it, was enthroned a Presence, shapeless, indistinguishable from the murky gloom.

---

* This synthesis strikes me as being really most remarkable. – A.H.

But I was not afraid. And anon a voice spake to me, saying: "O man of many wiles and inquisitive mind, it is permitted to thee to have thy will, seeing that thy will is good and not evil. And, forasmuch as wicked and fatuous anointed ones are minded to neglect thee, wasting thee, throwing thee away as worthless, forasmuch also as the Maker of thy stars will not have His good work spoiled and His keen tool rusted or blunted by disuse or misuse, therefore, employment is granted to thee such as thine energy deserveth and as thy mind desireth. For which cause, thou art put back in time; and several lives are given thee to live, and several deeds to do, and several fountains of wisdom are laid bare to thee, so that (being perfected by much striving) at a favorable occasion thou mayst fulfill thy free and perdurable destiny."

Thus having spoken, the Voice ceased. But I was alone, in the dark, very alert, inexpressibly elated, hugging huge joys in my superior mind; and my heart was throbbing like the tail of a lambkin in springtime drinking life from the ewe.

But the hall rocked slowly and more rapidly, with lamps and tones and the roaring of hurricanes and waterspouts and the vibrance of unmentioned and unthought-of music. And long tongues of white fire went before; and all the gods of Khem followed after in intolerable procession, Osiris and Isis and Heru the Child, and hawk-headed Ra in his splendor, and well-plumed watery Nu and Nut, and intelligent Ptah excessive in magnitude, and ram-headed Khnemu, and bird-like Khepera, and self-originated Tum, and feathered Shu, and lion-headed Tefnut, and Zeb the cackler, and Heru of the two horizons, and dark Set, and jackal-headed Anpu the way-opener, and ibis-headed Thoth the measurer, and Maat the straight, and Net the lady of heaven, and Sekhet the eye, and cat-headed Bast, and plumed Ansu with his flail, and mistress Ta Urt, and Hapi of the South with the papyrus, and Hapi of the North with the lotus, and Amen the Only One who has no second, and Mother Nut the sky his wife. And, all the while, I heard the shattering shaking of the sacred sistrum, denoting the presence of Divine Mother Isis, the Greatest of the Three.

But the Voice spake yet again to me, saying: "O man of many wiles and inquisitive mind, these are the forms of The

Supreme, at this time to which thou art come."

But I gazed on the assemblage of the gods, until my eyes were blinded; and, for a time, I saw no more.

Such, then, was the manifestation which I gained by magic art at Thebes.

I, Empedokles son of Polypemon, a Rhodian, have written this. My lord the king ceased from dictating these histories, in order that he might lead a squadron of his flying chariots, waging against King Artavasdes, who (audacious) has demanded tribute. And the Divine Herakles has gone with my lord the king. May unconquered Mithra, M.Z.L., P.S.U., D.O.M., S.H.C., M.E.L.F.,* prosper this undertaking. And I seal up the scrolls, impressing the wax with my lord the king's own sigil of the crab and the moon. And these scrolls are written fairly by me, and sealed by me, Empedokles, the scribe, by command of my lord the king.†

---

* I can only elucidate these majuscules by reference to the Henetian inscription containing the Mithraic Morning Litanies (*Corona Matutina Mitraica*) lately discovered by Mr. Rolfe at Tauricellium *(Torcelo)*: *"Manceps Zodiacorum Luminum — Pater, Sospitator, Unificator — Deus Optimus Maximus — Sol, Heros, Creator, — Mundi Expiator, Lustrator, Fautor."* — A.H.

† Several words in these documents are not to be found in my lexicons. On pronouncing them aloud, however, at a time when they worried me dreadfully, I discovered that they were mere phonetic transliterations, *e.g.* PEBOΛBEP is evidently "revolver," and I take OYAΔTΣ for "watch." Though, why Mr. Crabbe could not have continued to call these conveniences a "death-spitter" or a "fire-ball-spitter" and a "time-teller," respectively, is something of a mystery to me. Perhaps we shall be safe in assuming that his attention, to the form of matter which he dictated, varied in intensity from time to time. It does so with the best of us. Nec semper tendet arcum Apollo. I surmise that Mr. C.'s "death-parcels" were cartridges, and (from another indication in the papyri) it may he asserted that they were tipped with an article or convenience called a "dumdum." — A.H.

The Fifth Papyrus

I, KING *Balthazar of Moxoene, having been victorious once again over a barbarian people, and being wounded in battle, but not excessively, dictate these words to Empedokles, my scribe, to pass the time.*

Having seen, therefore, the vast white hall in the secret subterranean temple at Thebes teeming full of the whole hierarchy of the gods of Khem with all their relative appanages; and, having watched these holy ones departing with the indicible pomp and splendor of their coming; and, having heard the mystic voice which told me the meaning of these manifestations, warning me of my connection with the same: anon, I was left to ponder all these admirable happenings.

Now the hall was flooded with soft white light, as it had been when I first entered it with Amenemhat. And, as I meditated, standing strongly at my ease by the altar of blood-red porphyry, I was ware that white carpets of silk (covered with silver embroideries) were looped from column to column all round the immense circle, between each pair of pillars a carpet hanging from capitals to bases. But the embroideries represented the Assessors of Amentet: throned in state they were; and they judged the dead, allotting some to the blissful abodes, and others to the flaming house of Set who gnawed them with his teeth ever champing in expectation of fresh meals. And, while I gazed on these things, I remembered how that Amenemhat had spoken of similar carpets. But, when I thought of that priest of Tanis, I was moved to hold a council with the mind in my dear breast concerning many things. For it seemed good to me to recall events in order, so that (knowing the past precisely) I might understand the present and proceed securely to the future. Wherefore, I reminded myself of my godlike dismissal of Amenemhat at a time when I awfully needed a friend, of the ordeal of the scorching staff, of the overwhelming and wily inquisitiveness which impelled me to persist in spite of failure, of the mind-delighting reward promised to my perseverance, of the flying whirling wheels which swept me back through panoramas of Time, of the apparition of the godlike company of Khem. And I considered all these things, fully and turn by turn, before I laid them away in the cells of my memory, as sedulous squirrels store nuts in hollow trees, making provision for winter. But, when, at length, I was satisfied, I came down the steps from the purple altar; and, gathering my priestly robe from the floor where I had cast it at the beginning of the ordeal, I clothed myself, and proceeded to the cloistral antechambers in search of the truck of baggage which Amenemhat had trundled, from the outer future world, into that arena of untimed immortality. For I was convinced that I no longer stood in time where I had been, but rather more than nineteen hundred years prior to the life which I had left. But, of this, I had no particular or human certainty, but only a general or divine one, for my watch told me that barely eleven hours had elapsed since my entrance into the place; and I firmly prepared myself to find that those eleven hours included nineteen centuries, and that the land of Egypt (which I had left flourishing under the rule of Victory queen of the stalwart stately Anglicans) was now cowering beneath the talons of Roman Eagles. But, having wound-up my watch, and feeling very hungry, I refreshed my body with the provisions in my baggage, leaving nothing for mice. Thus I did, in the cloister behind the embroidered carpets.

Afterward, it seemed good to me to take such matters as would be useful to me in my new life, and to dispose of the rest, before emerging into activity in the sweet sunlight. Accordingly, under my linen robe, I buckled on my belt of beautiful death-parcels with my death-spitter in its proper sling. And, above that belt, I buckled on my broad belt with the well-placed pockets, so that the two belts (one above another) became like a thorax protecting my vitals. But, in the well-sewn pockets of the broad belt, I bestowed my watch, and a box of wax-matches,* and my gold and silver money, and my pocketbook with its beautiful pencil, and my Waterman's Ideal Fountain Pen, and my Foreign Office Passport, with the circular notes from my bankers, and eight notes each worth twenty-five ounces of gold. Thus having prepared myself, I laced the strong sandals on my feet, arranging the pleats of my robe conveniently to conceal what was underneath, yet leaving all things ready to be snatched-at in case of necessity. But there was nothing left, excepting my magic apparatus, and the truck and lanthorn which had come with me to the place.

But, on pondering the thing again, I was ware (from the carpets between the columns, and from a certain aspect of the porphyry altar), that the temple in which I stood was no longer a deserted temple, forgotten because buried by the lapse of ages, but actually a temple in daily use. From which portent, I also was ware that it behooved me to be ready to inflict my presence upon anyone (or at least to explain it plausibly to anyone) who by chance might totter in my direction, and, indeed, not to wait for such discovery, but to go at once in search of the society of articulately-speaking men, and to take my share in life as I should find it on the grain-giving earth.

For these reasons, then, I set my cabinet of essences and quintessences in a darkish recess, hiding it, in case I should need it again: but it remains there to this day. But I retraced my steps toward the causeway, recrossing the dark river; and, coming there, I broke my truck and lanthorn into pieces, and committed them to the swiftly-flowing stream. But I went on toward the light of the outer world, having the crystal orb (silver-banded with adornments of rose-crystals and blue-moonstones) hanging by its chain from my neck, and the silver divination-cup in my left hand, and in my right the magic staff with its silver chain twisted round my wrist. Thus,

---

* All these words: "wax-matches," "pencil," "Waterman's Ideal Fountain Pen," "Foreign Office Passport," and "notes," are written in English. — A.H.

I passed majestically through the antechambers; and a fold of my robe enshrouded my head, lest my silver hair and beard should bewray me to the shaveling priests guarding every portal. But they, seeing me emerging from the holy place with a holy and even mind and wearing priestly habiliments, were unperturbed; and, beside, the sight of the very beautiful instruments in my hands, and the *Word of Silence* in the ancient tongue of Khem which I gave them in my passage, prevented any doubts of me from afflicting their ingenious minds. But also, of course, I was receiving favor from the gods.

So, at last, I stepped up through the secret trapdoor on to the sandy plain under the full blaze of radiant Ra. And I at once perceived a difference. For the plain, with its low pillar on the spit of pebbles, was the same, but infinitely smaller; and, below me, where I had left desolate ruins, was a city heaped with mighty fanes and splendid palaces. I, Nicholas Crabbe, liegeman of Victory queen of the stalwart stately Anglicans, gazed with my live well-seeing eyes, not at puny Luxor, but on Thebes of the Hundred Gates, Menes' Thebes, Thotmes' Thebes, the capital of the Upper Land, the great metropolis of the south, in glory inconceivable, and yet not yet in its greatest glory.

For a time, I stood, musing at the wonder to which my wiles had brought me, and contriving many plans. For, it appeared to me, that (though I had done very well as a priest of Isis in extricating myself from the temple) the mind in my lordly breast was yearning for a wider more strenuous life, in which my wisdom and my power (but now considerable) might be used and (if possible) augmented. And, for this reason, it seemed well to seek yet another guise before entering the city.

But a certain remembrance set me searching the rock-strewn plain; and, by chance, about an hour before sunset, by favor of some god, I came to the cavity under certain boulders, where I had seen fit to hide a small teak-wood chest lined with aluminum, when I came to that place with my familiar Amenemhat. Now I am ignorant of the reason why I found it there, for the time when I hid it there is even now very far in the future. But, as I had found my baggage in the secret hall, with the food (which I brought from the era of Victory queen of the stalwart stately Anglicans) still sweet and fresh more than nineteen centuries before its actual confection, I was not then, and I am not now, disposed to vibrate the air with explanations of what no one can understand. It is enough that I found my teak-wood chest in the place where some day I shall no doubt hide it, and that its contents provided me with easy and beautiful garments wherewith I promptly endued myself, namely, a pair of brown leather boots, with a flannel jacket and trousers, and a silk shirt and socks, all of a very pale grey color, and a soft felt hat of the same hue but of the shape affected by Hermes.* But when I had clothed myself in these well-cut garments, I buckled my revolver-belt outside them, and hanged a leathern satchel, containing my crystal orb and my divination-cup, over my wide shoulders. But I kept the magic staff in my right hand to twirl and flourish by the way; and, so, I set out for the city.

A well-carved open chariot passed by; and the slave, driving, gazed curiously on my strange form. Around me, on both sides of the wide white road, brick-red tillers of the soil toiled with bent backs amid the emerald crops. Another chariot passed me; and halted a little further on for the naked charioteer to gaze upon me with jaw-dropped amazement. At the gate of the city, I saw fierce Macedonians on guard, clothed (as was the fashion of their race) with copper armor blazing like red gold, and kirtles of the well-cured skins of ponies, and great crested helmets on their heads, and long spears of tough ashwood in their hands, very brave to look upon. And, as I came near, one (the most righteous of men) said to his fellows: "I say, here is well-hatted Hermes!"

"Aye:" responded another: "and the godly youth goeth attired for this hot land in grey cloud-garments, shielding his tender skin from Helios his rays."

"Ho, stranger!" cried a third. "Stand thou, and say whether thou art god or man, and what contraband thou bearest in thy bag, and whether thou art friendly to the Pharaoh."

Now while the usual dirty little boys and loafers and inquisitive women were assembling, I realized that I had to

---

* All written in English. – A.H.

do with Argyraspides, seeing that the shields of the soldiers were laminated with silver; and, moreover, I perceived that they were offering me the *Sign of the Shield-rim.** But I used wiles, answering: "First tell ye me who the Pharaoh is, and why ye Argives serve the lord of Khem."

Thus I spoke: but deep-seated indignation swept from their hearts across their faces, even as Sihor's stream inundates the thirsty land in flood-time. And anon one chirruped: "O thou silly fellow! The divine Ayletes is the Pharaoh whom we serve."

"Ayletes?" I cried. "Is, then, Ptolemaios Dionysos the Piper lord of sacred Khem? And are ye Macedonians minions of the Lagidai?"

"Aye, stranger:" the blameless guard responded: "Macedonians we are, but no slaves of that Flute-player. Of our own will we serve Ptolemaios, for pay and for promotion. But, who art thou?" he continued. "Who art thou, who seemest first to know nothing and then to know everything? And why art thou thus garbed? And what bearest thou there?"

Then, indeed, I was wily: for I made them the *Countersign of the Shieldnavel*;† and I said, in a parable which he who has a grain of sense may read: "I am Karkinos Gampsonyx called Oypogonos, son of Kallikhronos, born of Nomadikos, begotten by Eypator son of Eygenes who sprang from the great race of the Selenidai. And I go thus garbed because I have a lordly mind to go thus garbed. And, in my hand, I bear that which is Life. And, on my thigh, I bear that which is death."

Thus I spoke. But the sentinels cowered before me, muttering among themselves: "He knoweth the great *Countersign*: Yet he is not of us, neither of present-born men, victims not masters of life and of death: but he is some god or hero out of the Netherworld." But to me they said: "Pass freely, O Karkinos Oypogonos of the multitudinous paternity, who art lord of life and death. And the Piper may stop thee if he will: but we will have nothing to do with it."

---

* The original has "ΑΝΤΥΞ." – A.H.
† The original has "ΟΜΦΑΛΟΣ." It is extremely humiliating to confess that I have not been able, so far, to trace this Sign and Countersign to any existing Rite. I am deeply pained and mortified. – A.H.

But I went smoothly into the city. And men cast wondering looks at me, because of my strange aspect; but, because I had been able to cause the insolent soldiers of the corrupt Lagidai to shrink from me, I was sufficiently admired. Now the sun was near his setting; and the mind in my breast earnestly desired to seek a small place of my own, near water, where I might rest awhile, watching for an opportunity of mingling advantageously with mortal men. For, indeed, I have ever had a natural longing to be near water, and useful to men. Wherefore, having found my way to the river, I addressed myself to an Argive colonist, and he was a master of barges, who (by chance) was seeing his barks laid up for the night. And from him I demanded the hire of a convenient barge, intending to sail downstream to the Delta, that (during the voyage) I might tranquilly estimate the wisdom which I had, and perhaps acquire more, and also take part in such adventures as the gods might assign to my treatment.

But the bargeman answered me, saying: "No barges, O lord, can pass down Sihor to the Delta, now. For the wild mercenaries of the Pharaoh have mutinied at Anteiopolis for an increase of wages."

"I know," I said, "that there are masterless hounds everywhere."

"But these, lord, are not masterless: for they serve Pyrrhos, one of themselves, a ruddy-locked barbarian, who has made Thebes (the sacred city of the ram-headed god) a byword through the Upper Land and the Lower, requiring of us (as tribute) whole meals of the milk of mice as well as a ransom of much gold."

"But the guards of the Lagidai —" I began.

He interrupted me: "Lord, they league with Pyrrhos; and a share of his spoils keeps them in their quarters while he bites our necks."

"But, why do not ye, Thebans, resist this freebooter?"

"There is no strength left to us, lord, since the dread Pharaoh Ptolemaios Lathyros sacked Thebes: whom may Set snatch, and his heart be eaten alive by slow-worms, hornets, and interminably-tongued chameleons —"

"Peace, fellow!" I snarled. "Nor soil shine Argive mouth with barbaric imprecations. And know that I will sail for the

Delta, though a myriad of outlaws be between here and there."

"Then, lord, thou wilt go alone: for no boatman will risk his life."

"Not for gold?" I inquired, shewing a handful of coins.

Then, indeed, the man wavered, curiously examining the money. But he said: "Oh, where were these well-minted pieces struck? For they are overround and too well-stamped to come from a barbaric mint. And, O lord, who art thou?"

But, being aware that he was as much in my power as though the knuckles of my first and second blooming fingers clutched the tender nose of him, and being desirous at length to make an end of bargaining, I answered him, saying: "Whom I am, thou shalt know on a fitting occasion: but, that I am to he obeyed, thou shalt know now. Let therefore thine eyes gaze in this direction,"

With which words, I stretched out my magic staff to the life-giving river, whispering a certain *Spell of Summons.* And the sons of slime surged up with great swirlings, the many-fanged far-sweeping crocodiles, while I slowly swayed my staff in rhythm with the enchantment which sang within me. But they came in cohorts from far and near, with huge eddyings of the dark-brown water; and they lay winking in close lines by the jetty, expecting orders from me their summoner.

But the heart of the bargeman became like dripping in a hot pan; and he said: "Lord, I perceive that thou art the Divine Hermes at least, with that wonderful wand: for none but thou, and only thou on a very important message from All-father Zeys, could do this thing."

To whom I gave a stern word, saying: "Be ware of opposing the counsels of Zeys, or of hindering Hermes. For the min-ions of Pyrrhos have no more power over me than had the Macedonians of the Lagidai. But, even as I command these sons of slime, so am I superior to all earth-stamping men."

"Dreadful lord," he answered at once, "take the best of my barges: for Nesamun my brother-in-law, who has more skill in boatmanship than I, shall indeed go with thee this minute in his own barge."

Having succeeded in my wile, I dismissed the Argive to see to the business. But I waited, watching the crocodiles having their teeth cleaned and blinking luxuriously, till I was tired of their musky exhalations. And, having given them leave, they returned to their stations in the slime. And anon, seeing that the barge was being prepared very speedily, I bade the bargeman that his brother-in-law should visit me; and to him I gave order that he should take a stock of provisions, buying also a slave-boy of lusty form and a mind incapable of fear, with other things which were necessary. Furthermore, I said that all was to be ready for sailing at dawn. And, having offered two quarter-ounces of gold of Victory queen of the stalwart stately Anglicans to the bargeman for his charges, he foolishly refused the same, abasing himself to the earth as before a god. But I, having ascended the gangway, entered my cabin, where I ate a melon and some cheeses and pigeons; and betook myself to slumber.

These things I did in Thebes of the Hundred Gates.

The Sixth Papyrus

*W*HEN Day with her white steeds was come (most beautiful to behold), and the dawn was yet cool, then indeed I examined my barge with its contents and its mariners. And I saw that Nesamun was a nimble and mightily powerful youth, and that Yokkho the slave was slim and very eager, both stripped for work, and of a brick-red color, with long black and white eyes, and closely shaven polls which they covered with a napkin as is the custom among the Egyptians. But they carried girdles in their bundles. And I saw that the barge was long and flattish, having two bulwarks. But there was a chief cabin in the waist; and the roof of it was like a deck: but the low waist was open. And, at the prow, there was a smaller cabin, with a deck above it, whereon a slave might stand to shove the barge off shoals and sandbanks with the well-handled pole. And there was a third cabin at the stern; and the steersman stood on the roof of it wielding the cunning steering-oar. But, in the waist, was a lofty mast, with triangular sail of woven reeds and the cordage relative thereto. And, having seen all these things, I inspected the baskets of provisions; and these were very grateful to the mind. For there was fresh bread, and much wheat (the marrow of men), and many cheeses, and fruits both fresh and dried, with jars of wine from Kos and Korinth, and vinegar, and condiments, and nuts. But, when I had given an order, all these things were stored in the fore-cabin. And I bade the boatman and his boy to take the aft-cabin for themselves, so that their smells might not come to me, as I slept in the chief cabin, or took the air in the waist, or on the main deck during the voyage. Not that they were in any wise disagreeable, being both healthy and naked and constantly washed: but so I willed it, for (at that time) my stomach heaved at the odor of all mortals. And, these matters having been settled, Yokkho pulled the gangway into the barge, while Nesamun pushed out on to the placid bosom of Hapi-hallowed Sihor. But, when they had hoisted the sail, a favorable breeze assisted the slow stream to waft us toward the distant Delta.

In this manner, I departed from hundred-gated Thebes.

But I began to ponder the past: for this always has been, and always is, and always will be, my singular habit, recounting in my dear mind every particular of the things which I had done, or which had been done to me, weighing their worth and import and possibilities, rejecting some to fall into oblivion, but storing others in my memory until such time when they might be used for my advantage. And, of all the things which I had done during the last two days, there were two things which I regretted. The first was that I had left my magic cabinet with the papyrus-enkheiridion at Thebes; and the second was that I had left my priestly robe and sandals in the cavity under the boulders on the plain. But, nevertheless, the mind in my noble breast bade me be of good cheer, relinquishing all matters, even greater than these, without a backward thought; and going forward boldheartedly in search of fresh adventures, and the more boldly as the more bare-handedly, seeing that greater wisdom is to be gained by the simple, and more blooming laurels are to be won by the absolutely naked, than by the trained philosopher, or by the heavy-armed. Furthermore, the divine ones inhabiting olympian palaces put into my mind an unmentioned and un-thought-of action. For I remembered the prediction of Amenemhat, how he said that within the month I should meet him again. For, since those words, Time had rolled back for me, so that it seemed that I was now actually living in the former lifetime of Amenemhat. And, also, it seemed that (if these things were so) the friendly priest would be performing his functions at Tanis in the Delta: to which place I, undoubtedly by the direction of the gods, was at that moment proceeding. Wherefore, taking courage from the thought that, though I had not all which I might have had, still, I had a great deal, to wit, the prospect of meeting a friend, the divination-cup, the crystal orb, and the magic staff, beside my arms and my money all safely stored in my cabin, to say nothing of the inestimable wisdom which I had so far attained, then, indeed, I became cheerful of heart; and set myself to take my pleasure from what was round about me.

For, as I walked about my deck, I saw the stalwart Nesamun poised like some grand archaic carving in carnelian jasper, at one moment lithe, and at another moment rigid, intent upon his business at the steering oar. And, at his feet, across the narrow aft-deck, Yokkho was stretched at length, busy with fishing-lines which trailed behind in golden Sihor. All around were the rolling waters, bordered with leaves like living emeralds; and, above, the great splendor of Ra flamed in the turquoise-colored dome of the heavens. Nothing broke the stillness, excepting ripples lapping about the well-carved prow, or when the slave laughed contentedly, drawing a silver fish from the stream from time to time and tossing it to flap in a heap below Nesamun's feet.

But when fishes enough for a meal for my crew had been caught, for fish is a food which my gorge rejects without even trying it, then I called Yokkho to me, demanding that he should soothe me with singing. And, having fetched a certain well-sounding harp from his baggage, he began to tighten the strings. But I saw that the harp was an old one, very dilapidated, and the gilding and the paint were both worn off, leaving bare wood to be seen. And also I knew it for the harp of a priest of Khem, though one of the glass eyes of the face on the base had fallen out, and the face itself was so broken and discolored that it was not to be deciphered either as of a god or of a man. And the slave-boy said that, having been rescued from a sunken temple-barge at Philai where he dived for it, the harp had been damaged by water. For which cause, he fitted it with new strings, the frame being still whole. And when at length he had tuned it, crouching on his hams and pressing it to his tender shoulder, then he opened his throat and began to sing. But his song was in a rude meter, with a pæan of praise at the end of every tenth strophe; and he would have continued singing even unto this day: for his song was as interminable as that endless song of future Galatia which

will be called Jean François de Nantes.* But long before
weariness prevented his hand from twanging the strings, I
myself called for silence, demanding the name of his ditty.
And he said that it was one of the folk-songs of the watermen
of the Thebaid. This, then, was the song which Yokkho sang:

Slowly return we
deeply deploring
great Hapi's anger:
we have enanger'd
Sihor's protector:
we must propitiate,
or we shall stare:
He is offended:
our nets go empty:
Let us lament it.

> Great is Hapi:
> worship Hapi:
> mighty Hapi,
> grant us favor.

Now let the Ueb
pour out the red wine:
now let the Kherkeb
offer our prayer,
that our petitions,
eager and earnest,
with a sweet savor
upward may fly,
mounting to Hapi
dwelling in Duät.

> Great is Hapi:
> worship Hapi:
> mighty Hapi,
> grant us favor.

---

* The title of this ballad is written in the French tongue in
  what I take to be Mr. Crabbe's own hand. "Galatia" is
  rather interesting, perhaps. — A.H.

Then will the dread lord,
dread lord of Sihor,
smell the sweet odor
and hear our prayer:
leaping from Eäru
amid the grain-fields,
and earthward flying,
the sacred Sahus
will speed his flight
to our rejoicing.

> Great is Hapi:
> worship Hapi:
> mighty Hapi,
> grant us favor.

Then he will fill
full, even fuller,
each fisher's net,
till inward trawling
we seize the prey;
and load our boats
with Sobk his food.
All will be purchased.
But we remember,
in our good fortune,
Hapi the Giver.

> Great is Hapi:
> worship Hapi:
> mighty Hapi,
> grant us favor.

We have offended;
and, on a sandbank,
we are held prisoners;
and the storm rages
tearing our sail:
winds blind us with spray,
while the sons of the slime
creep o'er our quarter,
each seizing victims

shrieking in vain.

> Great is Hapi:
> worship Hapi:
> mighty Hapi,
> grant us favor. . . .

But when I had made an end of his singing, I gave him a
small coin of no value to me, which seemed to him wealth
incalculable, he being such a simple little fellow. And, having
praised his pretty voice, a most innocent one and not by any
means shrill, I turned to Nesamun demanding a meal. For,
the sun being on his zenith, it was my pleasure to eat before
sleeping. And, having brought me cheeses and gherkins and
cakes of bread and fresh fruit and a jar of wine where I sat in
the shade of my cabin, the mariners went ashore and filled
their own bellies with the fish which they broiled in papyrus
on a fire. But, when they had bathed and returned to the
barge, we again set sail, Nesamun guiding the steering-oar,
and Yokkho fanning me with a palm-leaf where I slept in the
cool cabin.

But, while I slept, it seemed to me that I was wandering
near the Treasury of Dreams which overlooks the meadows
of Eäru in Duät of the gods. And the monotonous song of
the slave still hummed in my ears. And anon, as my manner
is in dreams, I found that I was all stark, without a single
stitch of clothing on me, having naught but my wings and
tail fixed to my arms and shoulders and legs at the back,
wherewith I swam in the air* like a beautiful expert seagull,
easily and enormously swooping. And I was flying finely
balanced over my former (or future) home in the kingdom
of Victory queen of the stalwart stately Anglicans. Which
place I have well in memory, having known it, in the life from

---

* Of course I suppose that it is fairly well known, now, that
  Mr. C. was the first living man of our era actually to fly of
  himself like a bird or an angel, and not like a libellulan in-
  sect in an Antoinette. The story of his (shall we say — are
  we quite justified in saying) accidental discovery of the
  slight physical development which enables this, need not
  be iterated here, I fancy. — A.H.

which I had come, and to which I infallibly shall return
terribly and invincibly armed with the wisdom of ages. But
I remembered the limpid river, and the little island with its
precipitous cliffs save at one end which sloped gently to the
water's edge and the wide-stepped quay. And I recognized the
distant river-banks, clothed with oak-forests and steep pine-
woods, purifying the air. And I looked southward to see the
river-mouth far away, kissing the lips of the innumerably
smiling sea. But I knew, also, the small old perfect fortress of
grey stone, which stood on the summit of that isle, where
were velvet lawns bestarred with daisies, and gardens of quaint
herbs and sweet old flowers, and the cedar tree, and the
ghent-azaleas, and the pergola furred with honeysuckle and
white roses and passion-flowers and dripping with amethys-
tine wisteria and asterial jasmine. And I saw the library of
ancient books for solacing my mind in wintertime when
pine-cones burn upon the hearth. And I saw my three well-
tailed kittens, the white and the yellow and the grey, frisking
round my tame white peacocks trailing pearllike prides in-
dignantly across the pleasaunces and neatly cobbled paths
which lead down to the boat-house. There also, I saw my
electric gondogla, and my flat-bottomed huge-ruddered sailing bragozzetto. And, too, I saw my sailors, John Marcus and
Ermenegildo Falier by name, the last telling horrible Venetian
tales to my three servants, Bob and Bill and Roddy, having
finished their day's work in my house and gardens. But I
swam in the air round and about the place, so near to the
flag of Saint George and the ensign of the Cinque Ports which
flew from my battlements that I could have touched the
bunting with my hand; and yet I was unseen by any mortal
eye. Wherefore I flew back to the Treasury of Dreams.*

And I saw the Master of Dreams summoning a certain
blameless Dream, to whom he said: "Go thou to such and
such a priest of Isis, who sleeps in a barge, near Koptos, on

---

* There is quite a considerable number of words in this really singularly and exquisitely lovely pen-picture of the
home of a hungry heart, of a lonely soul, which are written in English in what I unhesitatingly pronounce to be
Mr. Crabbe's own hand. It is quite unnecessary for me to
indicate them. — A.H.

River Nile; and try whether he will receive thee." And the Dream, having wrapped a cloak of pink and tinsel falsehood about him, leaped out through an ivory gate; and dived down toward me, asleep, in the cabin of my barge. But, because he could not find a foothold there (though he fought like a dog for it), he slank back to the Dream-Master, to whom he sulkily snarled: "Lord, there is that on that barge which prevents me." Whereat, the Dream-Master (having smiled and having dismissed him to his place) summoned another Dream, to whom he gave a similar charge. And the second Dream donned a cloak which seemed to be woven of dewdrops and the eyes of kittens or babies; and he leaped out of another gate, and pounced like a robin on my brow. And, with him, there entered to me Belmarduk the god of Assyria, very brave with fringed vestments and well-curled love-locks. attended by winged bulls and sphynxes and cherubs; and the heroes Gilgamish and Eabani came flatly smirking sideways in his train. But Belmarduk addressed me, saying: "By favor of the gods of Khem, I come to thee in a land which is not mine; and my message is that thou shalt be a king in Armenia, that is to say in Moxoene which is called Magurturgadash in Naïri." And, when he had said this, the traveler-god departed as he came. But, in my dream, I wondered very greatly, being overwhelmed with wave after wave of astonishment: even as a stranded ship is washed by waves pushed by azure-haired earth-shaking Nun, the lord of the ocean. For I was ignorant of the cause why any gods should visit me, specially a strange god, or why Assyrian gods should visit an Egyptian priest. And other doubts also assailed me. Wherefore, in my dream, I mentioned my perplexity to our holy Mother Isis, the wise goddess, whose priest I was, asking for news of these matters; and she instantly answered me by the mouth of Tefeu her messenger, saying: *"The god of Assyria came to thee: because the word hath gone forth in the hall of fate from the abode of The Supreme, the Dweller in the Innermost, Whose decrees nor god nor hero nor mortal can evade."* And the scorpion-headed god shewed the Sign of Life in token that the Lady of the Marsh indeed had sent him. But, having done this, he fled on uplifting wings to Duät of the gods which is above Amentet. Whereat I awakened from my sleep.

Such was the dream which I dreamed in my barge on sacred Sihor.

The Seventh Papyrus

*B*UT now the sun was near his setting, swathing the vast dome of heaven with arras of green and lilac and rose and burning gold. And, on the floor by my couch, the slave had fallen asleep, with the fan still in his hand, and his gleaming limbs stretched out, smooth, brick-red, decently folded. But, the air being cooler, I did not disturb him, but remained lying on the couch, pondering my dream. And, the more I pondered, the less I knew of the manner in which I might assist the fulfillment of the Supreme Decree. But, above all things, I was anxious to avoid the vulgar error of confusing particulars with universals, so as not to lose the fruit of any revelations which the gods had intended.

And, while I was thus meditating, suddenly I remembered a certain magic, by which one may learn a very great deal of the future; and it seemed to me that, in this way, I might test the prediction of my dream. But, indeed, it was the well-made body of my slave, straight, quickening, and apparently spotless, meeting my eyes while I thought on these matters, which recalled this magic from my memory: for it may only be done with just such an innocent one. Wherefore, being awakened, Yokkho opened his fearless black eyes and listened: whom I commanded to slip into the river, and to return to me fresh and clean. This he did. But I inspected him with the most careful minuteness from head to foot; and, having found neither speck nor blemish anywhere upon him, and his teeth sound and perfect, then I knew that he was worthy of my purpose.

But, having seated him on the edge of the cabin roof, with

his legs hanging down, for there the light was strongest, I placed his right hand on his knee, the palm being upward: whereon, with my Waterman's Ideal Fountain Pen,* I drew two squares, a lesser inside a greater; and, in each corner of the outer square, I wrote the Arabic numbers, Four Two Eight Six, with a Three between the Four and the Eight, and a One between the Eight and the Six, and a Seven between the Six and the Two, and a Nine between the Two and the Four; and, in the top of the inner square, I wrote the Arabic number Five: but, under it, I put a fair large drop of pure dichroic ink, purple-black, having unscrewed the top of my pen. And, when all this had been well-done, I bade Yokkho to bend the ridge of his supple back, looking attentively into the drop of ink, and telling me what he should see therein. But, standing below him in the waist of the barge, I looked up into his downcast eyes, very long and lucid and fixed upon the drop of ink. And the black-fringed eyelids gently winked from time to time in the ordinary manner: but, being a very obedient slave, his gaze did not waver from the palm of his hand.

Then, there came a moment when the winking ceased, and the eyes became fixed wide open but still looking downward. And, when I, with a low voice, bade him again to speak, telling the things which he saw in the drop of ink, then, indeed, he spoke as one who at a long distance speaks to himself, very gravely, very slowly, very solemnly, saying: *"The silver god, pointing at the galley, slays."* Then his eyes wavered, and again became fixed. And his voice continued, speaking single sets of words divided by intervals as before; and he thus said: *"The silver god, in the temple, taking the bow which sings. . . . The silver god, in the ship, speaking with the azure-haired god, on the white horses. . . . The silver god leading the golden goddess, from the dark. . . . The silver god, and the golden goddess, before many gods and goddesses. . . . The silver god, and the golden goddess on a throne. . . . The silver god, following the star."* Having said these words, which seemed to be nonsensical, he tired me. Whereat I smacked him, shaking his hand till the dark ink trickled over his thighs; and so I dismissed him to relieve Nesamun at the steering-oar.

---

* English. — A.H.

Thus I did with Yokkho, without gaining the wisdom which I expected.

But, during the rest of the evening, while the boatman was sleeping, I made no more attempts at explaining the past or foreseeing the future: for it seemed that this was not permitted. But I myself took the steering-oar, dismissing the slave to seek more sleep in the waist, by the boatman. And, as we sailed along, I watched the sky turning violet with an after-glow of rose-color fretted with green, which deepened into the clear dark heliotrope of night sown with innumerable constellations, surrounding the white-blazing serene moon. But, when the slaves had finished sleeping, they prepared a meal, and I refreshed my body with food and wine, while Yokkho returned to the steering-oar.

But I inquired of Nesamun the name of the city which we were passing on the right hythe, having seen a cluster of temples with their pylons and flagstaves and very many houses there.

"Lord," he answered, "it is the city of Khenoboskis; and, on the left, should be the lesser Diospolis of the Lagidai which we used to call Mutio. But, in the morning we shall water at Ptolemais Hermii, another city of the Lagidai."

"Our stay," I said, "must be a short one: for I wish to come to Tanis without delay."

"Lord, hast thou not heard of the mutineers at Antaiopolis, who bar the way?"

"Not my way, nor the way of the barge which bears me."

"Nor the way of thy slaves, then, who attend thee:" added Nesamun very quietly.

"Thou art not afraid?" I responded, inquiring.

"Nay, lord, for who can see with his eyes a god, unwilling, going either here or there. But I also can fight, if fighting be toward."

Now, when he spoke thus, I laughed without letting my memory be seen. For I remembered that his brother-in-law and partner had taken me for wing-footed Hermes, because of my strange aspect and the magic enchantment which I did with obsequious crocodiles; and I considered that the reputation of godship would do me no harm, But, looking also upon Nesamun, as he crouched before me in the open waist of the barge, more closely than I had looked hitherto, I was ware that he would fight well, as one born for fighting, being of a species different from that of other Egyptians. For he was a very mighty youth, in his prime, and his four bones were large and very long; and, although he had no muscles as youths of other races have, nevertheless his flesh was extremely firm and sinewy, and his skin healthily tanned and as smooth and polished as fine linen. Furthermore, I marked the immense force of his supple shoulders and thighs, and the strength of his loins and arms and deep-breathing breast. But, above all, I could read an indomitable character in the poise of his head and the carriage of his body, and specially in his fierce young eyes, which flashed so blackly and so whitely when his mind looked out on me. For which causes, I was not unwilling to have such an one on my side. And I opined that my own not-inconsiderable strength, and my wiliness, together with my magic and my arms, all assisted by the fearless obedience of little Yokkho and the intelligent force of Nesamun, needed not to worry about the resistance to be encountered.

But, nevertheless, I made my preparations. And, seeing another vessel coming up the river toward us, I bade my boatman to hail her and to ask for news of the rebels. Whereby I learned that, having been driven from Antaiopolis by Psalkos Memmaïdes (the Pharoah's general and governor of the lower Thebaid), they had sacked Hisoris, and were now holding the very place which I was intending to pass in the morning, that is to say Ptolemais Hermii. And, having mentioned that the rebel-leader Pyrrhos was the mightiest warrior ever seen in Egypt, the strangers scurried fearfully toward Thebes, adjuring us to turn and follow them: for, said they, to go downstream was to court an evil and somewhat protracted death.

Having heard this, and having ordered my slaves to sleep by turns and not to come within sight of Ptolemais Hermii before dawn, I rested tranquilly in dreamless sleep. And, waking while it was yet dark, we three bathed one by one, not disturbing the sons of slime, and also refreshed our bodies with food and wine. Which having been done, I instructed Nesamun and Yokkho for the fray, saying that they were not to concern themselves with anything, excepting the swift maneuvering of the barge, instantly and implicitly obeying my commands. And my first stratagem was to lower the sail, lest it should be injured in the battle which I expected. But Yokkho was to stand by with the cordage, ready to hoist the yard immediately when we should have pierced our foes. And Nesamun was to govern our course with the steering-oar under my directions. But I buckled on my cartridge-belt and loaded my revolver. And, when Helios Hyperion had driven the chariot of the sun about an hour above the horizon, we drifted on the current in sight of Ptolemais Hermii.

But, between us and that city, I espied a long and lofty galley, propelled by forty oars, hissing toward us.

A glance at the alert eager faces of my slaves shewed me that all was as I would have it; and, stepping into the waist, I inspected the advancing enemy. The galley was crowded with mercenaries from stem to stern. Red horse-hair streamed from their helmets. The shields of some, who were Rhodians, bore the rose of Rhodes. The others, as I learned later, were Karians. All wore white and blue kirtles girt with well-made sword-belts: but owing to the heat of the land and the feebleness of those who hitherto had encountered them, they neglected their greaves and body-armor. The rebel Pyrrhos (most righteous of men) stood on the prow, wearing a scarlet kirtle and a short purple military cloak. His helmet gleamed with well-forged brass; and a plume of red horse-hair sprouted therefrom. But the oars of the galley were pulled by enormous portly Nubians, rolling-eyed, blubber-lipped; and fiercely they snorted coming on.

"Stop, stranger!" shouted the blameless Pyrrhos.

"In whose name?" I inquired, dallying with my victim.

"In my name:" he answered.

"On what penalty?"

"Death."

"For whom?"

"For thee. Spear me this confounded babbler, O Orkhos:" he cried.

A spear hurtled toward me: but, at my quick command, Nesamun zigzagged the barge to let it pass, and held on a straight course as before. The galley swung athwart the stream twenty long paces distant. But I, raising my revolver and taking aim at the rebel-leader, bellowed: "Pyrrhos, I give thy carcass to the sons of slime."

And dark doom leaped from my finger and pressing palm, and sank into the socket of his eye. And his life withered in the seat of wisdom, so that his soul fled gibbering to the netherworld. But the carcass, heavily lurching, fell, purple and bejeweled, dully splashing into sacred Sihor; and crocodiles dragged down the shreds and tatters of its fatness with bubbling swirlings.

But the blameless mercenaries sucked in their breath during a full minute, being appalled at the sight of their leader turned topsy-turvy by a noise like the yap of a small dog. But Nesamun held my barge still, stem on to the galley's side and twenty long paces from it, ready to leap forward or backward at my word. But I said, very sternly: "Thus, O ye rebels, do I treat prepotence and audacity. And thus, also, will I deal with all, arrogant, who bar my passage."

And, so saying, I paused, while I reloaded my revolver, that they might evacuate their sites if they were wise. But, recovering from their amazement, they took to hurling javelins; and the rowers bent to their sweeps, turning the galley upstream and driving the dreadful ram against me. Then, indeed, did Nesamun give proof of his quality, nimbly leaping to and fro on his narrow station to avoid the hissing darts and (at the same time) wielding the steering-oar so dexterously that we circled round the cumbrous galley, always maintaining our relative position. But I, partly sheltered by the bulwarks, fired into selected eyes or ear-holes of the rebels, as their destinies presented the same to me. For the pure lust of fighting, which never before had really inflamed me, had come upon me; and I laughed hideously in bloodthirsty glee as my enemies fell to my hand. And those, in whose wet eyes my bullets quenched their blunt-nosed heat in fizzling, tossed their useless limbs when Death entered to drive out Life; and their knees slackened as they flopped into the river, where crocodiles anxiously scrambled for morsels of them. But my last shot slew two Karians, passing through their ear-holes, and also a Nubian in whose it remained. And the current threw the sweep, slipping from his dead hands on to the oars of his fellows, causing a shocking confusion, in the midst of which I recharged my revolver a third time.

But the rebel-helmsman was already a refection for the sons of slime. And, the galley having swung right round so that it now lay between me and Thebes, I saw that the mercenaries desired to escape upstream, being no longer inclined to have dealings with me. Wherefore, having sent fourteen in all of them to Osiris, I gave a word to Nesamun and Yokkho. And, instantly, the sail ascended to the top of the mast, while the boatman brought us about into a favoring breeze; and, as an eagle spreads his pinions having satiated his hunger with a prey, so we sped on toward Ptolemais Hermii.

In this manner I disposed of an impediment on sacred Sihor.

The Eighth Papyrus

*B*UT, as soon as the barge was going swiftly with wind and stream, Nesamun fixed the steering-oar, and came forward with Yokkho to adore me. And, having laid their two bodies (gleaming with wholesome sweat) at length at my feet, then they praised me in the Egyptian mode. But, when they rose up, we refreshed ourselves with cups of wine; and the boatman collected spears and javelins which were sticking in various parts of the barge, and stacked them in tidy bundles near the prow. But the slave brought sweet water for bathing a wound in my left forearm, which had appeared to be a deep one: but, when the drying blood was washed away, it was seen to be merely a scratch. And he bound it up, using the nimble tender fingers which had waited so patiently, during the fight, to hoist the sail at the very moment when I commanded afterward. But, when I had rewarded them each with a handful of Egyptian silver, I retired to my cabin, the radiant sun being near its height; and, anon, dark sleep embraced me.

And, once again I was disturbed by conceptions not of a restful nature. For, while my body slept, the mind in my dear breast concerned itself about innumerable ideas, asking unanswerable questions. It was quite clear to me that I indeed was living a new life: but I was not certain as to whether I was still a man, or really (as people opined) a god. And I laughed at the latter notion: because I never before had heard of a Yacht Club member (as I am, having compounded my subscription and never having been expelled), who also was a god of sorts. But, god or man, I supposed that I still had the right to put the address of the club on my visiting-card. And once more I laughed at the notion of leaving visiting-cards on Gajus Julius Cæsar, and Marcus Tullius Cicero, and the whole blameless gang of venal (but Roman) old-fogeydom, whom I actually might see in the flesh within a month, simply by crossing the unvintaged sea. But the scratch on my arm smarted, in what I took to be an ungodly manner: for I knew not then that the blessed gods are ever so much more sensible to pain than your mere man, having made men in a godlike image, but having given them only the sorriest fraction of a godlike nature. And the Whole is naturally greater than a Part of a Whole. But I persuaded myself that I was a man, at least so far. And, yet again, I laughed at the notions that I, a subject of Victory, queen of the stalwart stately Anglicans, was also an Egyptian master of magic, and, that I, a catholic of the Apostolic Latin Obedience, on whose agonies of cold and hunger and thirst and mind-maddening loneliness the foundations of Westminster Cathedral were laid, was also a priest of Isis. And a doubt came to me from I know not where, as to whether there were in fact any gods at all, beside those which men, are wont to make in their own idiotic image,* and (if, perchance, there ever had been gods), whether they had not all retired from business, to die at their ease, having grown so feeble that mortals could handle them rudely even before windy Ilion far back in the morning of time. Or, perhaps, the gods of the Argives had gone into partnership with the gods of the barbarians. For there certainly were gods in barbaric places, and my eyes had seen them; and I began to contrive new wiles for seeing them again one after the other, asking them to send me back to my own time, if I had a time. But I became displeased with the frivolous manner of the thought of visiting immortal gods who inhabit olympian palaces. And yet, I asked myself, why should I not visit gods, who had been visited by a strange god, even Belmarduk the god of Assyria with his attendant heroes. And that notion, that a god should have taken the trouble to come from distant Assyria to visit me in the land of Khem, convinced me that (if indeed I was not in truth a god) I was extremely important as a man, being certainly the sole representative of The Great

---

* I really cannot resist preserving this most pleasing pleonasm. — A.H.

Queen Victory, queen of the stalwart stately Anglicans, in the Egypt over which the Pharaoh Ptolemaios Ayletes ruled. And that idea reminded me of my Foreign Office Passport, and of the risk (which I was running) of being arrested as the possessor of an undecipherable document. But I scorned that; and began to contrive yet newer plans for going to see the Kolossos of Rhodes when I should have finished my business with Amenemhat at Tanis. And the last notion made me think of South Africa,* and the colossal man Umgugondlhovu (as the Zulus name the rumble of an elephant) whom I had left overshadowing that country, with the hybrid horde of I.D.Bs. and polemic georgics,† all the most righteous of men, who infested his vicinity. And the notion of an elephant reminded of a circus. And the notion of a circus gave me a foresight of the green and blue factions of Purity and Holy Wisdom striving in the circus at Constantinople. And, from Constantinople onward, notions came to me in crowds, notions of Turks, Bulgarian and Albanian atrocities, the traitors Gladstone and Asquith, the treaties of The Hague and Berlin, the German Empire, the Holy Roman Empire, Karl the Great, Rome, Pontifex Maximus, Saint Peter, strange gods, with whom I had no time to deal separately owing to a pressing engagement, but merely checked off their names as the procession hurried by. And, then, having come back to the notion of strange gods with which I had started, I bounded out of my dream.

And, instantly, to me there came the last words of my dream, namely "strange gods," said in a fat phlegmatic voice near by.

---

* It is perhaps unnecessary for me to mention that this papyrus simply bristles with words neatly written in English of course by Mr. C. himself. — A.H.

† This is the most cryptic allusion in the present fragment; and I must confess that it puzzles me sadly. I am given to understand that "Iota Delta Beta" sometimes signifies "Illicit Diamond Buyer," an obsolete species of South African criminal. But what kind of thing a "Military Agriculturist" is (for that is what Mr. Crabbe's Greek means), passes my comprehension. I have therefore rendered the expression by a simple traliteration of the original. — A.H.

To which the strong tones of Nesamun firmly answered, saying: "I have said that my lord is indeed a god. I myself am loyal to the Pharaoh; but I dare not stop until my lord the god bids me. And he is asleep."

"Let us see this strange god who journeys in a hired barge. Awaken thy god, O slave, and let us see him:" the fat voice wheezed.

But I, slinging on my revolver again, stepped out of the cabin. And, at sight of me, the boatman shut his full red lips; and leaned easily upon the steering-oar, as one whose part is well done. But I perceived that a royal galley lay alongside, which bore a very inquisitive Negro, richly garbed and of hideously inconvenient obesity. Whom I austerely addressed, demanding his generalities.

"I," he said, in a quieter tone, "am the Pharoah's private detective; and I stop all boats which come down-stream to satisfy myself that they are not sent by the rebel-mercenaries."

"These spears and javelins," I answered him, shewing the stacks, "are branded with the Rose of Rhodes and the Crane of the Karians; and they were drawn out of the holes which thou mayst see among my bulwarks: into which holes they first were hurled by the rebels. Judge, therefore, whether the rebels would thus have assailed their friends, or their foes."

"But, if ye be foes of the rebels, ye must have passed them by."

"That is true," I said: "for I encountered them above Ptolemais Hermii, where I slew Pyrrhos and thirteen of his gang; and so I passed them by."

"Doss thou say that thou hast slain Pyrrhos and thirteen of the mercenaries? Either thou art indeed a god, or a hero, or a very great liar. And, as I take thee for the last, I shall detain thee while I inquire into the truth of thy story. If it be true, thou shalt be compensated. If it be false, prepare to suffer certain torments."

Thus rashly he spoke, beating his ceruminous belly: but I, glowing with anger, said: "And dost thou, O mountain of impudence, think that I, who have outfaced a whole galley full of armed Greeks, will be stayed by any emasculate slaves of the Lagidai?"

"Hear the voice of the god, and give ear to long-armed

Psammy lord of apes!" the fat phlegmatic Negro exclaimed in a tone of derision.

But my blood boiled because my rather-long arms were mocked by a blameless black man; and the lust of battle inflamed me again, making my great strength as the strength of nineteen; and the ferocity of the long-curving fiercely-clutching claws of a crab inflamed the hands of me. For which causes, and knowing that it would take a better man than a bloated nigger to stand up to me, I bounded from my bulwark to the galley, terribly bellowing. And, alighting near my scoffer, I rent the well-toothed jaw from the head of him, and smashed the rest of his face to a purple pudding therewith. Also, tearing his fingers asunder like a rag, I split his right hand up to the wrist; and, so, I tossed him, devoutly hiccoughing his physical agony, as an offering to the sons of slime.

But I turned swiftly to seek another victim. And, on the prow, an archer stood balanced on long slim straddling legs, drawing a brass-tipped arrow to his ear: but its point was toward me. And him, complaining bitterly, I also sacrificed to the enchanted crocodiles.

But, being now well in the way of fighting, I snatched at my revolver; and, by chance, my hand touched the magic staff hanging from my belt. And the potency of it caused certain admirable events. For, first, my wrath cooled, and instantly died away: but I myself began to utter wily words in my usual manner, pointing the staff at the crew of the Pharoah's galley, and saying: "Ye have seen the dire fate which overtakes those who temerariously oppose me. Be wise, therefore. Stand not in my way: nor follow me too far.* But draw off speedily, lest a like doom should afflict you also."

But, when I had spoken thus with my mouth, I added the *Spell Which Binds* with my mind. And, being bound, they remained whimpering, but as still as stones: but I, returning to my barge, washed my hands and resumed my journey.

After this manner I did with the Pharoah's objectionable

---

* I simply can't help lifting this sentence clean out of Meredith's *Harry Richmond*; and I defy anyone to give a neater version of Mr. Crabbe's original, "ΟΠΩΣ ΜΗΤΕ ΑΝΤΙΣΤΗΣΕΙ ΜΟΙ: ΜΗΤΕ ΕΨΕΙ ΠΟΡΡΩΤΕΡΩ." – A.H.

private detective.

The Ninth Papyrus

NOW it seemed to me, when I pondered the thing, that it was a misfortune. For, when a wily stranger desires to pass through a foreign country for a certain secret purpose, it is but prudent for him to refrain from marking his road with homicides. Even my victory over Pyrrhos, though the Pharaoh would pension me for slaying his enemies, gave me notoriety instead of the oblivion which I preferred. But the matter of the face-marred Negro was indeed grave: for he was an officer of the Pharaoh. For which cause, I perceived that the blessed gods would have me in Tanis without delay, that I might find my friend there and perform my business in seclusion. For a man may seclude himself far more easily in a city (excepting in a certain city) than in the open country. So, for three days, I sailed in peace, resting my body, but contriving many new wiles.

But the possession of the barge and of the two slaves weighed upon me. For, having considered that I was going to a strange place, in search of one of whose existence in the flesh I had no actual knowledge, I determined that it is well (in all warfare) to provide a base for operations, and one which can he moved upon occasion. And it seemed to me that the barge and the slaves were precisely what I wanted. Yet I did not know whether they would serve me willingly at the end of the voyage for which they had been engaged; and, in a delicate matter, I will have none but willing and (indeed) devoted assistants. With these notions in my mind, therefore, I used winged words, questioning Nesamun and Yokkho while they piously shaved each other's heads. And I elicited that, when Nesamun's sister married the Argive bargeman at Thebes, the two mariners joined together in partnership, Nesamun being owner of the barge which I had on hire, and the three barges which we had left at Thebes being the property of his brother-in-law. Also, I learned that Yokkho was the son of another sister of Nesamun, both his parents being some time guests of the Divine Osiris in Amentet. Moreover, I learned that both were perfectly free to dispose of themselves as they pleased, and that on reaching Tanis nothing remained expected but that I should dismiss the youth and the boy with a gift, for they refused to take hire from a god: they, then, in the ordinary way, would convey another passenger upstream, returning to Thebes while I went back to heaven to attend to my godly affairs.

But, after I had heard all these things, and while I was weighing them in my mind, Nesamun and Yokkho crept nearer, laying themselves out at length on their faces very straight at my feet, and begging me not to send them away. And I, having considered their intelligence and fidelity not less than their agility and strength and quite singular comeliness, did not peremptorily deny them. For, in fact, the Nesamunity of Nesamun and the Yokkhoism of Yokkho were far from displeasing me.* Moreover, the words which Yokkho had intoned, when he looked into the palm-mirror, suddenly climbed out of my memory and buzzed at me. He, indeed, had chanted: *"The silver god, pointing at the galley, slays:"* and undoubtedly I (not old but silver-haired, and a god as they called me) had slain Pyrrhos and certain few on a galley, pointing my death-spitter at his eye. But that was only one of the things which the clear-seeing slave had predicted, being the first of his utterances; and, perchance, the others also would be fulfilled in their order. And I became sorrowful because I had smacked the clear-seer nor paid due heed to his sayings. But, calling on Memory for a really violent effort, I recollected the seven predictions, each in its turn, writing

---

* This sentence is exquisite in its justice. If we moderns only had the gumption to let ourselves be guided by the great natural law of Sympathy and Antipathy as naïvely as Mr. Crabbe appears to have done, how many failures, and (one can even say) tragedies, would be avoided. — A.H.

them in my hand-book; and I perceived that, next, the silver god would take a singing bow in a temple. Now, supposing myself to be the silver god, it was quite certain that I was about to visit a temple, seeking Amenemhat; and I opined that, there, I should engage in some adventure of a singing bow at the pleasure of the gods. Which adventure I began very eagerly to anticipate. But, meanwhile, Nesamun and Yokkho lay stretched at length before me in supplication.

And I determined that it would be greatly to my advantage to have the commodious barge at hand, as a base of operations, as a retreat, or as a means of retirement, should such be desirable. And I also determined that good slaves, who are willing slaves, are very hard to find, and (when found) ought to be cherished and used rather than rejected and wasted. And, lastly, I determined that these two, being well-made in mind and body, were very proper subjects for my magic arts, and likely to be of inestimable value. For which causes, I granted their petition. And, having bought their persons from themselves, paying two gold quarter-ounces to Nesamun for himself and one to Yokkho for himself, I bought also the barge and its apparatus from Nesamun for another gold quarter-ounce, all in the coinage of Victory queen of the stalwart stately Anglicans. And so we came nearer to Tanis.

But, during the last hour of my journey, I cut (from one of the Rhodian javelins) the little wooden emblem which none know save only the priests of Isis, without which none may penetrate the sanctuaries of temples. And I added it to the implements which I was to take with me on my quest of Amenemhat. And, having concealed all my other gear beneath the floor of my cabin in the presence of my slaves, in their view also (using my magic staff) I summoned the sons of slime, committing the charge of my goods to Nesamun and Yokkho, with a crowd of enchanted crocodiles for witnesses, whom anon I dismissed with the *Word.*

Thus we came to the last reach leading to Tanis which sits on both hythes of the river. But, skimming onward, we passed the little fane of Pasht, marking the site of the old city-wall which the hordes of Okhos had destroyed in the days when Nekt-Nebf was the Pharaoh. And we found a small quay below the city, secluded and abandoned, very suitable for a voyager desirous of privacy. But here my journey ended.

And, as soon as the barge was anchored, I sent Nesamun girded into the city to buy a length of fine linen, and to replenish my store of victuals and drink. Furthermore, I bade him to buy for me a necklace of heliotrope stones and a posy of fresh marigolds, for a new wile which I had invented. And, when the slave returned, I made a priest's surplice of fine linen, wherewith I vested my body, placing beneath it various convenient matters. But, when I appeared as a priest to them, I bade the slaves to clean the barge, and to pitch it within and without with pitch of Zakynthos (which pitch is the best), and also to keep it ready to start on a new voyage at a moment's notice either by day or by night.

Thus I spoke; and instantly I stepped ashore. But, when the two slaves popped their heads above the bulwark to observe my going, then, indeed, I rubbed the marigolds in my hand against the necklace of bloodstones which I wore, moistening the beads with the flower-juice; and, having made the proper *Act of Will*, I forthwith vanished away, simply becoming invisible at two paces' distance, and all in broad daylight. And this I did as very becoming to a god, and also to confirm them in fidelity, for a slave will not play his lord falsely when he has no certainty whether his said lord is here, or there.

In this manner, I came to Tanis.

The Tenth Papyrus

BUT I wended my way through the city, having taken my visible shape again in a dark entry. And I passed the walls and the gates, and the temples with their pylons, and quays thronged with merchants of all nations and slaves of all human color. And I saw the galleys of the Sidonians, and the light barks of the Sikels, with heavy merchant-ships from Rome, and Argive biremes and trading sloops. But a great quinquereme lay in the fairway of the mighty river; and it flew the royal purple standard of the Lagidai, denoting that a prince of Egypt was on board. And, everywhere about me were the insolent mercenaries of the flute-playing Pharaoh, standing in crowds: nor did any soldier stand alone, save the sentry on the great ship which swang at anchor in the current of the Tanitic branch of life-giving Sihor. Yet, great and busy as it appeared, Tanis had but a small part of the shadow of its former greatness when it was the chief city of the Lower Land. Slowly and surely had that greatness faded, as a well-painted wall fades unsheltered from the stress of storms in some northern land, when wind and rain wipe away the fresh pigment, leaving a tasteless thing behind.

But heavenly Ra poured down very hot radiance from the turquoise-colored vault of heaven; and the streets were crowded with evil-stenched mongrel folk, half-Argive, half-sons of Khem, mingled with the Hebrew hawkers who trot everywhere. And, because the mind in my lordly breast desired to pass a word with articulately-speaking men, I looked about for one with whom I might suitably address myself. And I selected a haughty Roman, wrapped in pride and a purple-bordered paludament, who surveyed the quays and the marketplace, while a slave sheltered his bare head with a sunshade of ostrich feathers. Whom I approached, intending to converse with him. And, coming nearer, while a squadron of Macedonians passed by, I heard the blameless creature muttering to himself in his own tongue, saying: "Gods! That men calling themselves soldiers should slouch in that manner! Perpol! But a cohort of ours would outmatch a legion of theirs!"

But I let the pride of race inflate me also, most superbly; and thus, in the Argive tongue, I saluted him, saying: "Hail, O senator. And how likest thou these mercenaries of the Lagidai?"

But he began to grow black fastidiously, because one unknown should have addressed him without introduction: but, when he saw how large I was and how assured my gait, he answered me in Latin, saying: "O man of the vast shoulders, whoever thou art, speak to me (I pray) in the language of Rome."

To whom I repeated my question as he wished. And he responded: "Indifferent well. But tell me, why dost thou (a stranger) dare to address me?"

"Thou," I said, "art not a god, that I should worship thee."

"But," he answered, "I am a Roman citizen."

Him I immediately coughed at, saying: "Never yet have I been told that Roman citizens are the gods whom men ought to worship."

Whereat, having blown off a little indignation, he laughed hugely; and would have known more of me; but I indifferently turned away to hire a litter in which I caused myself to be borne to the great temple of Isis.

But, when I reached that place, I began to walk very warily, making inquiry of the priest on duty in the portico. And, because the most wily way of dealing with earth-walking men, enmeshed with stupid petty deceits, is to be quite truthful and quite straight and never anything but bold, therefore, I instantly asked for my friend Amenemhat, priest of Tanis, who, being bound to me by sacred spells, would (with me) enjoy a mutual pleasure from a meeting. And, Amenemhat not being an uncommon name among Tanitic priests, if (perchance) my inquiry should bring to me one who was not the Amenemhat whom I desired to see, then I still possessed sufficient wisdom and magic apparatus for disposing of him in a suitable manner. On this account, I openly inquired for Amenemhat in the portico of the temple at Tanis.

And the watcher-priest answered, saying that Amenemhat was engaged in celebrating mysteries, and could not be seen at the moment. To whom I shewed the *Sign of the Peeping Thumb*, saying that I (also being a priest) would enter and pontificate with my friend. But the other still delayed me with gentle words, saying: "Sir, I do perceive that thou art a very notable mage and also an initiate priest possessing singular and admirable secrets: for, up thy sleeve, I see the silver chain which binds a master's staff to thy wrist. Nevertheless, our rites are so sacrosanct and so solemn that not even the high priest of Ra at Thebes may intervene in them. Wherefore, O master-mage, be propitious; and be pleased to repose thyself awhile in a cool room, refreshing thy body with fruit and wine: for the day is hot, and thou seemest to have come from very far."

But I agreed with alacrity, for my throat was twisted with thirst. Moreover, I saw something; and, beside, I well-knew the ways of priests, who always may be led by the nose by anyone wily enough to agree with them. And together we strolled into a cool antechamber, having an apsidal recess wherein we seated ourselves on cushions. And, over the recess, was carven a winged image of the Divine Ma, as above the Pharoah's throne, deep graven in the black rock of Syene and filled with fine red gold. But the watcher-priest, having named himself to me as Mensau, tapped the floor with his white ivory walking-staff; and acolyths of the temple, very straightly formed but plump, robed in fine linen, with their shaven heads roundly-shining and increasing the long blackness of their eyes, — these, indeed, brought trays of fruits and wines and a excellent beer of their own brewing. And, having laid them before us, they flitted away, leaving me alone with the priest. He seemed to be about my own age, whatever that may be: but he was straight in figure as the fragile Egyptians are, and his face was like smooth ivory, well-carved, wise and gentle of mien. And, having filled a cup of Korinthic bronze

(which is platinum)* to the brim with good red wine from a
well-chased Alexandrian flagon, he offered it to me. But I
chose beer: so he took it for himself; and, leaning toward me
watching him very warily, he began to speak, saying: "Health
to thee, O expected Wanderer."

But my wile was to lead him on, secretly compelling him
to shew me the way to the very root of the mystery, which I
had suspected, and now was assured of. Wherefore I, all
unmoved, responded, saying: "Health also to thee, O Mensau,
priest of Isis, who wearest the garb of a priest of Ptah
perchance for coolness' sake. And, as I perceive that thou
knowest me, tell me now how long will that other deny
himself to me."

"Dost thou then know me, O Nicholas?" he asked, sur-
prised, but smiling.

"Yea: I know well the Amenemhat who looketh out of thine
eye-holes. But thy form is strange to me:" I responded mag-
niloquently.

Thus I spoke. But the mind in my noble breast began all
of a sudden to tell me all sorts of things: so that I knew that
the form, in which I had known Amenemhat at Thebes, was
a form which I myself had given him by the merest haphazard
and in something like a violent hurry, having summoned
him from tiresome Amentet, to be my familiar, and being
unable to use him in the form of hot eyes and a jelly. And,
also, I knew that I never had seen him in his own form, which
his father and mother had made for him by the help of the
gods of his stars. And, having understood all these things, I
fell into a muse, because of the infinite number of causes and
effects which a seeker after wisdom must acquire, and arrange
in his mind ready for use at any moment.

But, even now, weighted and bedazzled as I was with
unthought-of wisdom, all was not quite clear to me. I, therefore, continued to speak, saying: "Nevertheless, O Amenemhat, though I know thee, and though I am beginning to know
thy real form which is other than that which I gave to thee
at Thebes, still, my mind is doubtful, not of the What, nor
of the Where. The dimension of Space is known to me: but

---

* Oh! Is it indeed? The statement (as it stands) is a little star-
tling though. — A.H.

what of Time? I understand the Categories of Substance, of Quantity, of Quality, of Relation, of Action, of Passion, of Place, of Position, of Possession: but I do not understand the When. Have I already lived and summoned thee from Amentet nineteen-hundred years hence? Am I living now another life nineteen centuries before I was born? Or is this all some dream and some weird vision in those secret halls of Thebes? Or what?"

"Nay," Amenemhat answered: "this is neither dream nor vision, but a special disposition of The Supreme, whereby thou, O Seeker after Wisdom, art granted experiences granted to no other man, as a reward for thy well-endured pains, and as a means of perfecting thee for some enormous purpose. And, to this end, I, whom thou hast known as a Sahu and an Osirian, have a message for thee, O Wanderer through the Ages. Doubt, then, no more: but take all things as the immortal gods are pleased to send them, always going onward cheerfully from one step to the next. For, know, that in Amentet, and in the Outer Immensities of Immeasurable Space, where The Supreme is, there is no such limitation as Time, nor any Impossibility to Him, or to Them His uncountable forms."

Thus he spoke; and again was silent. But I sat still, drinking the beer of Osiris, letting the wisdom of his words take root in my lordly mind. And anon I said: "This, then, indeed is the meeting of thy Theban prediction. But tell me, O Amenemhat, though thou didst expect me, by what means did these eyes of shine recognize me whom, formerly, thou didst see at Thebes with other eyes?"

"I recognized thee, O Nicholas," he said, "even at a distance, by thy stride and by the self-assurance of thy gait of the straightened knees: for no other man walketh as dost thou, as the owner and scorner of all worlds old and new. But, also, I saw the shape of the orb of divination in the folds of thy robe; and thou didst make the *Sign* and shew the staff of power."

And so we fell into more intimate conversation; and I told him all which had befallen me during my voyage down the river, of the slaying of that Pyrrhos (the most righteous of men), of the blameless* Ethiopian whose face I had spoiled, tearing also his hand (like a dirty rag) in twain; and I spoke of my two trusty slaves, and of all other matters which it was necessary for him to know. But, when I saw that he was not minded to make revelations to me on the instant, then, indeed, I determined to stay awhile with him, as a guest of the temple, pursuing my studies in the magic arts among holy mages whose business was none other, and waiting the pleasure of the blessed gods inhabiting olympian palaces.

Thus, then, I found Amenemhat in his body as he lived.

But, during this month of waiting on the will of the gods (for it was no more than that), a certain thing was done by me, at the suggestion and with the aid of Amenemhat, which I will set down here in its place. For, it being evident to both of us that my lot was to move through time, getting wisdom by living many lives in various circumstances, Amenemhat used to speak of the comfort which I should derive from constant companions throughout my wanderings. But I, knowing the sort of man which I am, and not by any means loving, used to respond to him saying, that it was not the perpetual companionship of an equal which would delight me, so much as the perpetual readiness of comely and trustworthy and affectionate slaves, whose services I could command at pleasure or neglect if I thought well so to do. But Amenemhat, having perceived the alert intelligent faithful minds and the pleasing and powerful bodies of Nesamun and Yokkho, inquired whether such as these would suit me. To whom I answered, saying, that I had them in my mind when thus speaking. Wherefore, Amenemhat suggested that I should perform the two magics called *The Soul-Loosening* and *The Life-Binding*, whereby the silver cords which tied the said Nesamun and Yokkho to their present forms might be loosed, so that (at a moment's notice) they might migrate to other forms of my invention, and, also, that by binding their lives to my life, the said slaves might accompany me into whatsoever other lives The Supreme might have in store for me and them.

But I, when I had pondered the matter, found it very

‡ This repeated use of these epithets "the most righteous of men," and "blameless" is, of course, obviously, an example of Greek irony. — A.H.

desirable indeed. For which cause, having obtained the con-
sent of the two, very gleefully given when (without any
concealment) I described the whole project to them, for
(beside being fearless and very eager for adventures) they
deemed me godlike, and desired nothing less than to be left
behind when I should go forward, then, having brought them
to a sacred part of the vast temple, where their screams would
be inaudible, I and Amenemhat did what was necessary on
the bodies, first of little Yokkho, and then of Nesamun, in
such a dexterous manner that they suffered not more pain
than they could bear without swooning: but I shall not
describe the process on account of a religious reason. Nor
could any earth-walking man, mage or simple, find out any
difference in them afterward, unless (by chance) he should
hap upon the tiny and almost invisible silver-colored puncture in the rosy breast-flower (but which one it was of their
breast-flowers I decline to indicate, for both breast-flowers are
punctured on both of them, yet only one puncture on each
of them is an exit), through which Nesamun and Yokkho
became able to leave their Egyptian bodies, and to follow me
through time, as easily as they could leave my barge by the
deserted quay and follow me through the streets of Tanis.

In this manner, I prepared myself and them for a new
migration.

The Eleventh Papyrus

*B*UT it was well that the thing was done when it was well-done. For, a few months later, the occasion for departure occurred.

Now I had been very diligently studying such magic of the Tanitic priests as I did not know, to fill up the interval until Amenemhat should be moved by the blessed gods to deliver his message. And, among other matters where improvement seemed desirable, it was put into my mind to try a new method of embalming the dear remains of the dead, which method (I believed and believe) not only prevents the mummy from shriveling and going black or dry or discolored in any way, but also preserves the exact freshness of appearance and condition which it had enjoyed while used as the temporary vesture of the soul, excepting the condition of life. But, because I found it unwise to make my experiments on the corpses of persons who had spoiled the pristine beauty of their bodies by overlong or overarduous usage, I and Amenemhat preferred those of such acolyths of the temples whose souls well-plumed Thoth had been directed to escort elsewhere without first afflicting their forms with loathsome diseases. But, because all the temples of Tanis supplied no more than two such corpses within the month, Amenemhat sent both wind-messages and ibis-messages to other temples of other cities stating our needs. And, when we had treated without emptying eight well-made blooming bodies, with imperishable quintessences of unmentionable virtue and in-conceivable fragrance, then we anointed them nine times in every part, under the nine proper stars, using a liquid un-

guent, preservative, which perseveres through all time and
disgusts worms. But the fame of our handicraft went abroad,
so that all the hierarchies of Khem desired to have their dead
acolyths mummied in the new manner for the benefit of the
temples. For which cause, it happened that I went to Alexandria in my barge to inspect a corpse so perfect that I brought
it away with me, intending to treat it; and, on my return, I
became embroiled in the streets of Tanis after this wise.

The priests attending Amenemhat had taken the beautiful
body from my barge and were gone on their way to the temple
of Isis. But I remained behind during a little while, inspecting
the diligence of my slaves, well-shaven, performing prescribed
purifications. And anon, later in the evening, I proceeded by
quiet byways toward the temple where Amenemhat awaited
me. But, on my way, I encountered a troop of land mercenaries, blameless Sithonians and Mygdonians, escorting the litter
of one of the Lagidai, a brother of the Pharoah's favorite wife.
And they were rudely brushing everyone from their path, not
being at all affable. But by chance, a certain aged philosopher,
Melkas by name, who taught daily in the porch of the
Serapion, was about to cross the road. His eyes were dim, his
step infirm, his pace tardy and grave. Wherefore, I tried to
help him into the shadow of a portico; and did so, but not
before a Sithonian, seeing the length of my arms, had yelled
at me, clipping the Argive tongue, "Ho, there, Ape-man, stand
aside before thy betters!"

But instantly divine anger inflamed my lordly mind. And
boldly affronting the mocker, I broke the crust of his blameless face to pulpy fragments with fist-blows, as a bear in
spring-time breaks a delicate egg. But the puny prince in the
litter ordered his guards to seize me; and half-a-dozen rash
Mygdonians hastened with an obedient start to obey. Then,
indeed, the fierce and frolicsome joy of Saint Aldate's or the
Cowley Empire on a Saturday night* came upon me, so that

---

* Written in English, in what I take to be Mr. Crabbe's own
hand. "Saint Aldate's" was, of course, a low acatholic par-
ish of Oxford, near Pembroke and The House, and much
frequented by monsignori and other catholic converts, and
I believe that no particular rashness can be attributed to
me for saying that there was also a slightly excessive music

I delayed not, but I simply smashed the first four faces using my left fist and my right like flails or sledge-hammers; and, snatching a falling shield and mightily sweeping with it, I shattered the shins of the others as they came on. Now, when they saw these things, the shrieking slaves fled, having dropped the litter. But I, by this time, had got into my stride, becoming very methodical in my fury: for which cause I determined to leave nothing important undone. Wherefore, I butted the prince out of his tangled curtains, and rolled him about with my feet in a pool of foul slime which happened to be near by. And, all things necessary having been accomplished, I went upon my way with a calm and holy mind. Nor did I bestow another thought to the matter. And indeed no one gave me news of it: for the city, in those last days of the Lagidaian dynasty, was a scene of incessant disorder; and a few messes more or less, found in the streets at dawn, were by no means uncommon. But, after four days, Amenemhat suddenly interrupted my studies, crying: "Fly, O Nicholas, to the secret chamber in the shrine: for the Pharoah's mercenaries are upon thee."

Thus he spoke. But I proceeded, without more ado, to the secret door; and, when I stamped on the right, it slid ajar, so that I could squeeze by, and sidle sideways along the narrow passage which led to the secret chamber. Now this secret chamber was a very wily one; and it was constructed after this manner: by the hollowing-out of one of the pillars which surrounded the shrine, but the pillar itself was (like all the others) carved into the similitude of an important god. And, inside the hollow of it (from the secret crypt beneath the temple floor in which I was), there ascended a very narrow ladder of twisted linen threads leading up into the secret chamber in the skull of the god. But, at the top of the ladder,

---

hall, called (quaintly enough) the "Empire" in the "Cowley" Road, Oxford. But I really feel quite unable to elucidate the allusion in this connection. Saturday-night is, of course, the eve of the day of the sun; and perhaps we have here some cryptic allusion to sun-worship, which (we know) was certainly of an hilarious and somewhat energetic character. *Cf.* Frazer's chapter on Osiris and the Sun: *Studies in Oriental Religion*, vii. 287-294. — A.H.

there was contrived a small seat like a saddle, so ordained that anyone sitting thereon in the skull, having pulled up the ladder, was very much separated from earth-walking men; and might (at will) speak through the orifice of the god's mouth quite safely, and also might see plainly all which happened in the temple, looking downward. And the place was used in the following manner. For the priests of the temple, being seated on the saddle and speaking awfully through the mouth of the god, delivered themselves of oracles imparted to them by the Divine Ones, or of revelations which they obtained in their trances or by sacred magic on account of a religious reason. Such, then, was the secret chamber.

But the lower part of the hollow pillar being dark, a studio of spiders, a thoroughfare of mice, and an abode of most holy beetles, I made haste to ascend to the saddle, pulling the ladder after me. And, being there conveniently ensconced, I perceived Amenemhat hurriedly entering the temple by the priest's door; and, having seated himself in his proper pulpit, he instantly began to intone the litanies, beginning in the middle so that an interrupter (I suppose) might imagine that he had been thus occupied for some time. He, therefore shook the sacred sistrum, saying:

"Homage to thee, O lord of the star-gods in An and of heavenly beings in Khez-aba, O thou god Unti more glorious than those gods hidden in Annu:

"Homage to thee, O Heru, thou dweller in both horizons, who, enormously striding, stridest over heaven, thou dweller in both horizons:

"Homage to thee, O soul of everlastingness, O soul who dwellest in Tattu, O Un-nefer son of Nut, thou lord of Akert:

"Homage to thee, in thy dominion over Tattu, the feathery crown is stablished on thy head, thou art the one whose strength is in himself:

"Homage to thee, O lord of the acacia tree, who settest the boat upon its sledge, who turnest back the ill-working friend, who causest the eye to rest:

"Homage to thee, mighty in thy moment, great god dwelling in An-rut-f, lord of eternity, creator of everlastingness, lord of Suten-henen:

"Homage to thee, who restest upon right and truth, O lord of Abtu whose limbs are joined to Ta-sertet, to whom fraud and guile are

hateful:

"Homage to thee in thy boat, who bringest Hapi from his source, on whose body light shineth, O dweller in Nek-hen:

"Homage to thee, O creator of the gods, O king of the north and of the south, O Osiris, O victor, O lord and ruler of the world in thy gracious seasons."

And, having met with no interruption at the time when he finished these beautiful imprecations, Amenemhat shook the sacred sistrum more loudly, and went on with the *Address to the Rudders,* saying:

"Hail, thou lovely power, thou lovely rudder of the northern heavens:

"Hail, thou pilot of the world, thou lovely rudder of the western heavens:

"Hail, thou shining one who livest with the gods in visible forms, thou lovely rudder of the eastern heavens:

"Hail, thou dweller in the temple of those with shiny faces, thou lovely rudder of the southern heavens."

And, because the expected intrusion of profane persons was still delayed, when he had chanted these strophes, Amenemhat shook the sacred sistrum very slowly and very solemnly, and continued with the Invocation of the Triads, thus:

"Hail, ye gods who are above the earth, ye pilots of the netherworld:

"Hail, ye mother-gods, who are above the earth, and in the netherworld, and in the house of Osiris:

"Hail, ye pilot-gods of Tasert, who are above the earth, and in the netherworld, and with the followers of Ra in the train of Osiris —"

But, when he had intoned these words, the quiet rattling of the sistrum and the monotonous drone of his voice were drowned by the clanking of arms, and by the blameless cries of mercenaries, appearing at the cedar portal of the temple. Whom Amenemhat, reverend of mien and very hierarchic, sternly confronted from his pulpit, saying: "Who dareth thus to intrude upon the sacrosanct shrine of Mother Isis?"

But the answer came from one, whom I (from my secret station) perceived to be an Argive of noble aspect, large of limb, and handsome, and very gorgeously appareled in golden mail with adornments of chrysoliths and the plumage of yellow cock-parrots. He responded to Amenemhat, saying: "I am called Agesilopodes, son of Golygosthenes, and I am a captain of the Pharoah's guard."

"And what doth Agesilopodes, servant of the Pharaoh, seek in these holy precincts?" Amenemhat continued.

"I seek the person of one Ape-man, whose trail we have pursued hither!" the Khrysaspid affirmed.

"Thou seest," said the priest indifferently, "how many persons are present occupying our pews."

"I see but thee!" quoth the captain: "but nevertheless I must search in the shadows of all the most secret recesses."

"The rule," said Amenemhat, "is that the sons of Khem may have free access to this oratory of our Lady of the Marshes, but not aliens, undesirable or otherwise."

"But the Ape-man whom I seek is guilty of sacrilege."

"Even in that case, he would have secure sanctuary here, unless he be pursued by the Pharoah's own sigil."

"Revere it:" said the captain, exhibiting his warrant.

Amenemhat had a prostration at the sight of the royal but tipsy flute-player's cartouche. But, having (by his wiles) caused the mercenaries to persuade themselves that they were on a bootless quest, he permitted the search to be made. Macedonians and Thrakians marched slowly round the temple, casting fierce glances into every dark place: but Amenemhat seated himself again in his pulpit, his knees closed and his palms upon them, his head up and his eyes fixed, as a hierarch who engages in holy meditation while expecting the imposition of his miter.

But I devised a new and perfectly frightful wile. For, having taken three wax matches from my box, and having frayed out the half of each match, wrapping the frayed part round the head loosely, as the men of my future race were wont to do when they desired to kindle tobacco in a gale of wind, then, indeed, I kindled them; and I dropped them, one by one and horribly flaming, from the god's mouth on to the plumed casques of mercenaries who (by chance) were walking just below. And their horse-hair crests instantly shriveled with appalling stenches, in flashes of fire which singed the soldiers' hairy faces, terribly, inexplicably: so that they fled, fearfully yelling, having a most hideous tale, about gods who vomit fire, to narrate to their awful comrades in their barracks.

In this manner, I dismissed well-greaved mercenaries (the

most righteous of men) from the temple of Isis at Tanis.

The Twelfth Papyrus

 BUT, when the place was clear, then, indeed, I waited where I was, till Amenemhat should leave his pulpit, giving me a signal to descend and join him. For he directed my actions at this juncture; and it seemed to me that he, being at liberty, understood what to do for my security better than I in my cell. But, after I had waited an hour, stiffness invaded my members and tedium my noble mind. Wherefore, seeing that the temple was deserted, and that Amenemhat still remained motionless in meditation, I came down from the secret chamber, retracing my steps, and entering the shrine by the priests' door. But, having approached my friend, addressing him softly by name, I perceived that he was indeed rapt in an ecstasy, and (no doubt) receiving a peculiar revelation from some god. At whose pulpit I stood, watching intensely, having no more fear.

And anon he came out of his trance, with the usual eye-rollings and shiverings and deep sighings for the long-unused breath. But, when his returning gaze lit on me, he began to sob very quietly in the manner of a man, shedding no tears; and that is the most horrible of all things to see. But I was aware, from these tokens, that he had had a revelation concerning me and portending a parting. For which cause I treated him tenderly, saying nothing.

And, at length, he descended from his pulpit; and, having led me a long way into the innermost recesses of the temple, into a large hall which I never yet had seen, wherein were numerous unheard-of matters, then, he began to speak. But his words were unwinged; and thus he said: "O Nicholas, the hour of thy departure is at hand. For, since the Pharoah's mercenaries have invaded this sacred place, it will be insecure for thee as also for us. For there will be a blameless guard continually about our walls; and, though thou mayst leave once by the secret postern, thou couldst not do so more than once; and it is not in thy nature to brook confinement. Also, as long as the guards remain, the shrine of the goddess will be deserted and her gifts wasted for lack of receivers. Wherefore thou needs must go. But, before thou goest, know that the well-feathered shiny gods have deigned to give me an order concerning thee and to send thee a message by my mouth, whereby thy mind may be enlightened about mysteries of the past and a foresight of thy future revealed to thee."

But I, hearing this, perceived that very fine solemnities were on hand. Wherefore I listened attentively.

And Amenemhat continued his discourse, saying: "Thou knowest, O Wanderer, who thou art and whence thou camest: but thou knowest not who thou hast been, nor who thou shalt be. But, these are the matters on which I am to give thee information. For thou, Nicholas the Third, called the Crab, who art come from the kingdom of Victory queen of the stalwart stately Anglicans, knowest no more of thine ancestors than the names of Nicholas the First who was father of Robert who was father of William who was father of Nicholas the Second who was father of thy gentle father James. Nevertheless, thou (having been brought backward through the rolling wheels of time) shalt know that it is the inscrutable will of the blessed gods to make thee aware of him who was thy primal sire. And he is none other than Laertes, lord of rocky Ithaka, whose wife Antikleja was the daughter of Aytolikos, whom wing-footed Hermes the Luck-bringer begat."

But I began to understand all sorts of riddles, and many mysteries indeed were being solved. But the priest was uttering his rede with the tones of one inspired; and I eagerly lent him both my ears. And Amenemhat pursued his revelation, saying: "Furthermore, O Wily One, thou art to know this. For, seeing that the much-enduring much-contriving son of King Laertes, having wandered far by sea and land during the ten years following after the siege of windy Ilion, set out once again on another wandering (but wherefore I do not know);

and was slain here, at the mouth of sacred Sihor, by young Telegonos, his own son and Kirke's (that awful goddess), ignorant of whom he slew, now, therefore, it is the will of those divine ones who have never lost their faces that thou, Nicholas called the Crab, shouldst pursue thy quest for wisdom reincarnate in thine original person as King Odysseys, undertaking a third wandering, the course of which is not yet known to me: but it will be known by me, and revealed by me to thee, in the moment when thou farest forth. For the thing is yet on the knees of the gods."

But, when Amenemhat had said all this, the Anglican portion of me suggested the placing of some term to such seemingly nonsensical ravings. For which cause, I said, as stolidly as possible: "When shall I, Nicholas called the Crab, find myself reincarnate as King Odysseys for the purpose named?"

And the priest solemnly answered, saying: "Thou art Odysseys, even now."

To whom I said: "I require proof of the truth of thy word."

But Amenemhat drew back a veil which was concealing a picture painted on the wall. And he said: "See here, now, O Wily One, for this is a copy of that portrait of Odysseys Laertiades which is in the temple of Herakles at Naykratis, a precious possession. Art thou like it, or does it resemble thee, O thou from whom it was painted?"

And certainly the piece did exactly resemble me, with my long arms and legs and my silver hair and my well-sunned skin and the shy fierce ruthlessness of my visage. But I was not overanxious to begin another life at that moment; and, for this cause, I would not be convinced: but I believed that the priest was deceiving me with a portrait painted from myself secretly, for I had never seen the portrait at Naykratis. But seeing myself likely to be brought to a full stop in the matter, I determined to use my magic art as a means of arriving at the truth.

And, casting a severe glance at Amenemhat, I withdrew my attention from him as one unworthy. But he waited, calmly, placidly, saying nothing.

But I took from my robe my orb of divination, of rock-crystal banded with silver with adornments of blue moon-

stones; and, having placed it properly, I peered into its illimitable profundity. And all within was blank and void. But I
made an act of will, willing to see the Naykratian portrait as
it was. And instantly it filled the crystal void. And, having
compared it with the picture on the wall, I was aware that
they were alike in every particular. But I gazed again into the
crystal, making another act of will, willing to see Odysseys
Laertiades in his habit as he lived. And instantly I saw him
there. And, having compared him with the picture on the
wall, I was aware that it was as like to him in every particular
as it was like to me.

But I returned the crystal to its place, and drew forth my
magic staff, signing the priest with it, and reciting the *Spell*
called *Compelling Truth*. And I inquired of him, saying: "Who
am I?"

And he answered me: "Odysseys Laertiades."

But I inquired of him again, saying: "Who have I been?"

And he answered me: "Nicholas, called the Crab."

But I inquired of him yet again, saying: "Who shall I be?"

And he answered me: "After many lives thou shalt be once
more Nicholas, called the Crab."

Wherefore I knew that these things were somehow so. And
I gave him leave to continue. He, then, said: "O Very Wily
One, proofs thou desirest; and proofs thou shalt have, of a
sort. Dost thou remember thy bow, the black bow of Eyrytos,
which none can bend save thyself or a god? And dost thou
remember thy sword, the sword of Eyryalos? I ask, for reasons.
For, after thy death near Sihormouth, thy weapons were
placed on the breast of thy corpse to go with thee to the
netherworld; and, when thy funeral-pyre was lighted, the
flames leaped up, and blazed, and died to embers: but thy
deathless soul was departed (where, I know not, nor dost thou
definitely); and there were no ashes of thy body: which things
are a mystery all. But thine arms and thy bow and thine
armor, having been forged by a god, could not perish. And,
now, thou art here; and they too rest here in the secret
treasury, waiting for thee to assume them again, O much-contriving King Odysseys, Sacker of Cities."

But, indeed, if any mind-perplexing doubt had remained
to me, this would have sufficed to dismiss it. For I was aware

that the prediction of my slave, Yokkho, when he said: *The silver god, in the temple, taking the bow which sings,* was about to be fulfilled. And I arose, following Amenemhat with a joyful mind.

But he led me into a yet larger hall, having row upon row of ungraven columns. And everywhere there were vast heaps of gold and silver ingots well-builded, with vases and cups and tripods of gold and silver and Korinthic bronze, which is platinum,* and sheaves of ivory-handed spears with adornments gold and chrysoprase, armor and shields of gold, elephants' tusks of monstrous dimensions, fillets of gems,

---

* This is rather worrying. Everyone knows that, before the reign of David, there was in Asia a plenty of a third precious and perfect metal: that Tyrians and Phoinikians founded and worked it till the reign of Salomon: that there were rich deposits of it in the Atlantis, where it was excavated, founded, and worked: that it was heavier and more valuable than either gold or silver: that it had most of the qualities of gold, but was something of the color of silver: that it was capable of high polish, the Romans using it for lamp-reflectors: that the Hebrews called it *Khasmal* = White Metal, and the Greeks called it *Elektron* or *Khalkolibanon,* or *Orikhalkon:* that it became rare through barbarian incursion and the submergence of the Atlantis: that it was imitated by a mixture of gold and silver by the Korinthians, the native metal (which they originally manipulated) being practically lost. Strabo (III.) and Pliny (Proem. xxxiii.) say that there was enough of this metal found in the sands of the Po in Trajan's time to form a statue of Augustus. Many other writers preserve its memory, *e.g.* Saint Ezekhiel Prophet, i. 4, 7: Homer, *Od.2 IIII. 71, XV. 458: Vergil, Georg.* III. 521: *AEn.* VIII. 402, V. 624: Martial, VIII. 50: Sil. It., I. 229: Stat. *Thebaid:* Juv. *Sat.* xiii.: Serenus Samm. *De Uenenis:* Serv. *Georg.:* Lamprid. *Heliog. Cf.* also Aristophanes' *Knights,* and Sophokles' praise of the White Metal (ελεκτρον) of Sardis with gold of India. But, even now I see no particular connection (excepting in Mr. Crabbe's mind) between modern platinum (which only exists, I am told, in the other hemisphere), and the undeniable White Metal (which the ancients called Elektron or Korinthic Bronze) which disappeared, I conceive, in the earthquake engulphing the lost Atlantis. The problem is a sadly distracting one. – A.H.

and ropes of pearls. But we passed through, into a smaller hall of a circular shape, having an altar in the center, whereon lay an enormous shield of silver, carved with various devices and set with crabs and moons in very pure nonagonal prismatic rock-crystals with balls of rock-crystal and blue moonstone. There, also, was a mighty helmet of the same, plumed with the lofty-waving prides of nine white peacocks. There, also, was a short sword, in a silver scabbard inlaid with similar rock-crystals and blue moonstones. There, also, was a vast black bow of a totally unheard-of material, with a quiver decorated like the scabbard and full of fear-inspiring arrows. There, also, on the altar-steps, were greaves of silver gloriously carven, with adornments of rock-crystals and blue moonstones, and a breast-plate with the back-plate and shoulder-pieces of the same so bespattered with moony gems that they resembled gigantic dewdrops on a frosty field seen in the clear of the full moon. And, also, a large bundle wrapped in white buckskin was lying at the foot of the altar.

And, when I had looked upon these things, Amenemhat thus addressed me, saying: "These are thy god-forged silver armor and thy god-carven bow and sword, O Odysseys. Take then thy bow and make a trial."

But, when I took the great bow in my hand, it quivered and thrilled, singing a marvelous mystic melody; and thus it sang:

"Hail King Odysseys,
  long hast thou left me,
  long have I lain here
  waiting in silence:
  wars loom before us:
  blood will pour over us:
  death flieth with us:
  take me, O Master,
  and slay as of yore."

But, having drawn a well-winged arrow from the quiver, I passed again into the great hall of the secret treasury; and Amenemhat followed me, holding aloft his lanthorn; and rays of light from it flamed upon a shield of burnished gold

at the far end of the hall. But, though never (to my remembrance) had I handled a bow since I, a little eager scolded and
mocked-at child, played my own solitary fantastic games in
the kingdom of Victory queen of the stalwart stately Anglicans, nevertheless I bended and strang the huge black bow of
Eyrytos with the skillful ease of an expert. And the back-bent
bow throbbed in my hand as though it were alive, itself taking
aim at the shield-navel. And the shaft sped forth, shrieking
and humming in the air, till it buried its length in the boss
of the burnished shield. And, having done what no man but
one man can do, I doubted no long but that I actually was
King Odysseys, the Wily One, Sacker of Cities, the Wanderer,
the grandson of Divine Wing-footed Hermes.

Amenemhat said: "Verily, thou art the lord of rocky
Ithaka."

And to him I answered, saying: "Yea: that I am."

But, returning to the inner treasury, I stripped myself all
stark, and put on the god-forged armor of yellow-haired
great-hearted Akhilleys, which, formerly, my agile feet had
won from Ajas son of Telamon, arming myself with the
glittering silver.* First, indeed, I put on the beautiful greaves
round my legs, well-fitting to the clasps. Next, I covered my
body with the white leathern kirtle having taslets of carven
silver about my loins, which Ares himself had worn. But I
clothed myself over it with a kirtle of silver mail. Next, I
placed on my breast and back and shoulders the corslet of
swift-footed Akhilleys, wrought by Hephaistos himself at the
behest of Thetis of the sea; and the silver shining of it went
to a great distance, as of the moon. And I hanged from my
shoulders the silver-sheathed sword, gleaming with moony
gems, and also the well-carven quiver of arrows. And, on my
head, I set the well-made helmet, crested with the lofty waving
prides of nine white peacocks; and dreadfully the plumage
nodded from above. And I took, beside, the bow which sings,

---

* Hitherto we have been led to believe that Akhilleys' armor
was golden, not silvern as here emphatically stated. Perhaps our error is due to the lamentable fact that all our
classical texts have been edited by tasteless and not highly
scrupulous Dutchmen, so far. I just throw out the suggestion. — A.H.

well-fitted to my hand, and then the huge and sturdy shield, whereon Hephaistos had wrought, in silver and rock-crystals and blue moonstones, earth, and heaven, and sea, and the unwearied sun, and the full moon, and all the constellations crowning heaven, the Pleiades, the Hyades, and the strength of Orion, and the Bear or the Wain which there revolves watching Orion, but it alone descends not into the baths of the ocean. But Amenemhat shod my feet with sandals of white leather, buckled with silver studded with moony gems. And he covered me with a great trailing mantle, of silver tissue lined with white fur, having a huge silver clasp of the crab and the moon. And the sheen of me reached to heaven; and all the earth around smiled in the splendor of the silver; and a sound like the trampling of men's feet arose. But I stood in the midst, gnashing my teeth, and my eyes shone like a blaze of white fire.

These things having been duly accomplished, Amenemhat left me while he went about my business: for, indeed, the occasion was one for operating very mighty and singular magic, whereby I, King Odysseys, might be sent on my new quest suitably attended and in kingly fashion, and not without my gear. But, when it was night, the priest returned to me contriving wiles; and he said that all things were ready. For he had prepared for me one of the temple-galleys, a stout ship builded in the yards of Alexandria, pierced for forty oars, twenty a side in a single old-fashioned bank. And he had manned the galley with rowers and slaves, whom he gave to me as a sweet guest-gift: but one Deythes was the master-mariner. And the galley rode at anchor in mid-stream, ready to sail.

But, at midnight, having gathered all my goods which were in the temple, and having rubbed my necklace of blood-stones with marigold-juice so that I became invisible, I went down with Amenemhat to my barge by the desolate quay; and I shewed myself without warning in my brilliant panoply to Nesamun and Yokkho. And, when they had finished their adorations (for they naturally adored the silver god), then, indeed, I and Amenemhat did the magic which we had prepared, giving to my two slaves new forms with new names, whereby Nesamun came out of his Egyptian body, becoming

Neandros, an Argive, and squire to me, and Yokkho came in turn out of his Egyptian body, becoming Thalos, an Argive also, and foot-boy to me. And the magic was done perfectly, nor was there any unusual noise.

But, when we had bestowed the evacuated Egyptian bodies upon the enchanted sons of slime, the mind in my dear breast was perplexing me concerning two further matters. For, I knew not what worthy gift I could give to Amenemhat as a parting blessing; and, also, I was aware that I desired to have something more in my slaves than that which they already possessed, to wit, their ingenious minds, faithful and fearless, which the gods of their stars had bestowed upon them, and the comely Argive forms wherewith I myself by my magic art had endowed them. But then, indeed, suddenly, a very singular and unheard-of thought illumined my noble mind, which bade me to use a most potent magic enchantment of another age (and I never had used it before, though I was fully competent in the circumstances), performing a sacred lavation, pouring a handful of Nile-water upon Amenemhat, and upon Neandros, and upon Thalos, saying over each in turn the *Spell of the Three Who are One.* Thus, then, I did. And the faces of the priest and of the slaves whitened, becoming strangely purified and thankful, unknowing. But I know all.

And, now that the time was come when I must part from Amenemhat, we two drew away to a darker corner of the desolate quay. But the haughty wise eyes of the priest were full of unshed tears; and he spoke in the secret tongue of the priests of Khem, saying: "Never, O Odysseys, shall we meet again, neither in this life nor in another, till the cycles of our opportunities shall be fulfilled. But to thee I give the galley and her crew, slaves; and I have placed a certain treasure in the hold for thy use and comfort. Take them, O friend, as a sweet guest-gift. And, so, fare thee well, O King Odysseys, whom may all gods of sea and land and air and sky have in prime and perpetual favor. And this is the message which I have in charge to give thee at parting: *From the Depths of the Dead, thou shalt win back the Treasure of Hades.*"

Thus he spoke; and, having embraced me, he went his own way.

But I ascended my barge; and, when Neandros and Thalos

had rowed me to my galley, I mounted the lofty poop, to see my goods brought aboard, and the empty barge sent adrift, for it was no longer useful to me. But I gave commands to Deythes, my shipman, that he should shape a course for Sihormouth and, so, out to the open sea.

Thus I did, leaving the land of Khem, and beginning a new quest.

The Thirteenth Papyrus

WHEN white Dawn was come, I left the small Pharos behind. Sihor had become brackish; and a favorable breeze drove us out on to the unvintaged sea. My galley was indeed meet for a king: for all her fitments were of cedar inlaid with silver and mother-of-pearl. Her food-service also was of well-chased ephesian silver; and her sail and her awnings were of thick white silk with vermilion bordures and fringes. Furthermore, my master-mariner, Deythes son of Kimon of Naxos, was an honest man, an islander, as well as a mariner of much favor with the Divine Ones who inhabit olympian palaces; and he had never lost a ship. Wherefore, being aware that my equipage was quite worthy of me and of my destiny, I was glad.

But, when I came to ponder Amenemhat's last prediction, I could not understand it; and it behooved me to understand it very speedily, in order that I might contrive new wiles and suitable: for, at the moment, I was sailing the open sea without a notion as to my destination.

For which cause, I tried my crystal orb of divination: but I saw nothing therein. But, having next refreshed my memory concerning the things which Thalos (who had been Yokkho) saw in the palm-mirror, I read in my notebook these words: *The silver god, in the ship, speaking with the azure-haired god on the white horses.* And that I might know more about this azure-haired god on the white horses, of whom the innocent eager slave had spoken, I performed the rite of the palm-mirror a second time, having summoned clear-eyed Thalos to me. But he saw nothing in the ink, though he gazed into it and sweated till he swooned from sheer exhaustion. But I was aware, having restored him and having given him to be treated tenderly, that a far greater magic was necessary to explain his utterance and the utterance of Amenemhat, to wit: *The silver god, in the ship, speaking to tile azure-haired god, on the white horses, and From the Depths of the Dead thou shalt win back the Treasure of Hades.* And, when the mother of Dawn, rosy-fingered Morning, was about to come again, bringing light to mortals and immortals, then my galley was alone upon the bluish-grey-green sea.

But I was resolved to try the *Rite of Thalattomancy,* which is most efficacious; and it may only be performed by a master and prince of the highest degree and most secret initiation and by a sacred ruler of the innermost light. To which end, I caused Nile-water and other proper apparatus to be placed on the lofty poop; and I made a proclamation to my crew, lest curiosity should overcome fear and obedience, that death in shreds (lasting some hours) would be the lot of an interrupter of my solitude in the sight of all. And, having bathed and arrayed myself in my silver panoply, I opened the rite.

Within the square of four pentagons, I drew the four concentric circles with white chalk on the lofty poop-deck, filling them with the proper names. Within these, I drew also the double circle for ebb and flow. And, within the last, I placed a dish of offerings to the seven sea-gods and the silver divination-cup brimming with Nile-water. But I stood between them, wearing the symbols of the Crab and the Moon: for the Crab is a watery sign, and the Moon is the Governess of the Sea. And, having called on the gods of the sea and the moon to be propitious, I burned aloes in a brazier, and I chanted the *Spell* which releases the souls of the drowned from their torments in the netherworld, providing the forms of birds for clothing them, and treating them to a taste of fresh air, so that (with their wings) they might veil the apparition of a favoring sea-god, an aboundingly holy awful sight not to be viewed excepting by initiates, as it is written: *It is not necessary for the novice to believe anything, but only to sacrifice his little pig.*

But the cries of my birds, rejoicing in freedom for an hour, came nearer and nearer; and they circled round me closely and more closely, till I seemed to be enclosed in a pillar like a cylinder of whirling wings. And, at the moment of sunrise, the spirits of the moon came knocking at the gates of the waves to summon the divine ones of the sea. But those spirits were of a great and full body, soft and phlegmatic, of color like a cloud, black, morbid, obscure, having swelling countenances and aspects ready to melt away like an exceeding great rain about the circles. And their particular shapes were a king like an archer riding on a doe, and a little boy, and a woman-hunter with a bow and arrows, and a cow, and a little doe, and a vermilion and silver garment, and many white horses having finny feet.

Then, I seized the cup of divination by both handles, crying aloud the magic *Spell*, and saying:

"Let him come in the boat. And the name of the boat is Assembler of Souls.

"Let him core with the oars. And the name of the oars is Making The Hair To Stand On End.

"Let him come from the hold. And the name of the hold is Good.

"Let him come lay the rudder. And the name of the rudder is Making Straight For The Middle.

"Let him come with the mariners. And the name of the mariners is The Divine Ones Who Have Found Their Faces.

"Let the master-mariner come. And the name of the master-mariner is The Divine One Who Has Never Lost His Face."

And I held out the cup of divination over the sea, flinging the water of sacred Sihor in a hemicycle of crystal drops as far as I could reach. But the cloud of birds moved away with it; and hovered above a billow with an agitated crest, which they surrounded with innumerably-feathered pinions. Whereby I was aware that a godlike form was manifesting himself in that direction. And, the dawn being fully come, I recited the *Invitation to the gods of the sea*, using the tongue of the gods.

Then, the answer arrived, very thin and clear, like a cock-crow far away in the stillness of a desert-night, saying: *Receive the azure-haired Earth-shaker from the sea.*

And the breeze instantly moaned and died; and the waves ceased from lapping against my galley. And my sea-birds made a great confusion in the awful calm, filling it with flashing pinions and plaintive whimperings, and settling into the shape of a dome all formed of beating wings, in which I on my ship and the tridentiferous god of the sea were enclosed, face to face.

The floor of the temple of this blessed vision was the marbled water of the rushing sea, frozen mute and motionless with awe. Throned upon white horses ramping along a curling-crested billow, was the form of wide-ruling sea-stilling earth-shaking Poseidon, king of the ocean, with his court of white-bodied nymphs of the sea attended by scaly tritons. And King Poseidon said: "Much is permitted to thee, O god-beloved Odysseys. For even I, forgetful of our ancient feud, am here to warn thee that severe ordeals of thine endurance are ordained. And my rede to thee is that thou speed to Delphi, there to have sure news of thy quest from the priestess of the Radiant Pure One: for we of the sea are ignorant of what may be intended."

Thus he spoke; and forthwith the vision dived in deep waters, splashing awfully in disappearing. But I was left alone upon the lofty poop. Wherefore, having summoned Deythes, my shipman, I gave him his course; and, afterward, I rested, for magic is much more wearisome than war. In this manner, I learned that the sea-gods at least were propitious to me, and (also) that I was to go to the shrine of Phoibos Apollon at Delphi, there to receive an oracle and a Pythian revelation.

But, when we had passed Patrai and were making Kirrha (which was the port of Delphi on the Korinthic Gulph), it seemed good to me to prepare a gift, meet to be given by me, a priest and a king, to the domestic prelate of Pythian Phoibos Apollon. For which cause, I took stock of the treasure wherewith Amenemhat had loaded my galley. And indeed it was a generous and a godlike treasure. For there were wedges of virgin gold, weighty, plastic, red as the hair of a lovely girl of Altino of the Heneti, with great cut gems in leathern sacks, and vases and lamps of Korinthic bronze (which is platinum)FI sadly fear that we must be content to take Mr. C.'s word for it. All the same, one can't help feeling a little exasperated at his reiterated emphasis of his statements, and at one's own utter ignorance of his real reason for being so insistent on a point which one is perfectly unable to dispute or even to discuss. — A.H. wrought about with foliage, and tripods of burnished gold fit to stand with those which limping Hephaistos made for himself, and chryselephantine images of gods the work of Pheidias and Praxiteles and Lysippos, and bales of tissues of silver and gold and vermilion, with other treasures innumerable. Moreover, there was a gigantic chariot all of silver, inlaid with crabs and moons in mother-of-pearl; and the spokes of its wheels were images of the heroes, mighty men of old, wine-companions and sword-friends of me when we beleaguered woman-mad Paris and his Phrygians before the walls of windy Ilion. And, poised upon the front of the rail of the silver-shining chariot, there was a silver image of Love, larger than life, blindfolded, naked, most alluringly proportioned, and his well-winged arms were spread abroad in the very act of taking flight. And there were four white horses, a well-matched team, to go before the chariot for the sake of custom: but their harness and caparisons were of white leather with adornments of silver.

Thus, then, I prepared myself for pursuing my quest on land.

The Fourteenth Papyrus

*B*UT, when we reached Kirrha, having harbored my galley suitably, I went on to Delphi with Neandros and Thalos and nine trusty-looking slaves, who carried a part of my treasure. But we were all disguised in sordid garments; and the treasure was concealed in filthy wallets: for I was prepared with a wile. For, indeed, I was willing enough, and even glad to offer gifts propitiatory to the Far-Darter, lest he still should cherish his ancient rancor against me: for time is of small account to the gods, but hatred may be an open fester forever. But, nevertheless, I (being myself a priest) did not intend to be skinned by priests of the Lord (of the Silver Bow), nor was I ready to let them suck me dry, as a fly is sucked by assiduous spiders. For the good shepherd only shears his sheep, leaving the skinning of them to the butcher.

Thus, then, I came to the fane in the laurel-grove; and I counted the glittering shields there while waiting for my turn: for there were many suppliants that day, seeking an oracle, and giving gifts of red gold.

And, anon, the warden of the treasury, the most righteous of men with the pleated regard of a not-very-gracious pig, bade me to advance and make my offering. But I grieved that men, of evil mind and turpilucricupidous, should have twisted the good mind of the gods to suit their own improper ends: for, whereas, of old, a suppliant's gift was made as a willing thank-offering after the Pythian nun had repeated the words of the god, now, indeed, the treasurer would have appraised my gift, before admitting me even to the narthex of the shrine where men may await the divine oracle. Wherefore, avoiding undue display of my actual condition, and (in fact) wilily simulating poverty, I began by making reluctant offering of a tiny golden ingot. But the blameless treasurer had a motion which made his miter slip down to one ear of his, discovering a corner of old skull red as a rotten bite of meat and giving his aspect something of dancing and elastic: also, he snorted very contemptuously, like a camel of sneering nostrils; and (seeing me to be clad in an old cloak and wearing no well-crested helmet but a shabby floppy hat such as my wing-footed grandsire Hermes loves to wear), he had a flapping of his fattish fingers, and cried out upon me, and would have sent me away. But I doled out gold in morsels; and, as a Kretan, selling embroideries or incised stones to some blubber-lipped carroty-headed chin-less alien who screams with spasms of fury, lies in wait to see what the fool will offer, so did I with the warden of the treasury, offering a little at a time, moaning prodigiously, till I wearied him of bargaining and gained permission to pass in.

And, at length, I stood before the hollow shrine, and I prayed to the son of Queen Titania that he would be propitious and easy of memory concerning certain former regrettable occurrences. And all was still.

The bards sat hard on their stools, anointed ones, ignoble, stinking, and perfectly contented, in an odious fraternity of dalmatics, listless, till such time when the shrieks of the Pythia should spinge them into vibration with verses.

Above the bards, the hierarch of Phoibos Apollon occupied a throne as archbishop, laurel-crowned, venerably filleted.

And, anon, the holy Pythian nun, standing on the fumy grating with her python coiled about her feet, ecstatic amid clouds of frankincense, shrieked, and moaned, and shrieked again; and her eyes glared, being fixed wide open.

The blameless bards sprang forth from their drowsing; and put on the allure of very intelligent men. The archbishop advanced an attentive ear of the rose of rotten flesh. And the inspired virgin chanted, in the Delian mode, with bell-like notes and simple cadences, delivering the oracle which the fair-haired god was whispering to her mind. But she sang in the language of the gods, intelligible only to masters alone among articulately-speaking men.

Thus, then, she sang; and the bards were dazed; and the filleted archbishop marveled vastly: for very rarely does the Pythia use the secret tongue in her frenzies.

Thus, then, she sang, as her ecstasy intensified, floating her up from the grating all rigid, as she stood on the willing air tenderly lifting her up on high. For far-darting Phoibos Apollon himself was uttering unwinged words through the mouth of his nun.

And thus she sang:

Time-straying Wanderer, sea-borne Sea-lover,
signed with the Crab and starred with the Moon,
priest of all crafts of god-lore and man-lore,
head corner-stone by base builders rejected,
castaway paladin, master of mysteries,
known in the future, renowned in the past,
now, in the present, thy quest thou pursuest,
god-confirmed, seeking the crown of thy wisdom.
    I smell, in the south, the odor of aloes
    and basil and thyme and verbena and rosemary:
    I see the black portal of Tainaron yawning:
    I hear the fierce howls of the three-headed hound of
       hell.
Where thou hast been, go again, very warily:
heroes shall compass thee, ghosts of the great
shall acclaim, and the high gods environ, thee.
    There is the golden crown of all wisdom:
    there, in dark Hades, accomplish thy questing,
    spoiling the god of the world of the dead.

Such was the Oracle of Delphic Phoibos Apollon.

But, when the Pythian nun swooned, having made an end of her singing, the blameless archbishop gushed hurriedly down from his throne, very ardent, very violent, the crupper under his dalmatic waggling with furies no longer to be concealed: for he knew the secret tongue; and he perceived that I must be a personage of superior quality, though assuredly he did not understand the full import of the message, which (indeed) could be known solely to the divine Bow-bearer and to me, the bearer of the singing bow. But, because (being a priest, and one of the most righteous of men) he hankered after the society of a person so openly favored by the god, he approached me, bent upon inquiries. And he made me the *Sign of the Master-Architect:* but I responded with the *Grip of the Ruler of Nine.* And he signed me with the *Word of the Knight of the Crab:* but I countersigned him with the *Word of the Prince of the Moon.* We embraced in the *Ways of the East and of the West.* Together we formed the *Symbols of the Peacock* and *of the Ravens both Black and White.* But, when he shewed himself to be a *Master of the White Stars,* I, in my turn gave him my token as *Lord of the Ultra-Violet Radiance,* further than which no mortal man can go in this direction. And I beckoned him to slink back to his throne: which he did, very sorrowful in his heart, and champing his ancient gums while borborygms of his belly went and came.

In this manner, I triumphed at the temple of Delphi, obtaining the favor of the god.

The Fifteenth Papyrus

*B*UT, having returned to Kirrha, I went up into the curved ship, and I sailed propitiously southward for Tainaron, dark, forbidding to strangers. And, while I was voyaging, I pondered the words of the oracle.

But, as I thought of these things, many remembrances crept out of my mind, crowding upon me: for, when I was a liegeman of Victory queen of the stalwart stately Anglicans, and also when I was a priest of Queen Isis in the land of Khem, I had been oblivious of many great and wily deeds which I had done in the morning of the world. But, now, I began to remember many things concerning lofty Ilion, and wars, and windy Fate, and my sometime comrades there; and the black bow of Eyrytos vibrated in my hand, and my glance fixed itself on the dazzling sheen of my huge silver shield; and the bow sang to me of implacable young yellow-haired Akhilleys, and faithful temerarious Patrokles his friend, and fearless ruddy-headed Neoptolemos his son, and magnanimous Agamemnon shepherd of the people and leader of the Argive hosts, and aged Phoinix who (when a boy) obeyed his mother, and proud insane Aias, and Aitolian Diomedes of the loud war-cry with whom I spied on the Dardanians and stole the horses of Rhesos king of the Thrakians, and Idomeneys the Kretan fierce as flame, and my own dear son wise Telemakhos, and, also, the blameless foes of the rolling-eyed Argives, to wit, pious runaway Aineias and accursed crest-tossing Hektor, and old Priam with his sons Lykaon and Kebriones and godlike Polydoros the runner, all blameless, and woman-mad Paris of the splendid body, and also equal-handed Asteropaios: nor was I unmindful of bandy-legged woolly-haired Thersites, the very ugliest man of all who came to Ilion. And, furthermore, my singing-bow began to sing to me, and it sang of the white-armed slave Lyrnessian Briseis, and of the inquisitive Deidamia, and of perfidious Klytaim-nestra wife of Agamemnon, and of unhappy Andromakhe, and of prudent Penelope, and of beautiful golden Helen daughter of Zeys the Swan.

But the mind in my lordly breast busied itself with causes and effects: for I began to understand many more things, and one thing specially above all things, this, to wit, that these heroes (my friends and enemies) strove as I strove, and en-dured as I endured, and contrived their plans as I contrived my very wily plans, all for a prize and a crown. And, further, it seemed to me that, in all my striving after wisdom, there was one branch of knowledge which I had not considered even rudimentarily: for, as far as I remembered, I had never permitted myself (as all other heroes permit themselves) to go stark mad for love of a woman. But that was chiefly due to my nature, which caused me to hide my soft and hungry heart beneath a hard and cruel armor of proof. Yet other men, not less brave (though far lest wily) than I, loved women, not coolly, as I had loved prudent Penelope (whom I always used most respectfully and kindly), but perfervidly and even hairily and with utter self-renunciation. And I began to wonder why my wisdom had omitted to take count of rather more than half the human race. And I began to wonder whether my comrades had gained certain rewards of wisdom by their madness which I, by my wily self-control, had not attained. For I suddenly remembered the old adage, *What I gained, I lost: What I lost, I won: What I gave, I have.*

Now I blamed divine Memory: for she was treating me in a scurvy and niggardly manner, doling out mere handfuls of all the wealth of notions and ideas which, from time to time, I had been used to store in her cells. For the wise man ought not to utter a judgment until he knows all the matter to be judged. And I did not know all. Wherefore I put myself to ponder the little which I knew.

And, one by one, slowly, and painfully, certain other matters were brought out and laid before my mind.

For I remembered that the oldest and the youngest and the most venerated and by far the most exceedingly powerful of all the gods is Love. And, also, I remembered that each one of us, who stamp on the wide-bosomed earth, is no more than a moiety and counterpart of a perfect human creature. For, very early in the morning of the world, Zeys Pampator cut all mortals in two, halving them, for a religious reason, and on account of their ineffable prepotence. Wherefore, having once been a whole being, and being now but the half of a whole being, all articulately-speaking men most fervently desire and pursue any other creature whom they take to be their lost counterpart, that the two halves may again be mingled and fused in one: for, as Plato definitely teaches, *Love is the Desire and Pursuit of the Whole.* For which cause, I was aware that all men and all women needed nothing more than this, and nothing so much as this, that Love should work out perfectly, each finding other, returning to the aboriginal nature. These things, then, occupied the mind in my breast.

And, moreover, I considered how that I was going (obeying the Delphic oracle) where I twice had been before, once alive and once dead, to wit, to the House of Hades, tremendous king of infernal shades, whom I was to despoil of his treasure and the crown of all wisdom. Yet, still, I knew not what that treasure and crown might be. And, having remembered thus much of the past, I held a sort of council with my noble mind, which determined me to despoil that king of whatever might seem to be of greatest worth in his kingdom.

Wherefore, having summoned Thalos my slave, bathed and purified, I set the magic mirror on his palm, bidding him to gaze therein, and laying a very strong spell on him so that he should have clear sight of that one thing of which I had no knowledge.

And his little body became rigid; and his long black eyes stared; and the sweet sweat oozed like dewdrops from his flesh, and he shook with fear, insomuch that I chained his arms and legs with my own hands as in brazen manacles, forcing him to do my will. And, when I refused him permission to swoon, then his rigors took him stupendously; and, being as rigid as a strung bow, he began to declare his vision, saying: *The golden goddess, sitting with her star-crowned brothers,*

in the dark, disdaining a victorious hero, and an unmanlike king,
and a shepherd beloved of goddesses, and innumerable warriors
contending among themselves. And then I could no longer hold
him: for limb-relaxing Sleep, the all-subduer, drew him from
me.

But I knew what I wanted to know.

For this utterance was all of a piece with the divination
which my same slave had made, when he wore a young
Egyptian body on the sacred river of Khem, saying: *The silver*
god, leading the golden goddess, from the dark. For who was the
golden goddess in the dark, but fair long-robed golden Helen
daughter of Zeys the Swan, dwelling in the unlighted House
of Hades?

And who were her star-crowned brothers, but the Great
Twins, godlike youths, Kastor the tamer of horses and Polydeykes the pugilist, star-crowned sharers of immortality?

And whose blameless homage was refused by Golden
Helen, but that of the victorious hero Theseys, and that of
sandy-haired old impotent Menelaos, and that of the woman-
mad shepherd Paris beloved of Hera and Aphrodite and
Pallas Athene most righteous of goddesses?

And for whom, but for Golden Helen, had innumerable
warriors, my comrades and my enemies, contended during
ten long years of war, and after?

And I asked of the mind in my lordly breast, saying: Who,
then, is the Treasure of Hades?

And my mind answered me, saying: Who but Golden
Helen, sought of all men.

Then, indeed, the mind in my dear breast bounded with
an unmentioned and unthought-of joy in thinking of these
things, and in remembering also the things which were to
come, to wit, the leading of the golden goddess from the dark,
the moving with her among gods and goddesses, and the
sitting with her on a throne.

In this manner did I find out the meaning of the Delphic
oracle and the spoil which I was to win from the king of the
netherworld with the crown of all wisdom.

The Sixteenth Papyrus

BUT I went to Tainaron, where the hollow ship lay at anchor in a little cove to the west of the headland, being too great to draw up on the black beach; and, indeed, at Tainaron there is no sand fit for such a purpose. But I came ashore on a raft made of spars and planks, which the slaves of my galley pushed before them swimming, thrusting the sea back with their strong legs. And the raft carried also my gear, and my silver-shining chariot adorned with crabs and moons in mother-of-pearl with its mystic charioteer poised on the front of the rail: but my four white horses swam lustily apart, having no fear of deep water.

Not every day does mortal man drive down in awful pomp to the dark House of Hades. And, indeed, I did not know the way: nor was there a sacrifice proper for so great an occasion ready to my hand. Wherefore, I mentioned the point in a prayer addressed to my grandsire, wing-footed Hermes, inhabiting olympian palaces; and he sent me a Dream, to tell me how to prepare for his coming. But the Dream said that I was to build up an altar of stones on a mound of earth, and to make a fire, and to sacrifice my four white horses to the areiopagos of the immortals; and, after the sacrifice, I was to feast with my crew; and, at moonset, I was to cast fresh fennel on a clear fire, having dismissed all the lusty slaves to my galley with a commandment there to await my return.

But, when I awakened, the sun was close above the distant mountains, all ruddy with his hard day's course and ready for the evening. And I bade my slaves to build up an altar, and to do all other things which the Dream had commanded me: but they were unwilling to slay the beautiful horses; and they coughed horribly when I did it myself; and they made no difficulty about thoroughly enjoying themselves at the feast when the sacrifice was duly done. And, in the midst of the sacrifice, a portent was vouchsafed to me: for the smoke of my burnt-offering was not blown abroad by the evening breeze: but it ascended straightly as a column to the sky above. And this I knew to be a very favorable omen, auguring that my sacrifice was accepted as pleasing to the areiopagos of divine ones who inhabit olympian palaces.

And, with a glad heart, I did on my shining panoply, the silver-shining armor of Akhilleys, and his god-made shield, with the singing bow of Eyrytos: so that I shone like the star which rises in autumn, whose resplendent rays shine among many stars in the depths of the night. But I slung my revolver on my body, in a secret hollow of my armor, having fed it full and made it ready to spit dire death.

But, when my mariners had cut me many faggots of fresh fennel, heaping the same in a stack apt to my hand, then, indeed, I dismissed them to the hollow ship, with a commandment to await my return, all as the Dream had ordained.

And, as soon as I was alone, I very eagerly began to cast choice twigs of fennel on the redly-glowing embers of my sacrifice. And the sweet face of the moon became pale and paler, as the face of a dear woman about to swoon; and she snatched up a few soft mists wherewith to cloak herself in her going. For black night was creeping up the vault of heaven to overwhelm her; and she fled before him, as a maid flies before a blameless Ethiopian slave, whose bestial nostrils snuffle as he capers meditating very evil deeds. And anon she escaped with her purity. But I sat down to wait: nor did sweet Sleep light on my eyelids, when I contemplated the Pleiades, and setting Arktoyros, and the Bear (which they also call the Wagon) turning itself and watching Orion, but it alone does not share in the washing of the ocean.

But soon there was nothing between me and the darkness, excepting the glow of my fire. And I, being very eager for an apparition, grasped the stalks of fennel by handfuls, flinging them on to the roaring blaze, till all the world was awhirl with the fragrant greyish-blue smoke beloved of my grandsire

Hermes, beneficial son of Zeys.

And, very far away, I heard a noise as of the noise of a single thunderclap. But I was aware that it was the clang of the great gate on lofty Olympos closing behind the wing-footed messenger who was coming in answer to my prayer.

But, while I was awaiting his swift arrival, I ceased not to feed the flame with the magic herb. And, suddenly, I became aware that I was not alone. For a Presence was very near me, but hidden by the clouds of scented smoke; and two glowing eyes were fixed upon me: also, from time to time, I caught a glimpse of horns and pointed ears very terrible of aspect.

Then, indeed, sharp Fear tried to lay her clammy hand upon my heart: as a boy of evil mind, desiring to annoy his bedfellow, slips a wet toad into the white armpit of him sleeping. And I said to myself, in the words of one dying: *I am about to see Pan.** For I remembered the adage concerning a man who is given over unto sweet white Death, of whom it is said *Let him see Pan.*† For, indeed, it is known that the faces of the dead shew one thing very clearly, and that is that they have found out everything which there is to be known by mortal man, and are satisfied, as we all have seen in the dear beautiful face of Diyllos: so that, in saying of such an one *He has seen Pan,*‡ it is signified that he is satisfied with perfect knowledge, having seen All. Wherefore, for the moment, I wondered whether the crown of my wisdom was to come to me (by the will of the gods) in this manner.

But the mind in my lordly breast instantly bade me to face fate with a brave and dauntless countenance: for which cause, I summoned all my boldness, fearlessly gazing upon the glowing eyes amid the smoke, being determined to know all which there was to be known, without counting the cost, and

---

* ΟΨΕΣΘΑΙ ΜΕΛΛΩ ΤΟ ΠΑΝ.

† ΒΛΕΠΕΤΩ ΤΟ ΠΑΝ.

‡ 'ΕΩΠΑΚΕ ΤΟ ΠΑΝ: I am reluctantly compelled to confess that I have quite failed to trace these illuminating adages to any source prior to the year B.C. 45; and can only recommend application to the erudite author of a treatise called *Dodo,* whose writings clearly demonstrate that he has at least a very fair working knowledge of their ideal content. — A.H.

meeting sweet Death unflinchingly and as a lover. Thus, for some moments, I eyed rustic Pan: for the silvan god indeed was looking upon me. But, as white Death gave no sign of approaching me, I remembered that I had no cause for fear, seeing that my veins were filled with the ichor of the immortal gods as well as with the blood of a man.

But, at length, Pan came out of the smoky cloud and stood before me, goat-footed, hairy. His voice, when he spoke, was like the sound of leaves lying in the forest which sigh when some wanton breeze disturbs their slumbers. And he said: "Now do I greet thee, O Stranger. And whence comest thou? And what manner of man art thou? Art thou violent and wild and not just? Or art thou hospitable, and hast thou a holy mind? For I rejoice to see that thou art not like other earth-trampling men, who incontinently die (a most foolish and reprehensible custom) whensoever as they set eyes on me, rendering themselves unfit for serious conversation, while I am a-weary of the prattle of the children of hills and streams and trees."

But I made audacious answer to the simple country-god, saying: "O Pan, folk say that I am both thy half-brother and thy step-father: for I am King Odysseys, the sacker of cities, and prudent Penelope (who was my wife) bore thee to Hermes, my immortal grandsire. Wherefore we should be kin of some kind, I and thou."

Whereat he laughed merrily; and he answered: "Thou thyself dost not believe that tale, O wily Odysseys: for thou well knowest that I am as old as Time, being own brother to great Khronos. Nevertheless, any god might indeed be proud to call cousins with King Odysseys. Wherefore, tell me, O cousin, whence thou art now come: for it seemeth that nephew Hades hath relaxed his grim ward of thee."

But, ere I could open my lips in reply, the rustic god cried: "Aha! Who cometh here? 'Tis young Hermes, as I live with goats!"

Thus he spoke. But I saw the grey-blue smoke-cloud broken by golden radiances flashing here and there. And, looking, we beheld now the golden wand, now the beautiful swiftly-flying limbs shod with golden winged-sandals, now the cloak of gold and purple tissue blown back from the body in flight;

and, anon, the youthful bird of heaven burst upon us out of the fume in all the inmarcesible splendor of nude immortality.

In this manner, I first saw Hermes, the Luck-bringer, my grandsire, a god.

The Seventeenth Papyrus

*N*OW that divine young one of gods came to me holding in his hand the halters of four white horses, all mad, incomparable in splendor, tossing their heads, and stamping with their feet. And Pan looked curiously upon us, while sprightly Hermes took me to his beautiful large breast, calling me Son and Child: for the heart of the youthful god was glad when he saw the goat-footed divine one with whom I stood as an equal; and the sheen of my silver-shining armor glittered with moony gems. And, first, he began to speak very eloquently (as his manner is), having a tale to tell of the cause of his lateness in coming.

For he said that the blessed gods, having sniffed the savor of my sacrifice with pleasure, graciously deigned to acknowledge the same by a gift. And, seeing that I had not hesitated to offer my only horses, those divine ones were pleased to send me another team. Wherefore, four heavenly steeds were selected from that godly stock which the indomitable hero Herakles won from King Laomedon. But, when quick-eyed though blindfolded Love had seen my grandsire about to descend bearing away beautiful horses, he had howled (that dire intractable boy), only for the sake of annoying, saying that steeds ought not to be sent to me, seeing that he himself (even Love) with his burning breath and wide-sailing wings was ready to come at my call to be my beast, my bird, my bearer of burdens and deep delight forever and ever. But, when Hermes persisted (for the thing was an order from the

All-father which must be obeyed), then Divine Eros had betaken himself to his bow and arrows, shooting through the bars of heaven's gate, so that more than nine times the halters had been severed, and the horses had gone free, galloping here and there, till, at last, being caught and herded safely out of range, they were led down to me, apparently docile and ready for the traces. Such was the apology of Hermes.

But Pan, standing by and listening attentively, saw how highly I was in favor with the gods of lofty Olympos; and he stooped, picking up a sprig of fragrant fennel, wherewith he touched my two eyes, saying: "Receive the power of seeing as the gods see."

And instantly he was gone, I know not where. But Hermes laughed, triumphantly merry, saying: "Thou, O my brave child, hast indeed won old Pan's favor: for few there be to whom he would communicate this virtue, a very signal one, as thou shalt know anon."

Thus having spoken, he bade me to prepare for my fear-some journey. But, while I obeyed him, he illuminated my mind with knowledge of the ordeals through which I was to pass: yet he could not tell me everything, for the time was short; and, as much of the rest as he might, he said that he would tell me by the way. For he was going with me as far as was permitted. But I went even gleefully, having so affable and so splendid a young god for my comrade.

But I yoked the white steeds to the well-wrought chariot, carven of silver inlaid with adornments of crabs and moons in mother-of-pearl, whereon was poised the silver Love, blind-folded, naked, larger than life, and just in the act of flight. But my grandsire examined my glittering armor; and, having approved it, he wrapped me in my great trailing mantle of tissue of silver lined with white furs and clasped with the signs of the crab and the moon. Furthermore, he gave me a heavenly amulet for my use and comfort, formed of two chalcedonyxes having the similitude of eyes set in the Sign of the Crab in a silver finger-ring, saying that I would need it on occasion. And he let me twist long stalks of fennel into a monstrous torch, three stalks with seven stalks and nine stalks, nineteen in all. And, having lighted it, we mounted my chariot, both I and the god.

Now the silver Love on the chariot was motionless and dumb, as the manner of gods is when they are made of metal: yet it evidently was a very potent and unheard-of magic, though neither Hermes nor I, Odysseys, wily and knowing as we both were, fully understood it, for the divine ones inhabiting olympian palaces had not manifested their will in this particular. For which cause, I stood in my proper place on the left:* but Hermes went to the other side of the flying Love, seizing the reins, and urging the huge white horses onward with the shouts of a charioteer. But they plunged madly forth into the cloud of fennel-smoke.

I closed my eyes, smarting with the murky reek. But the flaming fire-brand which I bore flared like a banner far behind me: so that, though I love sunlight as well as any man alive, I gladly and joyously went (god-driven) from the grain-giving earth to the netherworld, dashing into the secret adit whereby the souls of dwellers in daylight go down to the dark house of Hades. Thus, then, I went, to despoil the king of shades.

But we galloped on, at more than mortal speed, down the broad path, never slipping nor stumbling: for Hephaistos had shodden the heavenly steeds, and Hermes drove them, mightily encouraging them with shootings. And my fire-brand, fanned by the wind of the speed of my going, flamed on the pallor of dead men, terror-stricken, who were passing down the same road, like sheep unshepherded, toward old Kharon and his insatiable barge.

We came to the shelving river-bank; and the Old Man of Styx drove many souls from our path as the silver-shining chariot dashed irresistibly into the stink of the putrid stream. But my lusty horses swam swiftly to the farther hythe; and Hermes buoyed up the ponderous chariot with magic so that it did not sink. But we speeded on, over sandy desolate wastes, veiled in impenetrable gloom. Fast and faster tore those untiring stallions of matchless breed; and the whirling wheels span round; and chill winds blew in our faces, so that I wrapped myself shivering in my furry cloak. League after league we flew, through unpeopled wildernesses; and the earth

---

* But was "the left" really his proper place? — A.H.

became no more sandy, but thick with salt, which flashed back the gleam of my fast-burning torch, lying wide-spread on both sides of the narrowing way.

But when I (being inquisitive) addressed a word to my grandsire concerning the frenetic speed of our going, and what should come thereafter, and the salt which lay by the way, then, indeed, he answered me, saying: "The tides of hell are flowing fast; and, as we crossed Styx at the slack, so we must cross Pyriphthlegethon at the full, or we shall not win through: for none may traverse those dread streams excepting at such times. Nor can a man tarry upon the banks, by reason of the singularly putrid fumes arising. Neither may a man dally in this wilderness of salt, which is sacrosanct: for every grain thereof contains selections from the body of a dead man, and thus they are preserved against the day when they shall be required for use once more."

To whom I, without delay, spoke boldly, saying: "And what of those men who (by the sanction of the gods) have not died until after they have occupied several different bodies?" For I was thinking of Amenemhat and of Neandros and Thalos, and of the other persons whom I myself (from time to time) have metamorphosed.

But young Hermes responded to me, saying: "Know, O inquisitive wily and well-beloved child, that, in every body of a mortal, there is that which is beautiful and that which is hideous, just as, in every soul of a mortal, there is that which is good and that which is evil. Wherefore, it is the will of Zeys, the Father of all, that the evil and the hideous shall perish everlastingly, but the good and the beautiful blended together shall live in immortal palaces."

And it seemed to me very strange to hear such words of wisdom coming from a youth, whose cheeks of summer hue shewed not the tender mother of the vine-down. But he, Hermes, the powerful Argicide, fell again to urging the heavenly steeds, crying: "On, on, to the house of shady Hades!"

And the gloom before us was illumined with a dull-red glow, which shot up into the dark vault like a roof above our heads: for, indeed, we were rushing into the very abysses of the netherworld; and the light grew clearer and more fierce to us advancing. But, behind us, we left a trail of smoke from

my flaming fire-brand, and a trail of steam from the straining
stallions. And the cold wind died; and immeasurable flames
streamed upward from the river of fire, licking invisible
heights, flashing and flickering. And I heart my divine charioteer praising great Zeys with bated breath, for that we were
come at a propitious time. For, as we flew down to the
blackened shore, our wheels drove heavily among the crackling cinders; and the flames died, and evanesced: for, as the
tides of the accursed mystic river were flowing full, the flames
(which blazed and roared through ebb and flow) were hushed
in phosphorescent silence.

But my mighty steeds, mad by nature, plunged bravely in
the stream which bubbled and boiled with recent heat: yet,
because of their heavenly breed, they (already mad) suc-
cumbed not to the scalding flood, though they screamed with
terror and piety, as did Ares (potent in battle) when (wounded
by Diomedes son of Tydeys) he fell, covering seven acres, and
fled (bellowing) to Paieon (the surgeon of the gods) to be
healed of his hurt. But, when we were on the other side of
that flaming moat which surrounds the city of the dead,
Hermes assuaged the pangs of my mad horses with a holy
Spell which he contrived to remember just then, so that they
became much madder than they ever had been before and
went most valiantly onward.

Then, also, that same divine one of gods cried aloud to me,
saying: "If thou thyself canst remember any enchantments,
work them well now, O master of crafts: for this locality is
very fatal to miserable mortals as a rule; and already thou hast
escaped herefrom alive: but, for a third attempt something
extremely exquisite of magic will be found desirable."

Thus he admonished me. But I instantly recited aloud most
potent *Spells,* to wit, *The Spell of Sniffing the Air and Getting
Power over the Water in the Netherworld,* and *The Spell of Not
Dying Again in the Netherworld,** making the proper *Signs,* and
saying:

*"I take hold of air and water: I watch and guard the egg of the
great cackler.*

---

* These are well-known Egyptian enchantments, and Mr. C.
perhaps had them from the Rt. Rev. Amenemhat of Tanis.
– A.H.

"It groweth, and I will grow: it sniffeth the air, and I will sniff the air.

"It liveth, and I will live: I will triumph in the air and the water of the netherworld.

"Let the place of hiding things be opened: for I will not be treated with scorn.

"I will not submit to any violence: nor will I die again in the netherworld."

And, having thus composed and fortified my will, we continued to rage furiously onward.

Now the gloom of the place was very grey and terrible, insomuch that the mad heads of my horses were invisible to us standing behind them in the chariot, for a dense fog was enveloping the netherworld. And, anon, we found our way blocked by a great and monstrous wall which frowned blackly in the shade, wherein loomed a mountainous barbacan fortified with turrets and pierced by a tremendous gate. But the gate was guarded by unsleeping Kerberos, the hound of hell spoken of by Pythian Phoibos Apollon, barking at me with three ugly heads and gnashing the relative mouthfuls of teeth. Whom my grandsire appeased, silencing him with the *Word of Power.**

But divine Hermes began to warn me, saying that his business ended in the realms of shady Hades, his uncle; and he gave me to know that, in what more remained to he done, I must trust only in myself: but he bade me to be very wary regarding the mood in which I should find surly King Hades, biding my time and not precipitantly asking inopportune or excessive favors. And these were the mandates which he had brought to me from Zeys Pantokrator and Pampator. But, when he had said these things and embraced me, and when he had whispered a most pious and secret monition, then, indeed, he kicked off and vanished away; and his swift winged-sandals bore him again to the summit of lofty Olympos.

But I lifted up my voice, terrifically shouting to the warden of the gate. And a blameless titan peered over the battlements,

---

* "Down, dog, down!" is the exact (though perhaps somewhat colloquial) rendering of this particular *Spell. Cf.* Lucian. — A.H.

and brayed with the formidable degorgement of a trumpet, demanding of me the password. Whom I answered in the language of the gods, speaking one of the *Words* which Hermes had left with me, but I may not write it on account of a religious reason. And instantly the gate unfolded its enormous hinges.

In these circumstances, then, I came thundering in my silver-shining chariot invading the city of infernal shades.

The Eighteenth Papyrus

*N*OW I was all alone. And, before me on both sides, there stretched a sad-colored meadow, apparently interminable, thickly sown with flowers of pinkish pearlike asphodel. And no sky smiled above my head: but only an impenetrable dark-grey mist, which hung down also, like the curtains of a tent, at a very little distance on all sides of me. But the mind in my noble breast warned me to pause, and to ponder, and to contrive a few new wiles before going further. Wherefore, having abated the madness of my horses, I betook myself to deep thought.

And it appeared to me very desirable that I should not manifest myself to the denizens of that neighborhood, wheresoever they might be concealing themselves, without the full equipage and paraphernalia proper to a personage of my quality. And I very greatly wished that I had brought at least my two slaves, Neandros and Thalos, the one on account of his stalwart virtue, the other on account of his luminous innocence, and both full of grace, that they might serve me if need should arise. And I began to consider whether there was any magic whereby I might summon them to my side: for I already had done so many wonderful things by myself, and the heavenly gods had strewn themselves so entirely favorable to me, that I was not at any time daunted when confronted by what the purely stupid man is wont to cringe to as a sheer impossibility. For the minds of the prudent, indeed, are flexible. And a master of magic (who is thoroughly in earnest) may achieve unmentioned and unthought-of deeds, of course with the aid of the immortal gods.

But, while I was pondering these high matters, I saw two young boys, like twin-brothers, coming toward me across the meadow of asphodel and emerging from the obscurity of the mist. They were well-grown and in the prime of their age; and their gait betokened a very divine origin. Both were most sweet and gentle of aspect: but this one was of dusky hue, crowned with a garland of white poppies, and (in his tender hand) he bore a dark horn, from which (from time to time) he scattered a fine dust in the air, and an obsequious zephyr carried it away to fall on the eyes of mortals: but that one was of a candid whiteness colder than hoar-frost, such as I never have seen on the grain-giving earth either in marble or milk or the delicate flesh of the young in the clear of the moon, or the snow which falls in winter; and his pure candor was crowned with a garland of pinkish pearllike asphodel, and in his soft hand he bore a torch extinguished. Wherefore, I recognized them for dusky Sleep the All-tamer, and pale kind Death his brother, the twin sons of Khronos.

And now, indeed, the mind in my lordly breast spoke loudly, telling me what I ought to do. For which cause, I addressed a simple word to these divine ones; shewing the *Sign of Life*, engaging their aid by spells unutterable. But, when I had mentioned my desire of having with me Neandros my squire and Thalos my foot-boy, whose lives were bound unto mine, which itself was terminable only at the supernal will of the god, then, white Death (coldly smiling) turned away, saying that the matter concerned his brother. Wherefore, I made my petition to care-dispersing Sleep, saying the *Spell*: *"O Sleep, king of all blessed gods and of all men, if ever indeed thou didst lend an ear to mine entreaty, now, too, be persuaded; and I will own gratitude to thee all my days."**

And the dusky god also was favorable to me: for, having cast a pinch of dust from his horn into the air, it fell on the eyelids of Neandros and Thalos waiting for me in my hollow ship at Tainaron, so that their limbs were relaxed, and they submitted themselves to divine Sleep, who brought them straight to me in the meadow of asphodel.

But, when we three had ascended the silver-shining chariot,

---

* This is perfectly Homeresque. — A.H.

I gave the reins to my squire standing on my right hand: but my foot-boy attended me, eagerly clutching the rail behind. Thus, I, with Neandros and Thalos, swiftly galloped onward through the grey gloom, approaching the palace of shady King Hades.

And, having whizzed through its brazen portal, we drave horrifically into an immeasurable hall. And the awfully whirring wheels of my chariot, with the silver Love perched upon it, amazed the uncountable multitudes collected therein, insomuch that whimpering Fear took possession of all, and Rumor went squealing everywhere, whispering that some hero from out of the sunlight alive was invading the house of Hades. But I cared naught for the ineffectual gibberings of mere shades.

And I pursued my way to where I saw the great black throne set, with the very shady god enthroned thereon, and Queen Persephone by his side, and a court below him of the arbiters of the dead, Aiakos, Minos, Rhadamanthos, just, inexorable, most venerable, uttering immutable dooms for mortal men. And, near by, I saw also great-hearted yellow-haired Akhilleys, the greatest hero and faithfullest friend which the world has ever seen; and my heart in my dear breast leaped when he hailed me passing by, recognizing on me his glittering armor which I had won as a spoil: for, to have a trusty comrade in such a shady place is very good.

But, when I checked my chariot before the throne, then, King Hades (the most righteous of gods) sternly addressed me, saying: "Tell me thy name, O Stranger greatly-daring, and thy father's name; and say also how thou comest hither."

And thus I answered him: "O King of Tartarean realms and dreadful brother of Zeys, my father's name was James — may the gods grant rest to his gentle soul, — and I am Nicholas the Crab, client of the Muses and of far-darting Phoibos Apollon. But divine Hermes brought me hither, acknowledging me to be his own grandson, called Odysseys son of Laertes by all articulately-speaking men who walk in the sweet sunlight."

But the brow of blameless Hades became blacker than starless night; and he frowned so ferociously that even his shady eyes were shrouded. And he cried: "So thou art that much-contriving Odysseys, who aforetime camest hither and twice escaped alive. And now thou wouldst perplex me with a wily tale, mixing Was with Will-be and Is in a medley, and bearing a double name full of deceit. But doubtless that is part of thy evil purpose: for thy purpose cannot but be evil. Perchance thou hast it in mind to depose me, or even to steal away with my queen, divine Persephone. But, since thine overweening audacity has driven thee, foolish, to place thyself in my power a third time, thou shalt not now escape me." And he howled for titans to trammel me, as a trickster.

Thus he spoke. But, when I saw giants towering like mountains near me, in the gloom, then, instantly, I broke my necklace of heliotrope stones moistened with the juice of marigolds; and I thrust the two halves of it into the hands of my two trusty slaves, making the *Act of Will* for them, whereby they became unseen, even by Stygian gods, unknowing it. But I gave them a short command. And the stalwart Neandros started my horses, goading them again to madness in the twinkling of an eye, turning them, so that my slaves and my chariot went ramping out of the palace of blameless Hades like a flash of white thunder. By which means, both my slaves evaded the Tyrant of Tartaros. But, being visible and willing, I remained: for, as yet I had not done any of the wily deeds which I had come to do, and, moreover, there was no retreat for me till I had ravished a spoil from the king of the shades. Furthermore, I was not unmindful of the very pious and secret monitions which Hermes had whispered to me at parting, when he said: *Under-go to overcome.*[*]

And, so, I waited; and gigantic hands were thrust down out of obscurity, which seized me and shook me violently to and fro over enormous areas: so that giddiness nauseated me, and the eyes in my face refused to continue seeing, and my strength also rebelled and left me, and the utter darkness of oblivion settled upon me, shrouding the senses of my soul.

Thus, then, I began my ordeals in the Quest of the Treasure of Hades.

---

[*] I am almost inclined to say that this delicious epigram contains the whole body of Christian doctrine. But of course I speak under correction. – A.H.

The Nineteenth Papyrus

*B*UT when, anon, I had recollected my forces, I was in a pit, dismal, slimy, creeping with long cold worms. And great chains, also, were hanged to my wrists and waist and ankles. But, far above my head, there was a little window, very heavily barred; and, through it, there came a dull-red glow from the distant River Pyriphthlegethon. And the shrieks and moans of damned souls in mind-grieving torment elsewhere was the music provided for my entertainment.

As for myself, it seemed that I had been stripped of my armor, and (indeed) of all which I had brought with me from the sunlight; and, now, I was mother-naked, gyved also, and with no gear which would deliver me from my plight, excepting the knowledge of sacred spells which was stored in my mind, and a large quantity of natural strength which was stored in my body. But I rejoiced, seeing that I was unhurt, and as able as ever: because I was aware that I should have the greater fame when I should have passed through this ordeal. For there is not any greater renown for a man, while he exists, than what he shall have earned naked with his feet and his hands.

But, first, I gathered up the weight of my fetters, to try to break them; and, when I felt them to be as massive as the cable of my galley, then I let them drop again, not to waste time: for my noble mind began to devise insidious wiles. But, when the chains clashed against the slimy floor, I heard a sound of a drawing of bolts, and a brazen door was opened in my pit near by. And, to me, there entered a very gravely objectionable individual.

For she was a barren virgin of inconceivable antiquity, whose skinny arms were joined to her withered body by membraneous wings such as are the wings of bats and vampires and pterodactyls and all other flying dragons; and her slit mouth grinned disgustingly, having loose yellow fangs dangling from the dripping corners: vipers, also, writhed in the dankness of her sparse hair; and her hands were filled with torches and scourges. Moreover, what I took to be blood was oozing out of her pustulous eyeballs. And thus she said: "How now, O wily Odysseys! And art thou yet alive? For we deemed that the titans had shaken the life from thy white bones. And that, indeed, would have made our task an easy one: for we are not accustomed to torment live men here among the shades."

Thus she spoke: but the mind in my lordly breast bade me to treat this blameless Erinnys with affability while keeping her at arm's length, that I might gain a benefit from her conversation without coming to close quarters with her. For, when a female of this kind prevails, her audacity is more than one can bear without blasphemy; and, when she is affrighted or affronted, she is a still greater mischief to her house and city. Wherefore I said: "Hail, O divine one of goddesses, serpent-crowned, for I am ignorant of thy blessed name, or I would ask thee where we are."

But to me the most righteous of furies responded, saying: "I am night-born Tisiphone, a scratcher of earth-walking men after they are dead. But this is the dungeon where Pirithoos lay to be scratched by me during a hundred years."

Now there is nothing more terrible than such an impudent female as this. Wherefore, having prepared a wile, not to enrage her, but to delude her, by seeming to be overcome by piety and terror, then, I let my mouth gape like a fool's while I repeated after her: "A hundred years!"

But she began to be garrulous. But I watched for an opportunity of entangling her in her talk. And thus she chattered: "Yea, here indeed lay Pirithoos, son of Ixion, during a hundred years. For King Hades would not give him to sweet Death, so black was his crime. But, every night, we sisters three tormented his body as though he were dead, using fiery tortures and nail-tearings, until the decree came that his shade should repose in peace, being purged. But thou, also, O much-enduring Odysseys, will lie here, chained, purging thy presumptuous prepotence: but, not till after thy death, may we deal with thee according to thy doom, whatever that may be."

And, having thus enlightened me, the very excessive Fury suddenly left me, with extempore shrieks and a flapping of her skinny wings.

Thereafter, I forget how some days passed: for a prisoner may not reckon the flight of Time in the region of Tartaros, excepting by marking the ebb and flow of the fiery tides of Pyriphthlegethon. Moreover, I was occupied in my mind, reviewing all my store of magic wisdom and contriving many wiles.

And, by chance, one day, I became aware that I was hearing a song; and the sound of it seemed to come from very far away, sweetly, like the voice of a cicada drunk on dewdrops,* which, in the woods, sitting on a tree, sends forth a delicate lilylike voice.

Now, in the house of shady Hades (most righteous of gods), this is the condition of mortals when they are dead. For their nerves have no longer flesh and bones: but the strong force of burning fire subdues them, when first the mind leaves the white bones; and the soul, gibbeting like a dream, flits and flutters away. Wherefore, the souls of the dead cannot sing, nor do they attempt it, being occupied in shrieking with agony and fear. For which cause, I was vastly amazed to hear so very sweet a song, so grave, so quiet in tone; and, having summoned all my strength, despite the weighty manacles which trammeled me, I leaped up to the high barred window which looked out into the gloom. But I saw little more than that my dungeon was a pit in a rocky height: for it happened to be the hour of slack tide, when the flames of Pyriphthlegethon die down for a while.

And the wonderful song came more clearly from below, thrilling the darkness of black night.

But, when, anon, the voice was silent, I wedged myself (as

---

* One cannot help pointing out that the same poetic imagery as that used here by Mr. C. seems to have been adopted subsequently by Meleagros of Gadara. — A.H.

best I could) into the narrow alcove of the window, waiting
for the ebb of the tide, when I might see more plainly in the
light of the increscent flames.

And, when the flickering gleam of the fires leaped up, I
saw that my pit was a cell in a watchtower perched high above
the walls of the house of blameless Hades. But there was a
great gulf fixed below, and bleak meadows beyond, swept by
mists and winds of hell.

And, while I gazed, the lilylike voice began again to ring,
maidenlike, very solemn, and of entrancing sweetness. But I,
listening, heard it; and the heart in my dear breast thrilled
strangely: for it seemed as though Memory (that divine one
of goddesses) was opening yet once more certain chambers
in my mind, unknown, or unremembered; and I was aware
of treasures stored therein, whose very existence I had forgotten. But the simple song went sadly on, as though the singer
sat in patience waiting, singing only just to pass the time, but
always with hope, very faint indeed but never-failing, ever-en-
during, in the depth of her maiden breast. And thus she sang:

Once, a flower, in a garden where gold sunlight
flamed on all with its fervent splendor, flourish'd
stainless aye, from the tender seed's upspringing
to the snow of its yet-unfolded blossom.
When, at length, on its stem so straight and slender,
fragrant, delicate, fresh, this blossom budded,
men from near and a host from far came, each one
longing only to pluck and wear the full flower.
Came a stripling of noble mien and stately,
strong and clean as a sword. His bright eyes saw her,
shyly paused to admire, and pass'd in silence:
but she, pure as a priestess, ne'er forgot him.
Came a hero in triumph, wearing garlands
woven close with the glory of full-blown roses;
and he stole from her place the snow-white blossom —
rescued soon by the two who were her wardens.
Came a noisily-shouting dotard, jealous
for the bud, which he knew not how to cherish:
him, the lord of the garden fair permitted;
and he carried away the prize unfolded.
Came one mad with the scents of gaudy posies,

One who revell'd in robbing other gardens:
he, the delicate blossom, ravish'd: but she
never open'd for him her snow-white petals.
Last of all, then, the gods in grace restored her
to the pear, of the sunlit garden's splendor;
and the youth who, afore, had seen and loved her,
would have taken her: but dire Fate o'ertook him.
Still she blooms in a garden, where the winter
frost and cold cannot quench the golden sunlight
in her heart, nor the storms defile her whiteness:
waiting, till, on his breast, she bursts in full flower.*

And the strange sweet dancing rhythm made my pulses bound; and my breath came quickly in accord. For it was like a sudden-blazing thunderbolt illuminating the recesses of my mind; and I remembered the object of my quest, to wit, Golden Helen, who, when I was not much more than a boy, had watched me faring girded high through the ford of Eyrotas near windy Lakedaimon — Golden Helen, whom her star-crowned brothers (Kastor the tamer of horses and Polydeykes the pugilist) had rescued from the blameless hero Theseys carrying her away when she was a tender girl, — Golden Helen, whom King Tyndareys had given in so-called marriage to loud-shouting impotent old sandy-haired Menelaos, blameless, and blubber-lipped, — Golden Helen, whom woman-mad Paris had reft from her farcical husband, — Golden Helen, who had come again to me in the land of Khem, long ages since, pure as snow or fire, and always mine alone, — Golden Helen, whom black Fate had reft from me, when I died that time by the sacred river of Egypt, being wounded to death by blameless Kirke's son and mine, unknowing Telegonos.†

---

* I have managed (not without complacency) to render this exquisite (and perfectly pagan) ditty both literally and in its original hendecasyllabic or ithyphallic measure — a somewhat difficult task, and (perhaps) an audacious, in the light of Lord Tennyson's deplorable attempt "all composed in a meter of Catullus." — A.H.

† I fancy that I do not err in affirming that this particular incident in the lives of Mr. C. (*i.e.* King Odysseys) may be best studied in Haggard's erudite treatise entitled *The*

But now, indeed, I knew of a truth that Golden Helen was that very Treasure of Hades which I had come to win: for, by favor of Queen Persephone, she was safe in the netherworld, and only there, for in the netherworld there are no men capable of worrying a lady, but merely shades of men, who are quite negligible; and, there, she (being immortal) could live faithful to me and not altogether without certain amenities. Wherefore, with a great shout, I called her by name.

And she made answer, half-amazed and half-afraid, saying: "Who calleth me with the voice of one long dead?"

To whom I replied: "I am Odysseys, grandson of Hermes, victor over all sorts of people; and I am come here for thee, O highborn long-robed Helen whom I love."

Thus I spoke. But the golden goddess, filled with joy, said: "O Odysseys, I have waited long. But now where art thou?"

To whom I answered, saying: "I am imprisoned by shady Hades in a pit in one of his towers. But canst thou see me at any window, O Golden Helen, for I can not see thee."

She said: "I see thee not, O much-enduring Odysseys. But thou shalt soon escape and come to me: for, though it is not safe for me to go alone among the gods (married and unmarried) of lofty Olympos to plead for thee, and, though shady Hades doth regard me with disfavor, yet my twin-brothers (who are dead today in the netherworld where I can speak firmly to them) will be all alive tomorrow in the neighborhood of the immortals, such being their destiny. And they shall demand graces from my lordly sire Zeys Pantokrator."

Thus she spoke; and, incontinent, sped away about my business. But I, being refilled with hopeful ideas, felt my great strength increasing every moment. Wherefore, with loud laughter, I came down from the hollow window, beginning to break my bonds. Now, had I been on earth or sea, I should have used certain magic recipes known to me, whereby the bitter iron would have crumpled up in sheer bewilderment: but I wished it to be said of me that I had won the Treasure of Hades with my naked strength as far as possible, if (indeed) it should be permitted to me by the gods inhabiting olympian palaces. Wherefore, I set my sinews to work: for youth was

World's Desire. — A.H.

hotter than ever in my veins and my life was raging within me. And, having tasted the name of the golden goddess desired of all men, I made that my only spell; and then indeed I burst great fetters with my little fingers. And, with the same spell (and lusty loin-heavings), I tore at the staple inset in a flag-stone, dragging it from its socket. And, with the same spell (and a mighty swelling of my hardened body), I wrenched asunder the last hoop of iron; and stood free among my splendidly-shattered shackles.

Thus having delivered myself from bonds, I waited as patiently as might be. But none came near me; and, indeed, the mind in my noble breast would have bidden me to attempt the slaughter of anyone, even a blameless titan, who should have approached me, not openly coming as a friend. And my patience was tried during all that day, and the day after: nor did any voice of song cheer me.

But, on the third day, I heard someone buffeting the bars of my window; and a friendly voice uttered my great name. And, when I answered, a young and very godly face, crowned on the brow with a star, looked in upon me through the grating. And the half-immortal hero said: "Our sister, fair Helen, hath sent us to thee, O Odysseys, sacker of cities; and here am I, Polydeykes: but brother Kastor keeps watch below, for Father Zeys wishes to see what we can do unaided. Wherefore, we two are come to rescue thee: but Queen Persephone hath promised help hereafter, for Helen's sake whom she considers injured."

Thus he spoke: and indeed it was Polydeykes the pugilist, son of Zeys the Swan, who was taking my part. But, first, he tore at the bars of the window: but when, indeed, he found them firmly fixed, then he laughed, warning me away; and, with a boxer's blow straight from the shoulder, he drove the massive irons inward, so that they stretched out, becoming thin as threads with sheer amazement, until they snapped in twain in every direction and ceased from being bars. But I instantly leaped to the window, crouching on the sill, till star-crowned Kastor ascended. And, I having squeezed myself through the narrow aperture, the Great Twins bore me up, supporting me on both sides, till we touched the solid earth once more.

In this manner, I escaped from my dungeon in the house of Shady Hades.

The Twentieth Papyrus

*B*UT, upon the instant when we stood in open country at the base of the rock, there came a fearful whirring of the wings of blameless Harpies, beating down upon us, raucously screeching, calling titans and furies to their aid. But the Dioskoyroi laughed these bestial birds to scorn, and Polydeykes dashed his iron-studded boxing-glove into their ugly faces, whereat the ill-breathing wardens of the damned became melancholy, and fled back to their station on the wall, feeling much hurt.

But we went on through the murk, entering a secret chamber in the house of Hades, where were food and drink, corn-cakes the strength of men, with cheeses and the fat haunches of pigs, and honey-hearted wine. Here, also, by the arts of Queen Persephone, I found all my gear, and my silver-shining armor piled upon a bed, and baths of boiling water for washing. And having cleaned away my abounding sweat and slime, I anointed myself, coming out of the bath like to the immortals in person, and was visited by the shades of most accomplished barbers. But, when I sat down to a repast (not because of hunger, for, in that life I was not afflicted with the craving belly, pernicious, which brings so many evils to mortal men, but merely for the pleasure of eating and drinking with friends), then, indeed, godlike Kastor and Polydeykes served me as squires for a religious reason,* girding me again with my silver-shining armor glittering with rock-crystals and blue moonstones, which I won

---

* This night, perhaps, almost strike some persons as being just a little "thin." — A.H.

from Aias son of Telamon, in a foot-race, after lordly Akhilleys had left the earth.

Which matters having been concluded, the Great Twins
conducted me to the presence of well-disposed Queen
Persephone, who addressed to me unwinged words, saying:
"O much-enduring grandson of Hermes, always wily and
ready at need, my cousin Golden Helen hath persuaded me
on thy behalf; and I will protect thee as far as may be from
my shady husband's wrath. For King Hades bath a bitter
spirit, and is fain to do thee wrong, by reason that thou
already hast evaded him twice, and, also, that thou (by thy
wiles and a woolly sheep) didst cause to suffer much in mind
and to perish most miserably his sweet friend the Kyklops
Polyphemos. Nevertheless I will beseech the king to let thee
go in peace, for the sake of avoiding fresh wiles of thine."

Then came long-robed Helen, the divine one of goddesses;
and I read in her amber eyes that which told me (even more
than her song had told me) that she was mine now, even as
she had been willing to be mine in Egypt long before. Glowed
then the heart in my dear breast with love and joy; and my
very form swelled hugely with pride of conquest: for, not to
everyone of earth-trampling men is it given to win the love
of a goddess so true that she will wait for him during a
thousand years.

And so we passed into the judgment-hall of Hades, most
righteous of gods brooding on his shady throne: that that
which had to be done might be well-done with the least
possible delay. And, before the king, the judges were giving
dooms to the unnumbered dead, as usual. But Queen
Persephone stood before him; and she held my hand, and
said: "O king and lord of shades, it pleaseth me that King
Odysseys should retire forthwith from these dismal realms,
with his life, and with all else which belongeth to him."

But, at sight of me, surly Hades bounced and had a bor-
byrygm; and he quickly answered her, saying: "Such, O daughter of Demeter, is by no means my intent: but now I will toss
him into Tartaros, there to lie forever, on account of his
presumption in coming hither after having twice escaped me,
and also on account of the woes which his prepotence
wrought wilily upon my sweet friend, the giver of cherished

gifts, even the Kyklops Polyphemos who gave me this blooming helmet of viewless night."

But the holy queen persisted, saying: "Odysseys shall not
lie forever in Tartaros: for my cousin, Golden Helen, hath
persuaded me for his sake. Yet, seeing that he cannot go hence
without thy leave, I say let him fight a select champion for
his liberty."

But the shady king of terrors instantly assented, saying: "So
mote it be. And irrevocable doom shall come upon him when
he has been properly slain."

But the Stygian queen smiled in scorn, mocking a king so
foolish as to think that a woman, a daughter of Great Zeys,
could not find some crafty wile for evading an adverse chance
if necessary.

And the king cried again, saying: "Who, of all the heroes
here, will fight against Odysseys, grandson of Hermes, for the
honor of the house of Hades?"

And straightway answered him Attik Theseys the con-
queror of the Kretan Minotayr, and loud shouting impotent
old sandy-haired King Menelaos, and woman-mad Paris son
of Dardanian Priam, saying: "That will we do, O dread lord:
for, of old, we sought the love of long-robed Helen, to have
her after the manner of men and women. But she rejected us,
favoring Odysseys with her amber eyes, from her girlhood to
this day. Wherefore, we are ready to fight against him on thy
behalf, O Dominator of the netherworld."

And these three made their way to the front of the throne.
Now Theseys was a stalwart hero and a very worthy champion:
moreover, his very nose had gone black with jealous hatred.
But sandy-haired Menelaos was merely an aged screecher and
whimperer, blear-eyed, rheumy-nosed, scraggy, knotty as to
the joints, and unfit to be put to tussle even with a foot-boy's
slut out of the kitchens. And Phrygian Paris, once the comely
shepherd of Ida, was a flaccid obese weakling, exhausted by
excess, against whom I should have been ashamed to lift a
finger. So I said. But, from afar, there came a great bellowing
from Salaminian Aias son of King Telamon, very mad with
rage, saying that he would fight on the part of King Menelaos,
having also a private grievance to avenge, in that I had won
from him (on the plain of windy Ilion) the armor of glorious

Akhilleys. And great-hearted Hektor, son of King Priam, took up the cause of his wasted brother Paris, claiming the right of fighting against me because of the ruin which I worked on his house and city by my wile of the Wooden Horse.

But shady Hades sniggered, saying: "Not one of these three champions, who hold my honor so dear, shall be disappointed. Wherefore, fight each of you in turn; and let King Theseys fight first. And, if so be that no Odysseys is left in life to fight loud-bellowing Aias and great Hektor in turn, then, indeed, the blame will not be mine."

But Queen Persephone cried: "Now would it be foul shame to pit a single man, even though he be King Odysseys whom they call Peer of Zeys in Counsel, against three heroes so justly famous in battle, princes renowned throughout all time. Wherefore I, the queen, call for two heroes to fight side by side with King Odysseys, upholding the honor of Queen Persephone protecting him."

And, almost before the goddess had ceased from speaking, and, while King Hades was yet frowning in perplexity, Argive Diomedes the well-thewed son of King Tydeys cried: "I will fight cheerfully for the honor of Queen Persephone, and for my ancient friendship with King Odysseys, with whom, by night, I attacked the hardy Thrakians who wear their red hair bunched on the crown of their heads."

Then, indeed, the mind in my breast rejoiced: for I knew that, with my old comrade Diomedes (a mighty man of war) by my side, many very virtuous and proper deeds would be done against the hostile champions. But, while I wondered who would be my other sword-fellow and shield-friend, the voice of great-hearted implacable Akhilleys declared that his god-forged armor might in no wise go into battle, he being present, unless he himself fought by its wearer's side. But I knew then that I should not tarry long among the ghosts.

King Hades preened himself at the prospect of bloody war; and, seeing three sons of kings ready to contend with three sons of kings, he made no more ado, but began to embody the shades of these five heroes, furnishing them with bodies and limbs and arms and armor such as they had used in their very prime, when (living) they stamped on the earth the giver of grain.

Now it is not to be thought that I, when I saw such notable magic being done before my eyes, could (or would) refrain from offering also a specimen of my own proficiency. But I determined at once to let King Hades see how great a mage he had been minded to treat thus bitterly, and (at the same time) to comfort my friends and to secure respectful opinions from the inhabitants of the netherworld there present in innumerable multitudes.

Wherefore, seeing the ghosts of those five heroes becoming clothed with live flesh and about to be armed by their proper squires, I nobly refused the service of the Great Twins, star-crowned, when they would have prepared me for the fray. And the eyes of all, from highest to lowest instantly became fixed upon me. But I stood still, summoning certain forces within me, and silently saying the *Spell called The Summons which must be Answered.*

And, forthwith, Thalos my footboy (whose life was bound to mine) came from the misty meadows of asphodel, where he and Neandros and my silver chariot were waiting for me. Fearlessly he came, entering the judgment-hall of Hades, thinking of naught but his duty to his lord. And it was very strange to see a mere boy, mortal, but alive and very healthy, wearing his usual sandals and short mantle, running toward me through so vast a throng of naked shades. But the dead all made way for him, being beaten back and most dreadfully worried: for he was (as I was) immune against death by reason of my magic and also by reason of the grace of his own luminous innocence. And, having come to me, he went over the clasps of my armor in the usual manner, saying nothing. But, when he had done his service, he went (at my command) and crouched by the feet of long-robed Helen.

Then, again, I called, calling (this time) as Master.

And forthwith there came in Delphic Phoibos Apollon as Knight of the Sun, and Arkadian Hermes as Knight of East and West and North and South, and lordly Ares as Knight of Kadosh, and Lemnian Hephaistos as Knight of the Brazen Serpent, and Theban Herakles (who, they say, changed wives with Zeys) as Knight of the Sword of the East, all gloriously triumphant, and, also, beardless Dionysos as Noahite Patriarch, and pale Death and dusky Sleep as Princes of Mercy, and immortal Eros as Prince of the Royal Secret, each one giving me the greeting of his own degree. But to them I responded as Master. They seated themselves on the bench with the judges Aiakos, Minos, and Rhadamanthos. And I remember how that the shade of accursed Thersites, humpty-backed, blameless, took a mind-grieving toss from lordly Ares, having presumed (as his wont was) to thrust himself unbidden into the pews of his betters. And inextinguishable laughter arose among the shades, when they saw the staggering unhappiness of that chatterbox Thersites.

But, when all was ready, I took my place, having kissed the still brow of Golden Helen. But the touch of the goddess, though her mien was strange and unresponsive, put strength into my shoulders and knees, and placed in my breast the boldness of a fly, which persists in biting, although often driven away by a mortal man whose blood is its most delicate sweetmeat. For I burned with an insatiable desire for slaying, nor to surcease therefrom till all were gone who stood between me and Golden Helen. For I was in face of her, for pious reasons.

Thus, indeed, were the champions placed: at my side, I had great-hearted Akhilleys on my left, and well-thawed Diomedes on the right: but at the other side, renowned Theseys faced me, and keen Hektor faced Akhilleys, and sacrilegious Aias faced Diomedes. And we were to fight with spears and swords. But my wily revolver was ready to my hand; and long-robed Helen held my black bow, which sang of war and the slaughter of heroes till King Hades gave signal for the onset.

Theseys thrust his spear straight at my best eyelid, terribly shouting: but I raised my shining shield like a flash of white thunder, taking his point full on the god-made boss of it. And the heavenly silver rang true as a bell. But I, stooping, drove up with my own spear, which he (also) took on his shield. But, so mightily had I thrust it, that the head stuck fast in the metal: nor could I tear it again from the grip of his shield. He, then, noisily swang his targe aside, snatching away my weapon. But I dashed in, battering him with my own shield, till he was beaten to his knee. And, while he recollected himself, I drew my sword and lopped off his spear-head, pressing hard with my shield against his, and hewing at his head. But he, cunning, took my strokes on his well-crested helmet, while he fumbled for his sword. Nevertheless, his head must have hummed, for sparks fell thickly on all sides from every blow, as they fall from a red-hot horse-shoe smitten upon an anvil in a winter's night. And, when once more we were equally armed, we fell to fighting very seriously; and, for a time, neither of us gained an advantage.

But, suddenly, I heard a great sob on my right hand. For well-thawed Diomedes crashed to the ground; and all the netherworld shook at his fall, as a citadel shakes when thumped by a battering-ram. And, at the same time Aias son of Telamon leaped upon me, masked in blood, and bellowing like a hamstrung bull.

Now, hitherto, notwithstanding the gravity of our combat, neither I nor Theseys had let blood. But, when I saw scarlet Aias coming ravening upon me, and, when I sniffed the delicious odor of a hero's blood, then, indeed, I accomplished a certain wile. For I feinted downward, to draw the sword of Aias; and, lightening my guard before his eye (half-dimmed with streaming gore) could follow, I lunged upward, plunging my blade like an onion into the bellowing mouth of him, where a wound is particularly painful to a miserable mortal; and awfully my hilt thudded on the bones behind his face, passing right through his head under the brain and bruising the white bones at the back. And his teeth were shivered to splinters; and his two eyes gushed with gore, which he (gaping) made violently to spout also with a bubbling noise from his mouth and from both his ears and nostrils, drenching me with five purple fountains. But his knees relaxed; and he sat down suddenly backward, stretching out his two hands; and Death enveloped him in a pale cloud. In this manner, I lost my sword as well as my spear, being too much occupied to retrieve it from the badly-wrecked face of Aias.

And now one would have said that I was at the mercy of my own enemy: for Theseys all the time did not omit to hack at my head. But I caught his strokes on my shield till it was split in twain, and then upon my crested helmet studded with adamantine crystals and blue moonstones; and his blows were like the blows of a poleaxe wielded by a blooming butcher, or of a sledge-hammer wielded by a lusty smith. But, because I was unarmed and liable to reel giddily under the hero's onslaught, my noble mind contrived a new wile. And, diving upward under his shield (lest he should wound me in the back), I caught him round the ribs with my long arms, and began to crumple him up. He, indeed, having dropped his shield, smote once on my back: but it was only a half-cut, for my shoulder filled the sweet pit of his sword-arm, preventing him from giving either force or weight unto his effort. Meanwhile, I splintered his crackling ribs one by one, pinching him as ferociously as possible, and wrenching him hither and thither, with a heart full of pure joy, when I felt so renowned a hero as Theseys becoming like a broken basket of entrails in my arms. He, indeed, tried to stab me with his bitter steel, in the intervals when he was neither screeching nor gasping for breath with much hiccoughing. And, anon, having heaved him high above my head, (for he tired me), then I dashed him to the ground, snapping his big backbone with a noise like the quick tearing of linen. But he lapsed limply into a shapeless bundle of broken man; and his last breath shot out with a wet squeak, moistly whistling; and renowned Theseys was once more a shade.

But I sidled away from the carcass, looking toward my left hand, where the two great heroes and masters of perfect swordsmanship were fighting valiantly. And crest-tossing Hektor feigned to slip, half exposing his head: but implacable Akhilleys, for the nonce unwary, brandished his blade for a last terrific blow which should end the battle. But him Hektor overcame, eluding the shield which swang away to the left, and thrusting his own sword through the taslets of the breast-plate deep into the beautiful groin. Nevertheless, the end was not yet. For fierce Akhilleys, though wounded to death, finished the stroke which he had begun. And his sword came down irresistibly on Hektor's crested helm; and the horse-hair floated away on this side and on that; and the whole casque fell in two halves here and there, like the split shells of a walnut; and the head within, being divided in twain right down to the roots of the throat, flapped upon the shoulders like a halved pomegranate on a sliced stem. In this manner, fell together the two greatest warriors and the two most glorious heroes who ever stamped on the wide-bosomed earth.

But all voices were hushed at the splendor of the sight, grieving that the five famous sons of kings should so soon have ceased from sweet life, again becoming shades. And I, also, stood in silence: for I was still rather dizzy. But, all at once, shady Hades shouted from his throne: "This much-contriving Odysseys again hath tricked us by some magic wile. Ha, Titans, hold him!"

And, on the word, the enormous monsters lumbered in my direction. But all the shades began to gibber like bats, moaning with fear; and the shade of great-hearted Akhilleys became paler with horror, because of King Hades' treachery. But Thalos, my footboy, lithely leaped from crouching at the feet of Golden Helen; and, having snatched my black bow from her (but she gave it willingly), he thrust it into my hand, standing alertly close behind me with my quiver, ready to feed me with arrows. And, in an instant, I bent the great bow to the string, while it sang shrilly with joy, loosing the well-feathered shafts which swiftly hissed down the long hall; and they bit the eyeballs of the titans so that they yelped like whipped whelps in their displeasure, falling as great oaks crash earthward in storms, littering considerable areas.

But, as I sped the winged deaths on their way, I heard a terrible cry from the queen. But I, without turning round to her, was suddenly aware that I was seeing on all sides, both before and behind: for the eyes in my face, fearfully rolling, gazed in front; and, when I drew the string of the bent-back bow to my ear with my right hand, the two eye-chalcedonyxes in the magic ring which Hermes, my grandsire, had placed on my third finger looked out over my shoulder in the rear, warning me of danger from that quarter. And I saw shady King Hades, the most righteous of gods, about to dash out my brain with the gigantic key which fits the locks of hell.

But, leaping aside, I evaded the blameless coward's blow: but, in escaping from the god, I became far away from Thalos who bore my arrows; and my bow shrieked because I could not use it. Once more, King Hades struck at me; and, once more mightily leaping, I eluded the danger. Moreover, I saw, from the bewildered gestures of the shades, that they understood neither what was going on nor the reason of my marvelous agility. And, then, I perceived that the shady one had donned his cyclopean helmet of invisibility, whereby none but a god's eyes could see him. But I, being hard pressed, determined to use magic of another kind, such as I had found very efficacious against shady hustlers and bullies when I was a subject of Victory queen of the stalwart stately Anglicans. And, first, I praised rustic Pan and wing-footed Hermes, with wildly joyful acclamations: the one for his gift in the touch of fennel on the seashore by Tainaron, whereby I was able to see with the eyes of a god as well as with the eyes of a man, and the other (my grandsire) for his gift of two eyes more than the number allotted to olympians, to say nothing of miserable mortals: for, without these extraordinary faculties, shady Hades would certainly have gotten me again, and for good, and I should have lost Golden Helen for the third and last time.

Wherefore, I plucked out my revolver, as blameless Hades came upon me. He, indeed, had the air of being dreadfully worried, believing himself to be invisible, and yet finding that I was able to dodge him quite successfully. And, having pressed the well-made spring of my weapon with my palm, I pulled the beautiful trigger six times, afflicting the Shady One with a dumdum* in each nostril and two in the belly and one in each knee. But he, being a god, was unable to die, even though he had lost his ugly face: but all the same, he was extremely capable of feeling pain; and dreadful pain he felt. Now, as everyone knows, when lordly Ares was wounded by well-thewed Diomedes at the siege of windy Ilion, he hulla-balooed (as it is chanted in the canticle) like an army of ten thousand men all mad-drunk with beer. But, King Hades being of the elder generation of the gods, and (therefore) of far vaster bulk than his lusty nephew, the bellowing of nine-teen such armies would have been (to the outpouring of his godly griefs and pains) but as the wheezy puling of an infant to the thunder of immeasurable Ocean on a rock-bound coast. For, indeed, the very firmament of the netherworld was riven and cleft asunder by the thuds of his high-stepped

* I find several English words in this papyrus, written in what we will agree to call Mr. C.'s own hand. — A.H.

capers and contortions, and the bombilation of his vibrant vociferatings to my address.

But I, looking upward through the grateful fissure, saw clear heaven again, and the serenely-sailing Moon, and the glittering constellation of the Crab, and all the holy stars which kindly gaze upon earth-trampling men.

After this manner, did I work notable wiles in the house of blameless Hades.

The Twenty-First Papyrus

*T*HEN, the gods, divine ones inhabiting olympian palaces, whom I had summoned to see how a master-mage under-goes that he may overcome, intervened to protect me from further annoyance. For unspeakable confusion buzzed and boomed throughout all the house of Hades.

For the shades of well-born Theseys and of sandy-haired old Menelaos and of woman-mad Paris were gibbering with rage, seeing that I was free to depart with Golden Helen, the Treasure of Hades, as my spoil. And they shook their angry fingers at me, like fringes in a wind, being quite impotent: but Paris, unable to contain what there was of himself (so abounding was his ire), burst, over and over again, like a bad bubble in my vicinity. And he suddenly frittered away.

But, as I walked with the blessed gods, having Helen the Treasure of Hades beside me, we went to and fro, walking delicately over the monstrous wrigglings of titans, victims of my bow, as men pick their way among earthquakes, lightly leaping hither and thither. But the mind in my breast was contriving new wiles.

Then said Delphic Phoibos Apollon, the Knight of the Sun: "We have tarried long enough in the kingdom of twilight; and I yearn to go back to blazing noon. Return with us, O Master of Wisdom; and be sure of olympian welcomes."

Then said Arkadian Hermes Psykhopompos, the Knight of East and West and North and South: "Never yet have I led articulately-speaking men out of this place: but rather my business is to bring them hither when they are dead. But very gladly will I bear thee and thine away with swift-winged feet, O Master my child. Return, therefore, with us; and be sure of olympian welcomes."

Then said Lemnian Hephaistos, the Knight of the Brazen Serpent: "There be many dints and notches in thy silver-shining armor, and many of thy lovely rock-crystals and blue-moonstones have been shattered in battle, and what shall we say of thy nodding crest of the prides of nine white peacocks. But, indeed, my fingers itch to have thee in my smithy where I may restore thee. Return, therefore, with us, O Master of Arms; and be sure of olympian welcomes."

And, in like manner, all the divine ones spoke, very affably.

But white Death and black Sleep, being young, stood modestly aside: for the general rule is that the last may not come to man without an invitation, and that the first may come only at a particular time. And that time for me had not even been discussed by the authorities. For which cause, the pale god moved away, going about more pressing business: but the dark one lingered, lifting his horn of dust to tempt me. But, though I was not unwilling to receive the kindly gift of Sleep, the mind in my noble breast reminded me that many things still remained for me to do. Wherefore I addressed unwinged words to the blessed gods, saying: "Gladly, O divine ones, will I escape from this nasty neighborhood, and gladly will I visit the height of Olympos, bringing with me Helen the Treasure of Hades, and Love, the Crown of All Wisdom."

Thus I spoke, as we came forth from the hall into the misty meadows of Asphodel. But, behind us in the House of Hades, we left incalculable pudder and turmoil. For, beside the roars of the wounded, the innumerable shades of all the dead since Cain slew Abel,* being worried with pique and jealousy, were pouring themselves out helter-skelter, snuffling in clusters, whimpering and maudling and mumbling, waving themselves all over the place like streamers of seaweed, all in a most embarrassing manner. And it seemed as though my passage would be impeded by them, as by inextricable mazes of

---

* This is, or might very well be taken to be, an excessively nasty one in the eye for the obsolete delusion once called "Modernism." — A.H.

cobwebs.

Wherefore, I (to make an end) summoned Thalos, nimbly loaded with my gear by him collected and skipping after me; and of him I inquired whereabouts might be my silver chariot. Who answered me, saying that my squire Neandros was not ceasing from driving about the asphodeline meadows, being unseen, and keeping alert for my call: yet he knew not precisely where the chariot might be at the moment. And he mentioned his opinion that Neandros would be glad of a meal, not because he was dying of hunger as another youth would have died, famished (for his life was bound to my life, so that he lived while I lived), but just because it was the custom of mortals to eat at intervals. And inextinguishable laughter arose among the immortal gods when they heard the apt speech of my footboy.

Then, the Great Twins, impatient of delay, moved to the other side of their golden sister, as though to protect her from the mobs of gibbering shades: but I, on my part, uttered the *Spell* called *The Call Which Must Be Answered;* and, instantly, Neandros drove my silver-shining chariot toward us out of the imperscrutable mist. But the gods, when they saw that I was furnished with so suitable a vehicle with its equipage of four mad stallions of the divine breed of Laomedon, departed, flying up earthward through the riven roof of the netherworld, and thence onward to the height of Olympos. Thus the gods themselves were my heralds.

But I placed Golden Helen (divine one of the goddesses) beside Neandros in the chariot; and, when Thalos had mounted in the rear placing his beautiful bundle on the silver floor, I, also, was about to ascend to my place: but a very fearful occurrence delayed me. For the shade of woman-mad Paris, partly embodied again, darted toward us out of the mist; and his sufficiently-solid hand had been armed by shady Hades with the sword of dead Hektor his brother. Now had I been blameless Hades in these circumstances, I would have embodied the shade of Hektor and employed hint as my assassin rather than the feeble and fatuous Paris: but Hades was not at all wily. And the woman-mad one ran, gibbering frightfully, leering like a lunatic who after long seeking has found; and he, squealing (for his throat was not quite firmly finished), slashed as he passed with his blade at my harness, so that the snow-white leathern thongs were divided, and the reins fell severed from the hands of my charioteer. But the horses went madder, bounding upward; and careered (trace-free) to their native pastures in the rolling heavens, leaving us half-blinded by their hoof-sparks and (so to speak) fixed immovably below. And, every moment, the mobs of malignant ghosts surrounding us became more impertinently menacing.

But I, having won the Crown of All Wisdom (which is Love), and the Treasure of Hades (which is Golden Helen), and being unwilling to forego the enjoyment of my beautiful spoils, and remembering the word which Hermes had said by my altar on black Tanairon, lifted up my voice very loudly indeed, uttering the most mighty but two of all spells. And thus I said: "Hear, O oldest and youngest of all the blessed gods, sweet one, sly one, dire one, winged one, blind one, arch-archer, lord of unquenchable flame, thou who art somewhere in the rich state of heaven or on the grain-giving earth, for thou everywhere canst see and hear a man in affliction, hear now, and aid me in my need. Come, Love, come."

And, instantly, through the gigantic fissure yawning overhead, came the sound of merry childish laughter. And Divine Eros dived out of the darkness like a flash of ruddy lightning, folding his white wings to stand before us, lifting the bandage from his sparkling eyes to warm us with their radiance. And we, who had been shivering with ghostly cold and bound to the soil of hell a moment before, felt all our limbs a-thrill with life and joy and in our hearts a splendor at the coming of the bird of the gods. For he, indeed, was a very large and lovely boy, slim, and rounded, and so ruddy that his form had scarce been known within a fiery furnace of clear flame: but, when we saw the freedom with which he flung abroad his sprightly limbs, and his quick incessant movements, it was clear that he could have no rival in energy or strength. And, while we gazed, he was darting here and there, peering into my silver chariot's secret parts, having pulled out the pole and cast it away for inquisitive ghosts to sniff at and mumble. And even I stood amazed: for, notwithstanding my magic, I had not suspected that such marvels could be as those which Love laid bare. For, here, he pressed certain beautiful knops carven on the panels; and, forthwith, lids opened in the silver floor, whereunto he wept copious torrents of wet tears, because of foolish men; and, having closed the lids, he shewed us his ruddy young face wreathed with laughter. And, there, he ran his fingers over the bosses of other silver pallets inlaid with crabs and moons in mother-of-pearl; and other lids opened; and a fragrance as of smooth oil was wafted in the air. But all this, and very much more, was done in a moment of time.

And Love urgently charged us to mount to our places: but he was sprawling on his supple back, underneath, between the well-carved wheels, and belching streams of heavenly fire from his rose-red lips. But we four mounted, and clung to the rail: for the mighty chariot was beginning to hum and pulsate like a creature having life, so that (though I was not afraid, but rather exultant with joy unspeakable), I made the *Sign of Safety* from height to depth and from here to there, which is the test and the touchstone and the palladium of all white magic.

But the immortal god arose, sweeping the air once with his great white wings; and he swooped upward, diving into the very image of himself, larger than life, blindfolded, naked, most alluringly proportioned, which stood poised on the front of the rail, winged, and ready to fly. And the whiteness and ruddiness of Eros totally disappeared in the silver image of him, nor was the silver any longer hard and still, like silver, but smooth and firm and supple as young flesh, being alive in very fact and altogether godlike in potency.

And the silver Love hooted aloud in mockery of the gibbeting shades; and he swept back the air with his winged arms, as a strong swimmer slipping through the wavelets of the innumerable laughter of the ocean,* setting all mortal means at naught, needing neither oar nor sail saving his wings, winnowing the winds with those eternal plumes.† And the wheels of the chariot whirred astonishingly with the swiftness

---

* This ΑΝΡΗΙΘΜΟΝ ΓΕΛΑΣΜΑ is certainly a tag. — A.H.
† It is hardly conceivable that Dante Alighieri can have lifted these delicious phrases from Mr. C. The whole question is extremely perplexing. — A.H.

of our flight toward the fissure in the firmament of hell. But I, looking downward at the fearful ghosts, saw Kastor and Polydeykes catching treacherous Paris by hair and heels and slinging him into fiery Pyriphthlegethon. Awfully scorched was what there was of him when he scrambled out; and the Great Twins left him licking his burns on the bank: but they went back to the house of Hades, to serve the rest of that day in the netherworld for a religious reason, such being their immutable doom.

But the living silver Love bore us upward out of darkness. But I looked upon the walls of the vast chasm as we passed them by; and I saw the depths of rich earth's bosom all laid bare. Here were pockets full of white gold or korinthic bronze which is platinum* and of gold and of silver and of copper, and of iron, and of gleaming tin. There, were mounds of marble and porphyry and granite. Here, were rivers of chalcedonyx and jasper, and streams of rose-quartz and violet amethyst and rock-crystal and blue-moonstone and mysterious green-and-purple alexandrolith. There, were caverns full of buried and forgotten treasures. And, scattered everywhere, like the stars upon the floor of heaven, were very precious stones, in clots, or alone in glittering glory. But, above all these, we passed the pregnant soil of earth the cupboard of mortals, pierced in every direction by the juicy roots of herbs and trees.

I turned my gaze to my dear companions. The stalwart Neandros clung to the rail at the back; and his bold eyes stirred not from the god who had deposed him from his place as charioteer, for he was meditating an unmentioned and unthought-of work, which I will narrate at a suitable time. Thalos crouched on his hams on the floor, clinging with one arm to the straight legs of Neandros, but his other arm steadied the bundle of my gear. And, by my side, stood long-robed Helen, the divine one of goddesses. She was as purely white as the kernel of a nut; and her hair floated behind like a web of woven sunbeams. One gleaming arm round me, and the other on the rail near the feet of the silver Love, held her still. Her head was quiet and happy on my breast. Silent

---

* Oh, really! But this is a little more definite in its dogmatism. — A.H.

were her lips of coral. Eloquent beyond mortal words were her amber eyes: wherein gazing at my ease, I read of her pride, her meekness, her power, her weakness, her fidelity, her faith, her wisdom, her generosity, her pure unsullied soul, her worship, and her love. What she read in mine, I also know; and, that we two know it, is enough.

We were ascending from twilight to daylight. Not for nothing had those other divine ones gone before, announcing our coming: for the whole world was set agog to behold us. Heavenly breezes rustled down the shaft to refresh us with their clean breath. Little rills of sparkling water trickled over the cleft earth's lips in haste to greet us. And the forests bowed their green heads, like a canopy, above us flashing through the reft rock, as we reached the kindly-smiling earth once more.

In this pomp, I came triumphantly a third time out of the netherworld, with the Treasure of Hades and the Crown of All Wisdom. And Love himself was my charioteer.

The Twenty-Second Papyrus

*B*UT, when we had come to the beautiful plains of earth, there were spread before our feet (for us to walk upon) pleasaunces of emerald grass studded with jewels of daisies and bluebells and daffodils and buttercups and cyclamen, with swathes of poppies, and with splashes of pure gold crocus dropped straight down from the radiant sun. Then, indeed, I (as a mortal man) found a fit time when I might give way to human weakness: for a man who does godlike deeds must pay a price. And, because my head swam with weariness, and because every part of me ached from my sunned skin to my white bones, and because every sense of me was sickened by the slime and corrupt blood of hellish menials wherewith I was crusted from crest to sandals, then, I longed to be visited by barbers and clean slaves, and, also, I had a keen remembrance of the willing and alluring look which the young god with the horn of eye-closing dust had shot at me by shady Hades' hall, seeming to ask for an invitation. But I thought on these things particularly, as (with Golden Helen) I paced a soft meadow bloomed of violets and parsley, breathing the sweet air.

And Golden Helen perceived how it was with me: for two (who love) are one. Beside, being a woman, she needed but a single service from me, to wit, that I should never leave untold the never-to-be-outworn story of my love for her; and that (to me) was no toil, but a pleasure perennial. And, for the rest, she (the one women of women and the divine one of goddesses) had no other joy than that of caring for her lover. Wherefore, she sat down on a thymy bank in the shade of a may-bush: but I reclined by her side. Thus, we rested, during a little while, watching the slaves beginning to clear my chariot and my gear: for a cheerful brook ran by the place, sparing enough water for their work, but not enough for the cleansing of a man as well. But I intended, after resting, to seek a site apart, for my own embellishment. And, while these things were being done, a remarkable portent and a signal favor of a god were manifested, which I will at once narrate.

For, when we emerged from the fissure in the earth whereby we evacuated the abysm, it clapped-to behind us, just as did that other gulf which formerly yawned for showy Curtius in the forum of Rome.* And the living silver Love, my chari-oteer, folded his wings, while we paused to breath the upper air. But when we sat down to rest upon the thymy bank, his clear young voice, with a shout of laughter, called us by name. But we, starting, looked toward the sound; and the silver Love, poised all alive on the front of the chariot, bade us to come near and observe him closely. Thus we did; and the large volatile boy turned on his hips, spreading his quivering wings to balance himself; and he shewed us (and we perceived it) that he was girded about the reins with a fine silver chain, the two taslets whereof dangled down behind him as far as the rail of the chariot. And thus he chirruped: "Lady of Love, and Lord of the Lady of Love, give me leave to make other lovers happy in the intervals. But call me to serve you when you will, pulling the chain this way or that, having enslaved me and bound me to you by unbreakable fetters at present unseen."

And, with the word, the god returned to his position,

---

* This is valuable. I suppose "formerly" helps to date these papyri, at least within a century or so. But Mr. C.'s epithet for Marcus Curtius strikes me as being a little what I might almost term original. "Showy" hardly seems the just word for a hero. But, of course, Mr. C. wrote only a few centuries after the young Roman's celebrated header, which perhaps did not seem extraordinarily impressive to contemporary professionals. Distance does sometimes lend enchantment to the view, I believe. – A.H.

poising himself as before with wide-spread wings. But he came (a large boy's form of flesh, ruddy and white as roses, slender and splendidly rounded), out of the silver leaving his image behind him. And, leaping free with far-flung limbs and strongly-waving arms, he stretched himself out at length, swimming in the higher air out of our sight.

But my head began to whirl faster and faster. I saw Neandros and Thalos arising after they had adored the blooming god, and I felt that Golden Helen was conducting me again to the thymy bank. And, coming nearer, I heard the sweet sound of a syrinx of pipes, and the bushes rustled as though some divine one were approaching. But, instantly, the divine of goddesses cried out, saying: "Oh Pan! O obliging Pan!"

But the country-god pushed aside the branches, peering at us from the screen of green leaves, being shy in the quivering sunshine of noon. And, when he saw who we were, he came forth and greeted us; and he led us through the may-bushes to a little grove, on the bank of a deep stream, with a waterfall and a pool, and mossy-soft couches of moly in the shade, all of which (I believe) he invented at the moment. And, having gathered handfuls of the herb All-heal, knowing Pan eased me of my dinted armor: but fair Helen bathed me, and she bound the magic herb on my bruised and weary limbs. Then, indeed, I summoned benign Sleep, while Pan piped me a simple rustic ballad very soothing to the mind.

And there, in the grove, we rested during several days. For I contrived a new wile, which was that I would not hurry on my journey to lofty Olympos, but rather delay a little: for an unwilling guest has the greater honor. Moreover, I did not wish to appear before the blessed gods in a squalid or a sordid guise, but rather as a personage more accustomed to giving than to receiving, since I was actually a suppliant to great Zeys for the hand of his daughter; and it is the custom of gods and men to give the best gifts to well-seeming mortals. For which causes, I took my fill of rest, so that my strength returned, while my slaves (in the neighboring glade) polished my arms and my chariot as best they might, to make a respectable appearance. For magic is waived before Pan, and men must depend entirely on their natural powers in his presence unless the god himself suggests otherwise.

But, by chance, Hermes (my grandsire), passing by on a message, espied us one day; and he stayed his flight while he spoke with us. He said that there was much talk on the height of Olympos, because of our absence, and because the divine ones (witnesses of my acts in the house of shady Hades) had entered into a compact one with another to keep silence on those matters, so that the whole areiopagos of heaven might hear them (if I so willed) from my own mouth. Which was a very pleasant hearing for me; and, indeed, I thought it extremely nice and delicate on the part of the gods. But I answered Hermes meekly enough, saying that it was not for me, a mortal, to enter heavenly dominions in a manner unworthy of my grandsire. And my wile proved to be an excellent one. For Hermes, having had a word with kindly Pan, fled (swift-footed) away, presently returning with slow-footed Hephaistos and a portable smithy. For Hephaistos, being proud of the armor which he made for the son of silver-footed Thetis, was unwilling that the hands of slaves should renew its splendor. But when his forge was set up, in the neighboring glade, the divine artificer (out of admiration for me) deigned to employ Neandros and Thalos as his assistants instead of a parcel of kyklops of immoderate unsightliness: more, also, he let them learn several very important tricks of his trade, when he observed that they were intelligent workmen of ingenious and reverend mind. Such mortals, as a matter of fact, do the gods usually select, when imparting knowledge of the arts.

Thus, then, we passed the time, living on cheeses and nuts and blackberries and dandelions with the luscious milk of incontinent goats of amiable demeanor, while I continued to repose myself, cared-for by the divine one of goddesses and cheered by old Pan. He, indeed, entertained me vastly with stories of the youth of the world when Great Zeys lay hid in Krete and the older gods were yet unborn; and, at other times, he attuned his reedy pipes intonating quaint songs of the woodlands. And once, while long-robed Helen slept in the heat of the day, the knowing old god persuaded some dryads to come out of the oak trees in the grove to fan away the flies when I was dozing: but he himself sat among the reeds not far away, chatting with the cheerful little brown and silver river. They were very slim young girls (these dryads), with flesh as white as an acorn-kernel, with long smooth hair of the color of oak-bark, and shy green eyes of the color of oak-leaves, and excessively modest and timid of disposition. But, when fair Helen awakened from sleep, and spied the industrious little creatures, her sweet face flushed like rosy dawn, and she frightened the shy nymphs quite away by her bleak mode of thanking them for their care of me. Nor was I puffed with vanity: for I am not the only complacent mortal who has been an occasion of jealousy to a goddess.

But, at another time, while sweet Helen was washing her robes in the pool, rustic Pan took leave to inform me (as a friend) of her history during the previous ten centuries. And I will say that Pan was the only one of all the blessed gods who did not ascribe my own stories about myself, and about my future life in the kingdom of Victory queen of the stalwart stately Anglicans, to some one or other of my usual alto-gether-unexpected wiles. But Pan knows all. And he told me how that (when I fell dead in my former chariot, from the arrow of unknowing Telegonos, my son and that awful god-dess Kirke's), in Egypt, more than a thousand years before, then, the divine one of goddesses, Helen, had behaved very queerly indeed: for she shewed as much grief as though she herself had caused my demise. Pan said that many persons called her grief remorse: which is absurd. But, having vowed herself anyhow to my memory, she prepared to wander through time, mourning, until my coming again. And heroes and kings' sons without number sought her in marriage: whom having scorned fearfully (as far as so gentle a creature could scorn), she retired to find commodious seclusion on lofty Olympos. But, there, a certain Kyknos, a son (they say) of far-darting Phoibos Apollon, persuaded that god to de-mand her for him from Great Zeys. But the father and king of gods and men only confirmed (with a nod) the maiden's right of choice. Thereat, blameless Kyknos would have taken her by force, following the custom of Olympians: but her brothers, Kastor the tamer of horses and Polydeykes the pugilist, beat on his nose so very bitterly, that beef-eating Herakles wakened from slumber adding his shouts to the tumult. Which having been explained to him, he promptly tossed Kyknos to earth from lofty Olympos, breaking him. And Phoibos Apollon felt it incumbent upon him to take up the cause of Kyknos and to be extremely prepotent about it. But Great Zeys, upset by cow-eyed Hera (most righteous of goddesses), shrouded himself in black clouds, having decreed that the fragments of broken Kyknos must stay below to satisfy Golden Helen, and that she (the divine one of god-desses) must not stay above, being a cause of disorderly conduct among the young gods. But Phoibos Apollon col-lected the pieces of Kyknos, as many as he could find, where-with he made a new swan (that lickerish fowl), entirely black.* But Golden Helen, debarred from the height of Olympos, and her honor in peril from hairy men down below, betook herself further, even to the profundity of the netherworld, where the gods were austere, and men but senseless shades, phantoms of men worn out. And there she lived in exile, all for the sake of me, divested of godlihood, enduring ten centuries of sorrow, the inevitable penance for the glowing glory of her immortal inmarcesible youth.

But, having heard all these things babbled-of by rustic Pan one day when we dawdled together (and I could not learn them from fair Helen, for reasons of modesty), then, indeed, I held a sort of council with the mind in my noble breast. And I determined that, as far as I was concerned, she certainly should be rewarded for her grievous pains. For the best of women wants no more than a little true love; and well indeed did I know that that man is a blind besotted imbecile who, in pride or what-not, denies himself the pleasure of making a woman happy with what she wants, excepting (of course) for a religious reason. And, furthermore, I was aware that I myself was by way of owing a clearly-defined duty to the golden one of goddesses, in that I owed a debt of love to her, not only for her fidelity, or as amends for her wrongs, but chiefly because she had procured for me several pleasing and exciting and singular adventures, teaching me how to win the Crown of All Wisdom. The which debt I determined to pay forthwith.

Thereafter, I spoke not a word of these pious matters: but

---

* I cannot help citing Juvenal, *Sat.* VI., 165, in this connec-tion: *"Rara avis in terris negroque simillima cycno."* — A.H.

fair Helen was not unaware that I knew all that Pan could tell me, not as her accredited ambassador but as the trusty friend of us both. And, when I suddenly became very eager and insistent for nuptials, she would not deny me: but she mentioned that a bride ought to be brought from her paternal home to the house of her husband. Which doctrine I accepted. And I said that I would contain myself till her case and my case had been suitably pleaded before very-mighty many-named Zeys. That, then, was to be the object of our visit to the height of Olympos. For it pleased me better to go thus, on a matter of business, than merely to arrive, sleek, grinning, and complacent, to receive prizes and praises for athletic achievements and feats of endurance and wiliness, which, though most meritorious and praiseworthy, and valuable also, inasmuch as they gained for me the friendship of several very important gods (whose friendship is much preferable to their enmity), were, I affirm, rather to be classed with my ordinary habits than with my virtues.

Anon, cunning Hephaistos restored to me my shining armor of silver with adornments of rock-crystals and blue moonstones in all its pristine splendor: but he returned forthwith to olympian palaces. Neandros and Thalos also brought my silver chariot, polished in all its parts with a sheen like the full moon, and its secret recesses were well-filled with water and oil. But, when we had placed my gear therein, we said farewell to kindly Pan. And, in the cool of the evening, I led the divine one of goddesses to her place at the front: but I mounted by her side; and the slaves climbed up behind. But fair Helen pulled the fine chain by its taslet; and the whole chariot vibrated for sheer joy, panting and pulsating like a creature enjoying sweet life: for, at the same moment, young Eros dived out of open space, and the silver image of him started into perfervid life, boiling with force and merrily hooting.* But we, leaping forward with his beating wings,

---

* I cannot help remarking that this sounds rather awfully like what I might almost venture to term an ante-Christian automobile or motorcar, with its secret recesses filled with oil and water, its vibrations, its pantings, its pulsations, *and* its hooter on the front. If this conjecture of mine could be clearly substantiated, it would furnish a fresh ex-

skimmed into distance more swiftly than an owl in flight. All through the cool night we went at tireless speed: but, whether over sea or land, I cannot say. For, in good sooth, I was not aware of anything, save that the moon serene and the flagrant Crab smiled upon me from the dark-blue sky, that I was no longer dawdling but active and very strong, that Golden Helen was with me for good and all, and that Love was my charioteer.

In this manner, I set forth from the silvan grove where goat-footed Pan had been entertaining me.

---

emplification of the adage "Nothing new under the sun," I fancy. — A.H.

The Twenty-Third
Papyrus

*B*UT, when rosy-fingered Dawn had donned her saffron
robes, arising from her couch in the ocean to bring light to
mortals and immortals, then, indeed, we were nearing Tainaron, where lay the hollow ship with the shipmen expecting
my coming. And, when they saw us whizzing out of a dusty
cloud like a flash of white thunder (for, on the one side, the
hair of Golden Helen streamed behind us as streams a long
ray of sunbeams in no breeze, and, on the other side, my
mantle of silver tissue lined with white fur and clasped with
the Moon and the Crab in rock-crystals and blue moonstones
floated at large and at length beneath my towering crest of
the prides of nine white peacocks), and, when they saw
Neandros and Thalos, mysteriously lost, returning, and, when
they saw the large silver Love very much alive, and, when they
heard the gleeful whoopings of untameable Love and the
terrible whirring of the chariot-wheels, then, indeed, their
knees tottered, and their breath popped out, and their hearts
stood quite still for fear, so that their life left them, and pale
Death veiled their eyes.

But we lighted in the middle of the lofty prow, even as a
bird lights on the branch of a blooming tree;* and, when fair
Helen pulled the silver chain, instantly ruddy-white Love

---

* I would point out that the "vol plané" here described almost seems to resemble the showy but somewhat clumsy
mode of alterrament affected by the velivolors and aereo-
planes and dirigibles of the Fifth Georgian Era.

soared out of his silver image into the boundless empyrean; and thus we came to the end of our journey by land.

And now I was in a sort of quandary. For, knowing that I should need all my strength of mind and body on lofty Olympos, knowing (also) that rule of magic which says that a man of fluid temper (such as I am) can best collect a reserve of such strength from the sea, I had determined to go, by favor of azure-haired Poseidon, in my galley, from Tainaron in the south, by the Eyboik Gulph, to the small port of Myrai at the foot of mighty Mount Ossa in the north. But the rest of the journey would be made more splendidly, in my silver-shining chariot, by land.

But (such is the lot of miserable mortals, who forget to inquire the length of the life-threads, which the blameless Fates have spun for their fellows), I found myself, at the very outset of my voyage by sea, possessed of a huge well-benched ship with all its appurtenances in perfect order, but encumbered with the corpses of one-and-sixty mariners suddenly deceased, and a mere toy for the sea-gods. For which causes, I sat me down on the lofty poop, taking my dear head in my hands: and I began to contrive most astonishing wiles. But Golden Helen set by my side, like a true lover who knows when to speak to her man and when to hold her peace. But my two slaves waited silently in their places.

And, at length, it appeared to the mind in my lordly breast that the gods, divine ones inhabiting olympian palaces, are wont to deal with mortal men in this manner, shewing them singular favors so that they may be encouraged to expect (and, even, to insist on) a continuance of the same. For, as it is with a man, when he can do a certain deed very well, straightway he desires also to do it very often, for the benefit of the race of men and for all sorts of other pious and religious reasons, so, also, indeed, precisely, is it with the blessed gods, givers of good things. Wherefore, then, seeing that tameless Love had willingly bound himself (with a silver chain) to serve me and long-robed Helen, I contrived an altogether unmentioned and unthought-of magic: so that that ruddy bird of heaven might not have cause to complain that I let his blooming wings grow rusty with disuse.

Wherefore, I said unwinged words to Neandros and Thalos,

explaining to them what they were to do. But, first, having
pitched the dead mariners overboard to lighten the ship,
together we drew in the long oars, bestowing them tidily as
a rampart inside the bulwarks and fixing them there with
well-twisted knots. These things having been accomplished,
and the whole ship having been set in a new order, we took
a spare sail, white and vermilion, silken, with certain cordage,
out of the store. And, when we had ascended the lofty prow,
we fastened the wheels of the silver-shining chariot, fixing it
where it stood, immovably, in the middle of the prow, so that
a man might walk round and about it if he pleased, then,
indeed, we hanged the beautiful sail over it, and fastened the
same to the bulwarks, in the manner of an awning with
vermilion fringes. Thus, the splendor of the chariot was
concealed from the eyes of casual inquisitives: but the silver
image of Love emerged above the awning as a figure-head for
my galley: and the taslets of the silver chain about his reins
dangled down inside.

But Golden Helen pulled the chain of the silver image.
And, instantly, young Love descended into his image; and
the silver Love lived, flying with his tireless wings; so that the
great ship moved most rapidly across the frightened sea,
having neither oars nor other sail. But I governed the course
with the steering oar; and the divine one of goddesses was
near me.*

Now when I came again to hold council with my noble
mind, I was aware that (in winning the Treasure of Hades) I
procured for myself such a companion as I never had had
before. In sooth I have had comrades a many in my various
lives; and, among them I will name the most desirable Red
Heart of the southern sea, and the gloriolous son of Sycorax,
and the unchangeable George of the Roses, and timidly-false
Aubrey, and Hugh the priest devoured by hidden hatred and
envy and prepotence, and blind Karterikos of Bosporos, and
loving Vergilio, and naïve elegant Khekkhi, and also
Diomedes of the loud war-cry, and great-hearted yellow-
headed Akhilleys. Now, with a man, a man may fight, and

---

* I am given to understand that our own earlier hydroplanes
and hydrovolors had their motors situated amidships and
aft respectively. — A.H.

(at any rate) must quarrel: or there can be no true love, for love is not proved true until it has been tested by reconciliation after strife, preferably very bloody. And herein is the difference between a comrade and a companion.* For, with a woman, no man may dispute: but, if she has an evil mind, he may avoid her or annul her: but, when the gods, givers of good gifts, send to a man such a woman as he may fitly take for a companion, then, indeed, he becomes one with her, in that her ill is his hurt and her good his benefit. For it is very pleasing to the pride of a man to have a treasure to guard and to care for. And, until this time, all my wiles and all my wisdom had not won for me such a treasure. Not but what Queen Penelope had been a true wife to me while she had life on the earth: but, of those years there were twenty, when wars and the displeasure of certain blameless gods kept me away from her, so that (speaking with perfect respect to her face) I may say that she was a faithful wife and a most prudent housewife, but not by any means a companion. And, as for the quite-irrelevant matter of those divine ones of goddesses with whom I had intimate relations, to wit, deathless Kirke and Kalypso of the greasy braided tresses, who (I ask) can presume to talk about companionship when a man is imprisoned, with an awful woman, on a little islet surrounded by the boundless ruthlessly-smiling sea. But Golden Helen was altogether different from these three. Thus I meditated in my Love-sped galley.

But, coming to Khalkis, we stayed there, to procure sweet water and nutriments, before proceeding northward by the Eyboik Gulph. And hard-hearted envious Hera, that arch-mischief-maker among goddesses, sent me a horrid adventure, in the hope of impeding my progress.

For, while my slave Neandros was negotiating with merchants on the quay, loading the hollow ship with cheeses, and wheat (the marrow of men), and the flesh of bulls and swine, with herbs and dainty birds, and jars of oil and wine and beer, and casks of sweet water, I, with long-robed Helen, landed privately to view the city. For I had heard that Romans were

---

* I call attention to the extreme beauty and distinction of this original and (I sadly fear) little-realized doctrine. — A.H.

occupying holy Eyboia at that time, the island of rich vines, whence Elephenor son of Khalkodon led the proud long-haired Abantes in forty black ships to the siege of windy Ilion. And, neither in the future from which (for a religious reason) I had come, nor in the past from which also I had come, had I ever seen the conquering Romans in their togas as they lived, excepting once by chance in Khem. For which cause I determined to use this opportunity of informing my inquisitive mind.

And we too, therefore, happy as children who have found out a new game, disguised ourselves before we went to play truant in Khalkis. For fair Helen covered herself with a dark robe, veiling also her hair like a web of woven sunbeams: but I did on a tunic of grey wolves' skins having on my head a berreta of ferret-skins, taking also a very sharp sword and a pouch full of silver and gold. And, when we came to the landward end of the quay, a beak-nosed soldier armed in cheap bronze stopped us; and he demanded of us diplomas permitting us to draw sweet breath in Roman territory. For it seemed that the Romans, like locusts, were infesting the whole earth. I, indeed, began to try to edge in a wily word about a beverage: but the soldier led me to the guard-house to settle the matter with his decurion, who, also, was a dull boor amenable neither to words nor bribes. For I told him that my name was Ithakides son of Ithakos son of Ptenopedilos son of Kelainephes Polyonomos, and that I came from Egypt where I had been collecting antiquities: all of which was perfectly true and entirely misleading, simply because the lout was ignorant of the various uses of words. Also I said that the lady was my wife, sister of certain friends of mine by cognomen Asterostephanoi, who was taking a voyage for the benefit of her health and to visit her aged father in Thessaly. And that also was true. But it seemed that the decurion's duty was only to ask questions, but not to pay the slightest regard to the answers. And he would not take a bribe, because (I am sure) no one had ever offered him such a thing before, and he was dreadfully afraid. But he said merely that I must go to prison pending an inquiry.

And I, indeed, made no objection, being always greedy for new experiences, and, moreover, both I and Golden Helen did not restrain our laughter when we remembered who we were to whom such indignities were offered. Wherefore, having tucked away my natural ferocity, I was as meek as a clod: but I watched events with steady eyes. But I told fair Helen to go to a convent of the priestesses of Pallas Athene near the marketplace, there to wait till I should be dismissed without a stain upon my character. And, presently, the centurion himself appeared; and he would escort her thither: for he, indeed, perceived that we were persons of quality; and he said that, if nothing against me could be collected by the following day, he would give me a diploma valuable for all Akhaia. Also, he regretted my detention, assuring me that he himself was under authority. And, when he came back from attending the divine one of goddesses, we conversed, until I had emptied his mind into mine: but that was a pastime, and not a new labor for Herakles.

And, when Dawn (the mother of morning) was come again, and, when Helios Hyperion had driven the chariot of the sun to the height of heaven and was on the downward way toward his bed in the ocean, then, the Roman centurion (having found out no ill of me) gave me the promised diploma, setting me at liberty. But I hastened to the convent of the priestesses of Pallas Athene. But the portress said that the divine one of goddesses had been summoned to meet me at the palace of the governor of the province, whither she had gone at noon, with a plump of spearmen for a guard. To which place I followed her as quickly as possible; and the mind in my dear breast was full of dire foreboding. For I remembered certain words which the centurion had let fall in his cups of the previous night, concerning the sins of Roman governors in general, who bought their governorships by bribes, expecting to recoup themselves (for the outlay of a lifetime) by the crimes which a year of governorship made possible. Also, he had spoken of the governor of Akhaia in particular, by name Anthemius Cotta, saying that he was a Nouus Homo of coarse manners and huge wealth accumulated (no one knew how) in Asia, that he had bought his governorship, being possessed of a gluttonous appetite for the eels of Lake Kopais, greedily engorging the same without ceasing excepting to pant occasionally, and, that he was despised and detested, inasmuch as he cultivated Asiatic vices, filling his palace with females, slaves, guarded by black eunuchs.

But I found no sentry at the palace-gate, so lax is the rule of a luxurious governor. An elegant slave in a Persian miter, however, mentioned that Anthemius Cotta had finished the business of the day. And then, indeed, divine Rage inflamed me with the desire of horribly pinching and mangling; and, staring very starkly, I invaded the place without more ado. Crowds of feeble persons fell away from me, as I passed in frightful silence. And, suddenly, I heard the voice of Golden Helen moaning for me by name.

But I rushed toward the sound, tearing down a curtain, and running along a painted hall where a meal was spread. At the other end, a single Negro, armed with a monstrous curving scymetar, kept watch before another curtained door. His grinning head sprang to the right, and his blood-spouting carcass thudded to the left: but I passed between, passing to the divine one of goddesses.

She was at the far end of the chamber, back to wall. Two loathsome rolling-eyed eunuchs lay at her feet, blasted by her amber fires. But there were others, about to attempt an onslaught. And, before her, stood the Roman governor, a ceruminous personality, fatty and pustulous, and of proboscidean flaccidity. Upon whom I wreaked many most mind-grieving evils, saying nothing. For, first, I impaled him, thrusting my sword through his right shoulder, and spinning him (yelling) round by the hilt to face me. Next, having clutched a handful of his glabrous forehead and a large handful of his cataract of chins, I tore off his countenance; and threw it away. But he dropped on his belly, scrabbling the floor with tettered toes and fingers.

But the eunuchs were petrified with terror; and Golden Helen, seeing me near, was ready to swoon. Her, indeed, I bore (senseless) to a couch; and bestowed her safely while I finished the business.

The eunuchs had to turn the Roman governor face upward and to spit by turns into his rolling lidless eyes, while he winced, mewling with unlipped mouth. I drew my sword from its fat sheath, and flashed it through the eunuchs' necks, so that they fell asunder in a heap, but their heads rolled about the floor. I was minded also to carve Anthemius Cotta slowly into slices: but my gorge rose somewhat squeamishly. For which cause, I only cut the sinews of his knees and elbows, and heaped the carcasses of his slaves upon him, having collected their black heads: but I stuffed his own face into his mouth. And, being satiated with slaughter, I covered the mound with a door-curtain, lest the eyes of the goddess should be offended.

But her, I carried into the painted hall; and, having cleansed myself in several bowls of rose-water, I used the wine (which was there) to restore her. And anon we left the palace, being of an aspect so godly and terrific, that the slaves scuffled (catlike) to hide themselves as we passed by. But, hastening to the quay, we ascended the hollow ship, flying away as quickly as possible.

Thus I did, visiting Khalkis, a city on the island of Eyboia.

The Twenty-Fourth Papyrus

*B*UT, when my galley was in the open water of the Eyboik Gulph, we sat together upon the lofty poop; and the divine one of goddesses told me all her adventures. For, Anthemius Cotta, having seen her going to the convent of priestesses of Pallas Athene, sent her a message as from me, saying that I was an honored guest at the palace. And, when she (suspecting no evil) went thither, the governor offered her fair words, bribes, and violence, by turn, persuading her to submit to indignities. But she repulsed him, summoning to her aid the godly forces (inherited but long unused), which she possessed as daughter of Great Zeys Pantokrator. But, sooth to say, the sweet maid was no longer able to hold her own against fierce-passioned gods or men. Not that she would ever yield: but ten weary lonely centuries in the netherworld had weakened her high hereditary forces, so that she needed an ally. And, now that her peril was averted, she let fall a round tear, like a frightened child very anxious for a companion and protector. Whom I reverently consoled, swearing a great oath that I would ever be her faithful warden.

Now, if I had been alone, nothing would have pleased me more than going through Akhaia and Macedonia by land, seeking adventures, taking revenges, stultifying the Roman conquerors by the spells of magic art. Such, indeed, would have been a very convenient course for a Mage practicing the uses of his arts and crafts, and pleasing enough for a Master at liberty. But, since so great a god as Love had taught me, binding himself (with a blooming chain) to serve me, I was aware that service is as far above liberty as lofty Olympos is above deep Tartaros: nineteen times nineteen days, indeed, will a brazen anvil pass in dropping sheer from the one to the other. Wherefore, knowing how godly a thing it is to be a servant, I also bound myself with the chain of love.

For, it had been in my mind, even in voyaging by sea, to visit Opoyntian Lokri, for the sake of Aias the Less, who wore a linen corslet, and (though a mite of a man) was by far the best spear-thruster of all the Argives when we besieged windy Ilion. Also, I would have visited the steep fortress of Dios, north of the Gulph, and Antron by the seashore, and Pteleon couched in grass in its rock-bound bay, and rugged Olizon with the sea on both sides of it. But, for the sake of my timid maid, whom I bade to be comforted, I said that we would not risk anymore insults among the Romans.

For which cause, sped by Love's wings, we sailed northward, passing leafy Pelion on the left: but, anon, having come to the small port of Myrai at the foot of mighty Ossa, there we cast anchor in a secluded roadstead in the middle of the night. And, uncovering my silver-shining chariot, we untwisted the knots which bound it to the ship, and prepared it for a journey on land.

But I left my well-benched galley in charge to Neandros and Thalos, bidding them to hold it ready for me anywhen, but perhaps after a long absence. And when we had mounted to our places, the divine one of goddesses pulled the silver chain; and Love, our charioteer, lived in his silver image, and flew with wide-swept wings, hooting for joy because we were beginning the last stage of our journey to lofty Olympos.

Aurora, mother of morning, rose from her couch in the sea when we traversed the lovely vale of Tempe, fresh with glittering dew, where the night-mists rose from Peneys' diminished flood. Helios Hyperion, lord of light, looked from the zenith at noon when we began to mount the long slopes which lead to the peak of Olympos. Hesperos, star of evening, gleamed in the violet sky when we came to the little shrine by the Holy Well, beyond which no mortal foot has trod.

The priest came out, marveling that travelers should arrive at that hour: for most men fear the mountain after nightfall, believing it to be improper for them to go very near the paths which the gods tread in their nocturnal journeys. But he marveled still more, when he saw what manner of travelers we were, and the silver-shining chariot pulsating like a creature having sweet life during the first few moments after long-robed Helen had released our charioteer pulling the silver chain. But I and the priest led the daughter of Zeys the Swan to the guest-chamber of the shrine, there to pass the night: for we were unwilling to approach the abode of the blessed gods, disheveled and weary and stained with travel. But, after we had dismissed hunger, having supped, I indeed went out to pass the night in the open, keeping a vigil by my silver-shining armor with adornments of rock-crystals and blue moonstones, and communing with my lordly mind.

And, when the night was waning, and near was the dawn, and the stars had gone upward, and the night had advanced more than two watches, but the third watch was still left, then, indeed, I cleansed the dust from my monstrous chariot, burnishing the silver of it and the crabs and moons inlaid in lustrous mother of pearl, till it shone like a white flame. But the silver image of Love, larger than life, blindfolded, naked, most alluringly proportioned, poised on the front of the rail with his well-winged arms spread abroad in the very act of taking flight, this, indeed, I treated as a man would treat his own large ruddy son in a bath if he were a god. For I washed it all over with a sponge, going firmly into every crevice where dirt might obscenely lodge; and I dried it delicately with soft linen, polishing the smooth-gleaming skin and rubbing in soft oil with my hands. And, opening the secret recesses of the chariot, I poured in fresh water and oil, so that the well-carved wheels might freely revolve in courses. But I did also in like manner with my armor, giving it a radiance as of the serene and vivid moon in spring-time. And, having stripped myself to bathe in the ice-cold limpid water gushing from the Holy Well (for with pure body and pure mind the wise man approaches the blessed gods, then, indeed, I put on my glorious armor: first, the well-shaped greaves for my legs, covered with rock-crystals and blue moonstones and fitted with clasps: then, the white leathern kirtle with taslets of silver lapping about my reins, clothing my body above with my coat of silver mail, and the corslet on my breast and back and shoulders also of hammered silver plates with adornments of rock-crystals and blue moonstones. But I suspended from my shoulders the sword in its silver sheath and the silver quiver of arrows gleaming with moony gems. But, on my head, I placed the glittering helmet with a towering crest of the prides of nine white peacocks; and dreadfully the plume nodded from above. And I shod my feet with the well-made sandals of white leather, taking the great black singing bow well-fitted to my hand, and the great and sturdy shield bright as the moon. But I covered myself with the vast trailing mantle of silver tissue lined with white fur, clasped with the scintillating signs of the Moon and the Crab. And the sheen of my splendor reached heaven, when I stood stamping and gnashing my teeth: nor was I fearful of meeting my peer anywhere, even in the precincts of the immortals.

But, when golden-throned Dawn arose from her ocean-bed, I led the divine one of goddesses, fresh and pure as a pearl in a setting of red gold, to her place in the chariot; and I mounted beside her. But she pulled the silver chain; and young Love dived headlong out of heaven into his image; and the silver image lived, sweeping his wide wings, swimming in the higher air, with triumphant trumpetings and merry whirring of wheels, toward the wall of cloud which shrouds the city of the gods, the habitation of Great Zeys.

Thus, brilliantly blazing and swift as a flash of white thunder, I entered lofty Olympos.

The Twenty Fifth Papyrus

*T*HE HORA Eirene, warden of the gate, challenged us: whom Golden Helen answered, giving the password, demanding free passage as a daughter of Great Zeys. But Hermes, my grandsire, and the Great Twins, and boldly-steadfast Herakles, stood within the gate ready to greet us. Moreover, the golden streets were thronged with the beautiful children of gods and heroes, scattering amaranthine diadems. Thus, we went to the palace and the areiopagos of the immortals.

But King Zeys, the father of gods and men, sat on his clouded throne, with Queen Hera of the white arms (the most righteous of goddesses) who had hundred-eyed peacocks about her. But, on the right and left, were other thrones inhabited by all the gods and goddesses, whose courtiers were immortal youths innumerable having limbs of flaming whiteness and rayed hair. There, was Pan the lord of woodlands, and loose-haired Iakhos Dionysos the Son of fire washed by water-nymphs, and Phoibos Apollon lord of the silver bow, and Artemis beautiful queen of arrows, and tameless Pallas Athene of the dark Aigis, and blameless Aphrodite of the violet crown, and silver-footed Thetis unhappy mother of the noblest son, and even King Poseidon of loud-roaring white horses: but shady King Hades (the most righteous of gods) was absent for reasons of health, and his black throne gaped void. But my heart was leaping for joy in my dear breast: for I was aware that the fifth prediction, which innocent Thalos made when he looked into the palm-mirror, was in fact being realized. For indeed the silver god and the golden goddess were standing before many gods and goddesses.

But astute Hermes, the yellow-wanded luck-bringer and soul-guide, signed me with silence. He rose in his place among the glorious immortals; and began to expound my cause. Thus, then, he spoke: "O Father and King of gods and men, before this conclave of divine ones stands the steadfast goodly Odysseys, the much-enduring contriver of innumerable wiles, who claims as a sweet-guest gift the hand of Golden Helen, the exiled daughter of Thee the Swan, in honorable nuptials."

To whom Great Zeys responded, saying: "Odysseys, we know; and Helen, we know. But never before has one of the sons of men aspired to lead in open marriage a goddess, daughter of the race of the Kronides. Hitherto, indeed, passing (but nonetheless vehement) passions, or transient (but nonetheless perfervid) affections, have been the utmost relations between immortals and mortals. For we gods are severe, envious above others; and we grudge that immortals shall mate with mortals, when anyone shall take a dear wife or a husband: as when rosy-fingered Eos took Orion (that stalwart hunter), so long the gods who lived easily envied her, until chaste Artemis of the golden throne slew him, attacking him with her mild weapons. Moreover, the thing also is new: for, whereas, heretofore, gods and goddesses have loved mortal women and men in secret, now, this Odysseys, boundless in audacity, openly demands a goddess-bride before all the court of heaven. Wherefore, lest we be captured in some snare of this notoriously-wily one, we require that eloquent Hermes (his sponsor) shall give good and sufficient reason for such artless candor, such ingenuous presumption."

Hermes came down from his own throne among the divine immortals, passing the throne of radiant Phoibos Apollon, the bright one, the pure one, crowned with the sun in his splendor; and he took thence the lyre which he himself had made for the master of the music, fashioned out of the hollow shell of a crab like polished translucent amber and obsidian, from which sprang the silvery horns of unicorns to the olive-wood cross-bar, pegged, and fitted with nineteen strings.

He came down, to the clear blue ætherial floor studded with golden stars, in the sight of all, like a princely youth in youth's full bloom whose youth is very graceful, the largest and lithest and loveliest and wisest and most innocent ever seen, smooth and lissome and gleaming as living ivory, and his bare head crowned with clusters of honey-hued curls and a nimbus of sunbeams.

He came down; and cast (to the floor, by his feet) his purple mantle, — by his agile feet, shod with golden-winged sandals, — and laid his golden wand upon it, he lightly standing poised on one fair foot; and he rested the other on a stool, bending his sprightly knee.

He held the heavenly lyre on his thigh with his hollowed arm, leaning toward till it could not help kissing his beautiful youthful breast; and with a quill, he tried it note by note: but it sounded, deeply thrumming beneath his hands. And the young god sang under the notes of the lyre, a doubly-thrilling intonation, making an extemporaneous attempt, as full-grown boys at feasts sing with different voices, rivaling one another in turn.

He sang; and, at his song, my spirit reeled, so strong and passing sweet the strain. One universal smile it seemed, of joy beyond compare, unutterable gladness, imperishable life of peace and love, exhaustless wealth, illimitable power, the cup of health brimful, and bliss immeasurable. Such was his tone.

He sang; and, at his voice, my spirit lived again, that youthful heavenly sunny voice, which welled from his open well-sunned throat, not shrill like a boy's nor clogged like a man's, but full and vibrant, true as a bell, loud as gigantic trumpets, deep and clear as a limpid river, now high now low from middle notes ranging, strong and resonant as the voice of an ever-young god who is both boy and man, warbling unearthly melody around and above and between and below the golden warbling of the lyre.

He sang; and the faces of all the immortals became diaphanous with unimaginable radiance; and the steady godly eyes gleamed like fixed stars at the rapturous magic of his singing. For he sang of arms and the man, the deathless song of the man so ready at need, never so strong nor so fierce nor so terrible as when he (naked) fought fearful odds and a losing battle back to the wall, who wandered far and wide after he had sacked the sacred citadel of Ilion — the deathless song of

much-contriving much-enduring Odysseys, and of all the
deeds which ever I had done since the distant day when I, a
great boy, met Helen, the divine one of goddesses, a tender
girl, who watched me faring girded high through the ford of
Eyrotas by rugged Lakedaimon; and of the doughty deeds
which thenafter I did at the siege of Dardanian Ilion. He sang
of my wily contrivance, the Wooden Horse, whereby at length
we Argives took the city: of the wanderings of Golden Helen,
and of mine: of our meeting again in torrid Egypt and our
wooing there, and of how there I died, slain by unknowing
Telegonos my own son and Kirke's of the awful braided
tresses. And, in a solemn slow low descant, he sang of how
that was the first time, and the last, when ever I lay in the
pure arms of Helen, being dead.

He paused; and the immortal gods wept softly, at the
sadness of his song and the cruel fate which drove us ever
here and there apart. And it was dusky eve.

He bowed his beautiful godly young breast for the lucky
horns of the lyre to kiss again; and his wonderful fingers
skillfully wielded the quill which awakened the delicate voice
of the strings. And he sang of my far-future birth in the
sea-girt island, kingdom of Victory queen of the stalwart
stately Anglicans: of my sordid squalid lot there; and of the
wily audacious ferocity of the deeds, which I did in contempt
of all men, to deliver myself and to soar.

He sang of how I, grieving in mind because not one single
honorable friend or companion came near me, but only
rogues and tosspots and false traitors, set out to wander in
strange lands, studying all divine mysteries and magic lore,
seeking for wisdom everywhere. He sang of my marvelous
deeds, summoning ghostly souls from the dead and bending
them to my will: of how, in Egypt, I half-failed in the ordeal
of the scorching staff, and of the consequence which befell.
And, there, his sacred strain leaped, leaped like one who meets
a sudden slimy toad sitting very still upon his way, leaped,
and was still.

And the immortal gods kept silence. Night flung her violet
mantle round the dome of heaven; and she pinned it with a
star. But those resplendent faces scintillated like many moons
in the violet luminous sheen, intense, immovable.

He took the lyre close to the warmth of his well-spread breast in the hollow of his shoulder uplifting his stainless throat, singing with the well-struck strings. And he sang jewels five words long, which, on the stretched forefinger of all time, shall sparkle forever, singing of my long fall backward through the rolling wheels of time: of my vision in the secret subterranean shrine at Thebes: of my voyage adown the sacred river of Egypt: of my coming to Tanis: of my doings with the hierarch Amenemhat; and of my flight to the open sea.

He sang of my magic invocation of the azure-haired earth-shaking lord of ocean: of the apparition of King Poseidon amiably-minded: of my going to the shrine of far-darting Phoibos Apollon at Delphi, and the oracle chanted by the levated Pythia: of my meeting unafraid with Pan, and his goodly gift of clear-seeing.

He sang (and his cadences rippled) of my furious drive down hill, over the rivers of cold and of flame, for the third time into the world of the dead.

He stretched out all the slim lithe strength of his ivory limbs, lambent and supple and warm with refulgent youth, to the heavenly lyre. His fair throat poured forth a stronger canorous strain, thrilled with unspeakable splendor. And he sang of the singing of Golden Helen in exile: to whose sweet anthem, all the blissful court, from all parts answering, rang.

He sang of how I escaped from fetters and dungeon: of how my wiles and my audacity and my endurance, sneered-at or scorned by men, made great gods glad to serve me: of the fight of the six champions, sons of kings and mighty heroes all. And Herakles, glory of Hera, burst into boisterous blub-berings, inasmuch as he had had no part in so finely finished an affray.

He sang of my treatment of titans: of the wounding of shady Hades of recording mind, inexorable king of the land of the shades. And all the gods and goddesses cried aloud, beating on their blessed knees, because of the sheer stupen-dous magnificence of my audacity.

He sang so divine a song, that even fancy's ear records it not, and the pen must pass on, leaving a blank: for, nor mortal speech, nor even the inward shaping of the mind has color fine enough to paint the sweet great strain of his nectar, flowerlike, fertile of song. He sang of my wonderful journey out of the netherworld: of the swift death of my shipmen, fearful, when they saw my mysterious coming: of my lonely voyage in my uncared sail-less galley over the windless sea.

He sang the cause of my coming, which was Love, the Crown of all Wisdom.

He sang of the sturdy unswerving indomitable force, reward of my wiles and my audacity and my endurance, which had brought me bearing spoils, even the Treasure of Hades, from out of the deep and the shade, to the height of the peak of lofty Olympos. It was Love, all-conquering Love.

Such was the close of his marvelous melody. And, as the last tone thrilled, strong as a proclamation, Echo caught the strain, repeating ever lowly, and more low, from sphere to sphere, LOVE . . . Love . . . Love . . . Love.

Rosy-fingered Dawn, crowned with auroral coronal, flung wide the gates of day: Hellos Hyperion began to drive in scintillating splendor across the sky: the rays of the rising sun splashed beams of golden light over the clouded throne of the Father and King of gods and men, when Hermes finished singing thus for me before the areiopagos of the blessed gods.[*]

---

[*] It would be almost improper to attempt to pick out the multifarious quotations which adorn this extremely lovely poem. Those of us who had the privilege of Mr. C.'s acquaintance in his recent life cannot but admire the stupendous erudition which enabled him to blend the Bible with Homer, Dante Alighieri with Meleagros of Gadara, etc., etc., etc., with such perfectly chiseled facility. — A.H.

The Twenty-Sixth Papyrus

*B*UT King Zeys Pampator sat up, and said: "What, O divine ones inhabiting olympian palaces, think ye now of this Odysseys?"

And they answered: "He is a hero."

But boldly steadfast Herakles rose from his throne, saying, in a voice even louder than Stentor's: "He is worthy of a chair in our college of immortals."

And the gods and goddesses sang together, making the *Sign*, "So mote it be."

But the Lord of the Lightning and the Dark Cloud spoke again, saying: "What, O divine ones inhabiting olympian palaces, think ye now of Golden Helen?"

And they answered: "She is a spoil well-won."

But chaste Artemis, beautiful queen of arrows, rose from her throne, saying: "Let the hero wear his spoil."

And the gods and goddesses sang again together, making the *Sign*, "So mote it be."

But I saw that there were some who did not join in the voting; and one of those was Queen Hera of the white arms, the most righteous of goddesses; and another was blameless Queen Aphrodite of the violet crown: the first, because it is bitter for a woman to be supplanted in her husband: the second, because of jealousy on account of Queen Helen's transcendent beauty.

But the Father and King of gods and men said: "It pleaseth us; and so, we, of our own free will, command that it shall be."

And, saying this, he nodded with his immortal head, so that I might be encouraged. For the nod of Zeys is the greatest pledge among the immortals: for his pledge, even whatsoever he shall sanction with his nod, is irrevocable, not false, nor unfulfilled. And, in the sight of all, he drew me from Golden Helen's side, out of my silver chariot, where we had been standing together during a day and a night enraptured with the singing of Hermes. And he breathed upon me, so that my mortal nature was blown away from me: but I bathed in the breath of the god, being soaked in the source of the fire of eternal youth, the prime and flower of strength; and such red blood as was in my veins was sublimed, giving place to crystalline ichor, very pure and limpid, such, to wit, as flows in the veins of the blessed gods: for we eat no bread, nor drink gleaming wine, wherefore we are bloodless and are named immortals.

And, while I was yet encompassed with the thick clouds of the god, beautiful dark Sleep was permitted to light upon my eyelids; and I slept, as a sweet boy sleeps, dreamlessly.

But, when, at length, I awakened, I was in another place. And Phoibos Apollon, lord of the silver bow, and strenuous Herakles whom not Hera but Eros could conquer, were come to conduct me to the marriage-feast. And they spoke of many things: saying that the immortals were rejoicing in the happiness of so wily a warrior and so fair a maid, save only the lord Hermes who (after his long singing during a day and a night) was curing a relaxed larynx, and also shady King Hades who was raging horribly on account of painful perforations, and swearing that neither I nor Golden Helen need ever think to expect hospitality from him again. So, with mirthful minds and smiling lips, we set out all light-heartedly.

The divine one of goddesses was brought by her Great Twin Brothers, star-crowned Kastor the tamer of horses and Polydeykes the pugilist. But, before she came to stand with me at the throne of King Zeys, then, indeed, divine Memory illumined my noble mind, shewing me a remembrance of a most graceful *Spell*. And, instantly, I stooped to the limpid river which flows through the clear-blue ætherial realm, taking a handful of crystal water, a sacred lavation, wherewith to sprinkle the maid whose hair was like a web of woven sun-beams, saying the *Spell of The Three Who are One*. And all the immortals bowed their radiant heads, greatly admiring the magic.

But, after the nuptials, we feasted, eating purple ambrosial jellies, dainties, such as Zeys-nourished kings eat, with savors of unblemished hecatombs, and quaffing foaming flagons of nectar distilled from the apples of heaven and flavored with roses and rosemary: till, at last, rustic Pan threw nuts on the floor, for Love and Desire and Sleep and Death and Hyakin-thos and the cupbearers and other children to scramble for. But, when we had drunk a last cup to Hermes the Luck-brin-ger, I led Queen Helen to the palace which mighty Herakles had lent to us. For that hero was shewing himself very friendlike to me, on account of my wily deeds and my long endurance of evils, since he also had done deeds and suffered intolerable evils in his turn. Moreover, the said hero was very well-mannered and able to rule himself, wherein he differed from many of the immortals. And, beside all these things, he was the most married man on the peak of Olympos: for which cause, no doubt, he was excited about my welfare.

In this manner was the Crown of All Wisdom confirmed to me, when, having been chaired in the college of immortals, I led Queen Helen, the Treasure of Hades, into sacred matri-mony, in the presence of the gods of Olympos.

The Twenty-Seventh Papyrus

WHEN, at length, we were alone with Love, then, indeed, Golden Helen kissed me.

I, in sooth, had kissed her in the house of blameless Hades, before the combat of the heroes: but she had not returned the sweet embrace. And now she told me the reason: saying that it is an immutable law that an immortal goddess, who kisses a mortal man in honorable love, thereby fulminates him. Wherefore, when (in Egypt) I was warring against the five nations, more than a thousand years before, and when Telegonos wounded me near the blooming groin with his dark arrow, then, sweet Helen (mad with fear and love) kissed me, staying me in her arms in the battle at the mouth of sacred Sihor. Of which arrow-wound, I should not have died: but, of the kiss, her first, I died. So, lest I should again be lost to her, she had not kissed me in the house of shady Hades. But, now that I was immortal, as was she the divine one of goddesses, Golden Helen kissed me.

And, anon, she said: "Lord king and husband of me, seeing that we rejoice in happiness, being immortal and mingled in love, so that we have no desire unsatisfied, let us be merciful to one who hateth us and kind to him who has wronged us: for, indeed, it is not right continually to be enraged in one's mind."

But this was a most strange saying, whereat I wondered gravely: for such ways had not been taught to Golden Helen, nor were they known at that time. And then I remembered the grace conveyed by that most mighty magic, the sacred lavation and the *Spell of The Three Who are One*, which, in a mystery, I had been moved to work upon her before our nuptials. And then I was not affrighted by anymore amazement.

But she was embracing my knees, continuing to speak, saying: "Go, now, dear lord and husband, faring immortally to Khalkis in holy Eyboia; and take also sweet white Death with thee. And, having entered to Anthemius Cotta the Roman governor, let the pale god draw from his breast gently the torch of his life, quenching its flickering flame, so that his body may rest from its torments. For he is unfit to continue alive and in health. But, though he would have despitefully used me, I am unwilling that he should writhe much longer in anguish, being irremediably mutilated."

Thus she spoke: but I kissed the pitiful maid again, rejoicing at the grace which was replenishing her. And, having summoned kindly Death, together we went, faring invisibly from lofty Olympos with the speed of a thought: for we immortals in nowise appear visibly to everybody. But, when we came to Khalkis after the middle of the night, when night is darkest, then I took the divine white child, silent, garlanded with asphodel, by his frosty hand leading him; and, so, we entered the chamber of the Roman governor, plain for all to see.

He lay upon a bed, mangled and shapeless, moaning in the throes of his torments. But, when the slaves, physicians, watching beside him, saw me radiant in silver armor with adornments of rock-crystals and blue moonstones, and the pale young god purer and colder than glittering frost, standing in presence manifest in an aureole of moonbeams, then they fell on their faces and were much afraid.

But I addressed the moribund, saying: "Uneasy Anthemius, know that Queen Helen, daughter of Great Zeys, whom thou didst use despitefully, wills to release thee from these earthly pangs which are but a just penance for thy crimes. Nevertheless, the divine one of goddesses bids thee to enjoy the blessed rest of death, gaining remittance of sufferings."

Thus I spoke; and I uttered the *Spell* which unchains the soul from the body. And white Thanatos stooped, with his tender young frigid fingers drawing the torch of life from the Roman's bloody breast; and, blowing upon it, he extinguished its flickering flame. And Anthemius sighed, and was comforted, retiring to the world of shades.

But we returned to the peak of Olympos, before he had reached the netherworld.

*N*ow, when we had dwelled in the palace of Herakles during the full course of the moon, then, indeed, Great Zeys ordained to employ me in a certain duty. For it is the custom on the threshold of the immortals that, whoever shall be raised to the rank of a godly hero and endowed with immortality, must visit in person the courts of strange gods, announcing his own apotheosis and receiving recognition. Wherefore, the cloud-compelling son of Khronos bade me to prepare for my progress: but to astute Hermes was assigned the task of inscribing letters-patent for exhibition to all barbarian theocracies.

For, as do earth-dwelling kings, each having power and dominion over his own people, so also do the gods, each having power and dominion over his own worshippers. And, upon occasions, disputes arise among the various dynasties inhabiting the wide-rolling heavens, and wars and fearful conflicts follow, when the high gods fight among themselves for lordship over the hearts of men. In which quarrels, the divine ones of the Argive race are ever to the fore and very ready at need: seeing that the nations of the Argives are wont to stablish colonies, daughter-cities, in barbarian lands, crossing the unvintaged sea, whereto they carry a sacred fire from their mother-city; and they pray not to the strange gods of the barbarians among whom they dwell, but to the familiar gods of their dear motherland. Furthermore, the strange gods of the barbarians sometimes send solemn embassages of heroes to the king of gods and men, bearing complaints, because their rites go unrecognized by the Argives inhabiting their domains. Then, indeed, Great Zeys, having taken counsel with the olympian immortals, returns a just decision in like manner. At other times, dire complications unexpectedly arise, when the strange gods send plagues (perchance of rats or dragons), or pestilences (perchance of bad blind boils), or even famines, to punish the prepotence or the impiety of their blameless barbarians; and, by chance, one of the Argive colonists perishes by reason of the scourge. Then, indeed, loud-thundering Zeys inflames himself with mighty wrath, when his dear Argive folk fall victims to the clumsiness of the indiscriminating gods of the so-sinful barbarians; and he exacts a compensation. But the immortal gods love not to war overmuch among themselves, their battles being terrific and the issues not unusually thankless.

And it chanced that, at the time when I reached my chair in the college of the immortals and of my blissful nuptials, that there was a matter of feud between us and the theocracy of Juppiter Stator. For the Latin gods, very stolid, very bu-colic, were claiming the worship of the whole Argive race throughout the earth. And they, rash and overweening, al-leged that, as the fair Argive land had submitted to their bloody Romans, so, also, Olympian Zeys ought to acknow-ledge as his blooming suzerain their Capitoline Juppiter.

For which cause, long-enduring and tiresome and tedious conversations of high diplomacy were striving to adjust the dispute without appeal to the arbitrament of war. But a regrettable incident was likely to occur at any moment: for Ares, bane of mortals, weary of the arts of peace, paraded himself daily wearing shield and sword; and boldly-steadfast Herakles, weary of the arts of husbandry, was carving a collection of most mind-delighting clubs; and my own sweet cousin, Perseys of the sea, the most renowned of heroes, weary of the arts of love, was all agog to meet monsters more worthy than pterodactyls in deadly strife. Wherefore, the Father and King of gods and men bade me to visit, first, those strange gods who were known not to be unfriendly; and, then, to proceed to Rome: so that, returning to Olympos directly from the court of Juppiter Stator, I might bring back the very latest account of the negotiations.

And, having embraced me and Queen Helen, very-mighty Zeys gave us our charters fairly written out by cunning Hermes, my grandsire, who first brought letters and the art of writing into the Argive land.

Thus, as an immortal, I began to go about the work of the immortals.

The Twenty-Eighth Papyrus

*B*UT we ascended the silver-shining chariot inlaid with crabs and moons in mother-of-pearl, a wonder to be seen, Love being our charioteer; and we flew afar to the remote regions of the skies, gazing (from time to time, and with certain thoughts) on the grain-giving earth below.

Now there were certain dynasties of gods, such as those of Anahoyak and Nippon and Serica,* with whom the Olympians dealt but rarely: for they were of a secretive nature, nor did they exactly welcome guests from afar, but rather did they slam the door of divine hospitality, excepting when rare embassages brought news of very grave matters. And, indeed, no such embassage had been sent from lofty Olympos across the streams of ocean since Pantokrator Zeys sent pious Deykalion announcing his accession to the throne of Khronos. For which cause, it was not deemed necessary that I and Queen Helen should fare so far to visit divine ones whose very names cannot be written in the Argive tongue.

And, first, we came to the court of the gods of Assyria. There, indeed, we were mingled in friendship with the Seven Magnificencies, Anna who rules the Assyrian sky, Ea who rules their earth, Mulge who rules their abyss, the three rulers of their sun and their moon and their air, and Belmarduk the god. Beside those, we were mingled in courtesy with their fifty great gods, and their three hundred heavenly sprites, and their six hundred earthly sprites. Also, I held converse with

---

* Mexico, Japan, and China, I presume. — A.H.

their heroes, Gilgamish and Eabani, the same who came to me in Khem; and, while I admired their most artificial beards, the mind in my lordly breast grieved, because (though brave enough and strong) they seemed to me to be but curly and oily bullocks or gladiators in comparison with Herakles or Perseys or Kastor and Polydeykes, and the other well-bred heroes of Olympos. But I held very wily conversation with Belmarduk the god, gaining certain wisdom which need not be written down here.

But we journeyed on to the court of the gods of Iran, immortals who bear the strangest of names, such as Ormuzd whom we Argives call ΦΩΣ or Light, and Ashem or ΑΛ–ΗΘΕΙΑ meaning Truth, and Vohu Mano or ΕΥΝΟΙΑ meaning Good Sense, and Khshathrem or ΕΥΝΟΜΙΑ meaning Power, and Armaiti or ΣΟΦΙΑ meaning Obedience and Haurvatat or ΠΛΟΥΤΟΣ meaning Perfection. But chiefly was the mind in my dear breast exalted with pure joy when I came, radiant in my moonlike sheen, into the presence of Great Mithra. For the unconquered god of the Iranian sun looked upon me so earnestly, with wise young eyes of such transcendent candor, that I was moved to know as much as possible from him. Wherefore, I gave him the *Sign of the Father of Warriors.* Instantly he replied, signing me with the *Sign of the Father of Bulls.* I gave him the *Sign of the Father of Lions;* and he signed me with the *Sign of the Father of Vultures.* I gave him the *Sign of the Father of Ostriches;* and he signed me with the *Sign of the Father of Ravens.* I gave him the *Sign of the Father of Gryphons;* and he signed me with the *Sign of the Father of Perses.* I gave him the *Sign of the Father of Suns;* and he signed me with the *Sign of the Father of Eagles.* I gave him the *Sign of the Father of Falcons;* and he signed me with the *Sign of the Father of Fathers* which is the summit of the twelve. But, because I was ware that I had come upon my master, I made myself obedient, gaining such wisdom as is not lawful to be written, nor even to be uttered, on account of a religious reason.

But we journeyed on to the court of Benares; and, having shewn my charters, we departed as speedily as possible. For it would have been a shameful deed, to have exposed Queen Helen to the evil communications of a horde of riotous brutes, apes, reptiles, abortions, frightful malformations, greasy with rancid butter, dripping with fresh blood and mildewed with stale, interminably-headed illimitably-armed innumerably-nippled smirking bestialities, at whose amorous activities even Olympians were wont to say Phy. For which cause, we just went to Benares, and we just came from Benares.

But we journeyed on to the mountain of Sinai. There, at its foot, we stood silently, during the space of a night and a day and a night, revering unmentioned and unthought-of mystery.

But we journeyed on to the court of the gods of Khem. And Mother Isis being amazed to greet one of her priests and a master of masters of magic in one who had risen to the rank of a hero and immortal of Olympos, of her own free will released me from the oath which I swore to her before Amenemhat the priest of Tanis: for (as she said) it seemed that the Supreme had dispositions regarding me otherwhere. And Ptah the Pain-lessener explained why he neglected my torments in the ordeal of the scorching staff: saying that there was a law in Khem, made by Ra himself, which ordained that no alleviation of pain should be due to a mage who, willingly, should accept the ordeals of wisdom's way. To whom I answered wilily (reserving a private opinion of my own); and I said that the laws of the master were good in the eyes of the servant, and that this law was particularly to be praised: for, had I been rendered able to hold the scorching staff, I should not have fallen backward through the rolling wheels of time, regaining Golden Helen, the Treasure of Hades, nor Love, the Crown of all Wisdom. Which answer was greatly admired. And so, for a little space, we dwelled with the well-mannered gods of Khem, amid the groves and fountains of Duat, hunting with holy cats and kittens by night on the banks of the Nile, and by day among the dark hills of Amentet. Moreover, having withdrawn our shapes from the gaze of mortals, we visited the temple at Tanis, where, formerly, I had done many wily deeds. But my friend Amenemhat had submitted himself to white Death; and I saw his form at Philai, conveniently mummied in the manner which I myself had invented. For the eyes of immortals, peers of Pan, obey their particular desires, seeing (at will) through stone or wood or any other substance, excepting the substances whose names and virtues and properties are known only to masters who have the proper spells for using them. But I obtained as a sweet guest-gift from the gods of Khem, that they would clear kindly with dead Amenemhat (till I myself could provide for him), lightening his dreary lot in tedious Amentet as with frequent cups of cream. And, I must not omit to mention that, while we were still over Egypt, Queen Helen would have me go with her one day to Nilemouth: for, having once innocently slain me there, with the kiss of an immortal goddess given in honorable love to a mortal man, the gentle mind in her fragrant breast persuaded me that she owed me an amend. And there, indeed, having openly kissed me on the lips, she hid her rose-red face on mine while she whispered a secret joy. For I lived again in another.

But we journeyed on to find the court of the gods of the sea-girt island, the kingdom of Victory queen of the stalwart stately Anglicans. And, at length, we found, indeed, the sea-girt island: but there were no Anglicans, nor venerable Victory the queen, nor any gods at all. Instead, we saw the place to be infested with a rabble of pygmies, some black-hairy, others sandy-hairy, all cannibals, obscenely naked, painted blue, inarticulately howling, whose hag-toothed breastless females mutilated their innumerable slain abominably. Moreover, they were worshipping very bad devils, dwarves, giants, furies, hobgoblins, and other dubious monsters, with hekatombs of idiot boys and girls, bandy-legged, hairy, knock-kneed, stunted, scraggy, whose throats they tore with sharp stones, stretching them out stark on cyclopean boulders, or else with twisted-ozier baskets of human shape, fifty cubits high, which they stuffed full of babies and enemies, burning them alive with fire, to the music of screeching. From which horrors we flew away with Love, having laid hideous enchantments on those barbarians in relief of the earth which sustained them.*

---

* The writer would seem to have hit upon some remote
parts of Wales, or perhaps Scotland, to which Roman civilization had not penetrated. This is rather unfortunate. for
the general condition of the "sea-girt island" *cf.* Co-
drington, *Roman Roads in Britain,* and Mr. Haverfield's

But we journeyed on to the court of the gods of Scandinavia. For I was very desirous of seeing Baldur the Beautiful, and of lifting the hammer of their Thor; and my desire was not ungratified. Baldur, indeed, was a comely youth in a crude gaunt-boned pink-fleshy way, such as I have seen a many of among the Argives: but he could not be named with Hermes of the golden wand, or with any of the olympian immortals, lacking the effulgent limpidity and transcendent agility of mind without which a fair body and sprightly limbs are merely dull and devoid of spiritual quality. And, as for the so-called ponderous hammer of Thor, it was as a feather in the wily knack-knowing hands of the man who had burst the fetters of Hades. But the other gods and goddesses of Scandinavia offered us a disgusting banquet of fishes and bones of beeves half-charred, half-raw, whereon they themselves browsed, gnawing interminably, and washing down the gobbets with bucketfuls of fiery potions, wherewith (anon) they drowned themselves in drunkenness, stertorously dropping on sleep in the slime where they fell. For which cause we left them while the night was dark.

But we journeyed on to the court of the gods of Rome, where Great Zeys maintained Nestor of Gerenia, lord of chariots, that very wise and ancient hero, as his embassador. And, in the vast palace of Capitoline Juppiter was the abode of the Olympian embassage, where, for a time, I dwelled with Queen Helen, being Nestor's guests. But it seemed that nothing could stay the division of counsels among the immortals any longer. For the Latin gods, implacable, boundless in audacity, persisted in claiming the sacrifices of all pious persons who dwell on the wide bosomed earth: nor would they listen to most interesting conversations, being tribeless lawless homeless fanulloni, disguised in the shape of their betters, having not the most rudimentary notion of the difference between meum and tuum, and loving nothing better than strife. And day by day they inflated themselves to

amazingly luminous monographs on *Roman Britain.* At the same time, we must not forget that the Scotch did really worship demons originally, which is why their descendants have jumped at Puritan theology, as Mr. Chesterton expressly demonstrates. — A.H.

bursting with overweening fury, desiring to obtain a monopoly, spurning the just and moderate claim for supremacy by prescriptive right made by Olympian Zeys. Yet knightly Nestor, pleasant of speech, the clear-voiced orator of the Pylians, from whose tongue flowed discourses more sweet than honey, bravely strove to find some ground of agreement. For he still hoped that his conversations would avert war.

And, being over Rome, it seemed to me fitting that I should pass certain words with that blameless senator whom I once had seen at Tanis. Him, indeed, I found (by certain simple magic) to be called Gajus Gargilius Gnipho;* and to him I addressed myself without delay, entering his palace on a moonbeam, at midnight, radiant in my silver splendor, in stature and in aspect very much more than mortal. For the fellow had comported himself rather too superciliously, when he saw me as a stranger in the land of Khem and not very flourishing of appearance. But, when he saw me in Rome, he fell flat before me, quaking with terror, babbling obsequious deprecations with a rust-hot tongue. But I, having twitted him with his former blindness to my divinity, so severely that he wished himself unborn, gave him sundry comfortable words: whereat, of his own free will, he vowed a blooming shrine to me at his villa near Caere, with a flamen and two casmilli of free birth, and a weekly sacrifice of two white sea-gulls and a crab, as long as the world should endure men. For thus anxious are rich mortals to purchase the inattention of the immortals.

And, by chance, one day, it happened that, when I returned from going to and fro, alone and unseen, among mortals in the city, hearing the speech of men, on entering the palace I found old Nestor lying stunned in my antechamber. And, instantly, terrible Fear invaded the mind in my breast on account of Golden Helen.

But, rushing forward, inflaming myself by the way, I found her in her chamber, gagged with a silken cincture, and struggling in the arms of truculent Mars. Him, indeed, I dragged

---

* This is valuable for testing the authenticity of these documents. *Cf.* Hor. *Ep.* I. vi. 59–63: "Gargilius . . . Ithacensis Ulixi." The importance of this can hardly be minimized. — A.H.

about the room, as one drags an impatient bullock from the altar before his bloody turn, twisting him; and I dashed the blameless god to the floor with not-innocuous concussion. But, having released my faithful wife, I bade her to go to Nestor in his need, and to heal his ill: for she herself was unharmed, excepting for certain bruises of her lilylike skin which she took from the grip of the ruffian. And, for these, I made him pay a just price. First, indeed, he rose from the floor, black in the face with rage. But I cursed him thereto in good and concise Latin, while he stood all amazed, being too stupid to think of me as aught but an Olympian speaking the limpid language of gods and Argives. And I rejoiced in my lordly mind, at my faculty of venomously-scathing invective, when I saw how I could exasperate him with my tongue. For the language of immortals is voluble, and the discourses in it are numerous and varied; and vast is the distribution of words here and there. Moreover, whatsoever word one shall speak, such also shall one hear; and, whatsoever deed one shall do to another shall be repeated with interest upon oneself. But, when my lickerish swashbuckler had winced sufficiently, we took to our swords. Now Mars was a war-god whose habit was to supervise slaughter from his cloudy citadel, descending to massacre fugitives, and to glut himself with human gore: but he personally was no more than a slow and clumsy warrior, able (certainly) to overcome mortals by sheer weight, but no match whatever for an immortal hero skilled in wiles and expert in all the arts of war. Wherefore, having dug him well in head and foot, I began to beat him, abominably bruising his paps. But he bellowed with pain; and fought wildly, exposing his tender places so that I carved him at my pleasure. And, when, hacked to shreds, he was ready to fall apart, he took a great toss from me, hideous in immensity, being pitched from the window of the palace into the city beneath. But his atoms fell sprawling in the forecourt of his own temple crushing the Flamen Martialis as flat as a corncake. But the Romans took it for a portent; and were filled with forebodings of evil.

Then, Queen Helen begged me to bear her away from the sullen court of the blameless Latin divinities, returning to the peak of Olympos, where the star-crowned Twins would guard her honor during my absence, if absent I was obliged to be. Even wise old Nestor agreed that conversations must end here, and war begin.

But, first, I demanded audience of Juppiter Stator (the most righteous of gods): whom I told of the crime of his son, and the penalty paid, demanding also the usual compensations. Whereat the blooming pretender was very angry, and made a menacing pass at me with his thunder. But, him, indeed, I mocked most shockingly, flinging at his feet a bunch of fat fingers hewed off blameless Mars, and giving him warning, on the part of all the immortals of Olympos, to prepare for war. But he, too late, cowered, and was for offering satisfaction, saying that he would make an agreement concerning the heavenly dispute, desiring not the enmity but the friendship of us Olympians.

Whom I superbly answered, saying: "Talk now no more of agreements, O thrice-and-four-times accused pretender and new god. For, as there are not faithful leagues between lions and men, neither have lambs and wolves an according mind, but ever meditate evils each against other, so it is impossible for us and you to contract a friendship. Long, indeed, have we striven to treat your pretensions leniently, in accordance with reason: but ye have presumed on our forbearance, mistaking our gentleness for weakness, and crowning your bloody folly with a crime, an outrage wrought by a dastard on a daughter and on an embassador of the king of gods and men. But now it is time to make an end of you. And I go forthwith to lofty Olympos, to rally against you the hosts of the splendor of Zeys."

Thus I spoke; and having by magic called my silver-shining chariot, I led to it Queen Helen, and Nestor the Argive, who was not to be left to the mercy of Juppiter Stator; and, when they had mounted to their places, I placed on the floor the sword of atrocious Mars, intending to take it as a trophy and a perpetual memorial. But I, also, was about to ascend beside them, when there came heavily prancing certain blameless divine ones, squalid of demeanor and agitated of aspect, offering gifts on the part of the Capitoline god, and begging for a little respite. And I, having relieved my blooming mind by speaking fierce opinions to them, and being not at all times implacable but rather inclined to urbanity, actually did delay for an instant, revolving the whole matter in my mind, and waiting to hear what might be proposed. But, even while I tarried thus, my godly eyes clearly saw revengeful Bellona, sister and pander of Mars, beginning to harness the hounds of war to her chariot round the corner.

Then, indeed, I turned upon thievish Mercury the messenger, an apelike imitator of my wing-footed grandsire, saying: "Return, O messenger, to Capitoline Juppiter, to whom do thou tell all things openly as I charge thee: so that all the gods of all the wide-rolling heavens also may be indignant, even if he (clad in impudence) still dares to deceive any of the immortals. Let him not (doglike as he is and not godlike) ever hope to look in my face again as an equal. I neither will join in counsel nor in action with him: for having already offended me, now he will try to deceive me. He shall not again overreach me with lying words. Enough for him once to do so. But let him perish in quiet: for Great Zeys, no doubt, has deprived him of reason. Hateful to me are his gifts, and himself I value not a hair."

Thus I spoke: but my heart and noble mind were delighted in my breast. And, having ascended my silver-shining chariot, Queen Helen pulled the chain; and faithful Love flew away with us as swiftly as a bird or a thought. But my great black bow began to sing very gloriously of war, as we left the Super-Capitol, making bright the eyes, hardening the body, and kindling flames within the mind: for fierce-hearted Bellona pursued us, over the breadth of Apulia to the unvintaged sea. But being loathe to fight with a bloody female and (moreover) a blameless Latin one armed with a bow which to mine was but as a toy, I loosed my death-bringing shafts backward against the hackles of her blooming war-hounds, throwing them into confusion. And she, cursing obscenely, turned, retracing her difficult way.

In this manner I did deeds, wily, and also audacious, visiting the courts of strange gods who bear rule over barbarians.

The Twenty-Ninth Papyrus

*B*UT the way in which we Olympians went forth to war was on this wise.

King Zeys, armed with black clouds and white thunder, sat throned in the areiopagos of the immortals, collecting his forces, assigning commands and stations. For, as when some hairy barbarian (devoid of reason) was wont to prance minaciously in the vicinity of the flowing-haired ingenuous Akhaians, or as when some city (jealous, or what-not) warred against its neighbor or some bumptious young colony against its staid and respectable mother-city, all the other Argives were wont to mingle themselves hilariously together against the foe, so, also, when the Olympian gods are menaced, each one (from the highest to the lowest) and including the heroes takes up arms in defense of his dear motherland.

But King Zeys, whose joy is in the thunder, bade golden-wanded Hermes to summon from the house of shady Hades the shades of innumerable heroes who had not attained immortality; and these were as unnumbered as are leaves and flowers in their season: nor could I number them, did not the Muses, daughters of Zeys of the dark and holy Aigis, put into my mind the names of some who came at call to lofty Olympos. For, when the Olympians go forth to war, then the shades of heroes are called from the netherworld, and are endowed with bodies. But, if they stolidly permit themselves to be slaughtered in battle, they lose an opportunity of attaining immortality and return as shades to the house of

Hades for at least another hundred years. Such, indeed, is the law. But I remember that these were called from the nether-world, to wit, yellow-haired fleet-footed Akhilleys, and daring Patroklos his dear comrade, and red-haired Neoptolemos his son as brave as his father, and horse-taming Diomedes, and Phoinix dear to Zeys, and blameless Telamonian Aias the Great, and Lokrian Aias the Little, and great-hearted Iphitos, and Abantian Elephenor breathing fury (whose hair flowed behind), and high-hearted Erekhtheys, and godly Eyryalos, and Agamemnon shepherd of the people, and warlike Agap-enor, and stalwart Diores, and pious Polyxeinos, and Meges peer of Ares, and large-souled Oineys, and gold-haired Melea-gros, and Idomeneys the famous spearman fierce as flame, and Meriones peer of the man-slaying war-god, and goodly tall Tlepolemos the Rhodian son of Herakles, and Philoktetes the cunning archer, and glorious Eyrypylos, and unflinching Polypoites, and fleet Prothoos, and sage Antenor, and high-stepping Pandaros, and fluent Talthybios the herald, and comely Sthenelos, and the lusty cheerful stripling Simoeisios, and well-greaved Tydeys, and noble Hypsenor, and glancing-eyed Diokles, and innocent Pylaimenes, and Mydon the squire, and that nymph-born shepherd Boykolion, and haughty Bellerophon. And these, being summoned, gathered with speed.

And, as the many tribes of well-plumed birds, wild geese, or swans or long-necked cranes, or even blooming bustards, on the Asian meadow by River Kaystros, fly hither and thither enjoying their plumage, and (with loud cries) settle ever onward, and the meadow resounds, so poured forth the many tribes of warriors, with Theseys the most righteous of men, from the house of Hades; and they joined with the immortal heroes, lion-hearted Herakles, and my own cousin Perseys of the sea (the most renowned of heroes), and Kastor the tamer of horses, and Polydeykes the pugilist, and magnanimous Iason with his nine-and-forty generous marine Argonayts, and with others quite innumerable whose names I have not written for a religious reason: all mingled together manning the walls of lofty Olympos.

Then came forth from their well-built golden palaces, Ares the lordly stormer of battlements, and Phoibos Apollon lord

of the silver bow, and his chaste sister Artemis the Archer
wearing the moon. And bright-eyed Pallas Athene cast off her
rainbow-hued garments which she herself had woven; and did
on her armor for battle. And, about her shoulders, she put
the terrible Aigis, which knows neither age nor death,
whereon wave a hundred taslets of pure gold, all deftly
twisted, and each worth a hundred oxen: whereon, also, is
Panic as a crown round about, and Strife, and Valor, and
horrible Onslaught withal; and thereon, also, is the grisly
snake-haired head of Medoysa the Gorgon, a portent dreadful
and grim. And upon her virginal head, she set the two-crested
golden casque of fourfold plates bedecked with the men-at-
arms of a hundred cities. And she brandished the great stout
spear, wherewith she vanquishes and demolishes all with
whom her immortal sire is wrath. But Hephaistos, the glorious lame god, sweated in toil, busy about the bellows and the
anvil in his house of bronze, imperishable, starlike, far-seen
among the abodes of the immortals: for he was forging
thunderbolts, with arms, and armor.

And, anon, came running the Hora Dike, warden of the
cloudy gate, bringing news that the Latins were approaching
in battle-array.

But, instantly, we were pouring out, like wasps who dwell
by the roadside: whom silly boys are wont to irritate, inces-
santly harassing creatures possessing cells by the wayside, and
causing a common evil to many. And, as when thick snow-
flakes flutter down, born in the æther and chilled by the blasts
of Boreas, so, thickly streamed forth brightly-glittering helms
and bossy shields, with strong-plated corslets and nastily-
pointed spears. And the sheen thereof filled the heavens near;
and the world underneath winked at the flashing of gold and
silver and at the noise of the trampling; and our teeth gnashed
together; and our eyes blazed like so many flaming fires.

But wing-footed Hermes and wind-borne Iris flew, like
unseen arrows, the one to azure-haired Poseidon lord of the
ocean, the other to blameless Hades lord of the netherworld,
always collecting reinforcements. And gallant young Love,
ruddy, naked and invulnerable, rushed with me into the
mellay. For no shafts are more deadly than Love's.

And the war-chariot of King Zeys the Scarer thundered,

awfully rolling along by the polished colonnades of palaces, bearing the father and king of gods and men to the forefront of the fray.

But King Quirinus was leading the heroes of the Latins, all blameless of course, with Aulus master of knights on the left and Furius on the right, with Herminius in the rear. Turnus served under King Quirinus, with Mamilius prince of the Latian name. Under Aulus, served Metius of Anxur and Astur lord of Luna. Under Furius, served showy Curtius, the forlorn hope. These were all the most righteous of heroes. But the Latin gods preferred to look on, sullen, from the rear, in what they fondly deemed to be security.

Thus, immortals were matched against pseud-immortals.

The Thirtieth Papyrus

T HEN the Father and King of gods and men thundered appallingly from above, and, from beneath, the sea-king Poseidon set the vast earth shaking, even to the tops of her blooming mountains. And the brazen voice of impetuous Ares resounded through the press of battle; and bravely-steadfast Herakles strewed the Latin heroes in swathes, sweeping his club here and there, shattering shins, causing the marrow to spurt from spines, so that knees became loosened; and sweet Death in a white cloud enveloped them while life left their bones. But the lord and lady of the silver bows rained down their hot arrows, which hissed into wet eye-sockets, forcing-in the pupils, and going forward into the backs of the heads: so that many heroes sat down without warning or thrones, stretching out both their hands for nothing. And blissful Pallas Athene smote many, with her spear, where a puncture is particularly painful: so that they panted, spinning round and round upon the point like cockchafers, writhing, holding their interiors in their hands, until white Death veiled their two eyes wanting life.

But I, on the battlements, saw naught but brave Horatius, heard naught save his personal challenge to me, felt naught save the blows which he delivered to my address, touched naught save him, smelt naught save his delicious blood and sweat mingling with ichor of the immortals. For I drove my bloody spear into his shield; and pinned it to his arm. But his spear tore away my silver helmet crested with the prides of nine white peacocks. Then, indeed, I leaped upon him with my sword, protecting my head with my fluttering targe. Nor

did he abide my onslaught: but he retired pace by pace; and
a shower of sparks burst out of his armor as I shattered it bit
by bit. But, perceiving that he was on the very verge of the
wall, I hustled him so horribly with my great glittering shield,
that, stepping back, he fell for nineteen days, reaching the
bountiful earth at length in the form of a thin red rain. But
I recovered my silver helmet, running sidewise at Furius, who
was pressing the red-haired boy Neoptolemos son of implacable Akhilleys; and him, too, we hustled from the summit
of the wall. But the stripling laughed; and he fought beside
me, fighting as I did, shoving with very weighty shields, till
we had cleared a little space: for the assault was keen.

But Pallas Athene of the terrible Aigis came whirling along
the open way in her war-chariot, shouting aloud and frightfully in the Orthian strain. And scores of the blameless Latins
she squashed to pulp, or hurled from the height. But then,
indeed, when one might have begun to think about victory,
suddenly I heard the voice of Queen Helen calling me by
name. To whom I revolved like a flash of white thunder.

But the divine one of goddesses was flying toward me in
the pleasure-chariot of white-armed Hera the queen, woven
of golden thongs plaited tightly, with pole and wheels and
yoke and harness of gold. And peacocks drew it, flying on
large wings colored of cinnamon and ebony, with quivering
crests and necks of shining blue, and waving golden prides
which gleamed each with a hundred purple eyes. She cried to
me as she came: for a faithful wife (being troubled) thinks
that no one but her dear husband can relieve her. And she
said that constant Regulus, and Scipio the African, and Gajus
Martius of Corioli, were attacking on the north, having scaled
the wall: whom Queen Hera and the goddesses were with-
standing, as best they might, with golden tiles and paving-
stones and jars and bowls and stairs, hurled from the blooming towers.

And I heard the saying of Queen Helen, with those who
fought near me; and, instantly, we ran roaring to repel the
invaders. And yellow-haired Akhilleys the bravest of heroes
ran with me, and red-haired Neoptolemos his son, and
Idomeneys strong as flame, and Diomedes of the loud war-
cry, and magnanimous Iason, and glancing-eyed Diokles, and

golden-haired Meleagros, and my own cousin Perseys of the sea (the most renowned of heroes), nine in all. But we, ravening with fury, fell upon the Latins; and I myself engaged Titus son of Tarquinius, a gallant enough hero, who (after some striving) took a toss from me into the sea, the abode of fishes, where eels might eat him, nibbling the white fat round his kidneys. But only implacable Akhilleys remained alive beside me, having his breath upon the height of Olympos, with glancing-eyed Diokles who became my sweet friend, and also Perseys the immortal hero. And all the might of the Latins was surging round to the north wall; and Titus Manlius of the golden collar was leading them. But we three fought grimly on.

Then leaped-up in her might Strife the rouser of hosts. Then Pallas Athene sent forth a cry. And Ares shouted, terrible as the blackness of storms. Then came Artemis of the silver arrows and the echoing chase, and Phoibos Apollon darting afar. Then the Father and King of gods and men came lamping and toning terrifically from above. Then came Hermes the Helper.

And shady Hades, lord of the netherworld, leaped from his black throne, bursting his bandages, in terror lest the earth should again be riven by King Poseidon irascibly rolling great billows about: so loud was the din made by us immortals. And, at King Zeys' behest, King Hades gave up a new host of heroes to Hermes the Helper, Lysander and Leonidas those dirty-knuckled Lakonians, and Alkibiades and Nikias the Athenians, and Macedonian Alexandros, and lacerated Prometheys, and thirsty Tantalos, and wise Telemakhos my son and prudent Penelope's, and unknowing Telegonos my son and Kirke's of the awful braided tresses, and Teykros the bowman, and belted Orion, and gigantic Tityros, and even the blameless Dardanian heroes of Ilion to fight for the gods of lofty Olympos, to wit, Hektor of the glancing helm, and pious runaway Aineias, and Amphios of the linen corslet, and Asios prince of men, and Hippothoos skilled with the spear, and well-legged Phorkys, and uncouth Nastes, and Sarpedon counselor of the Lykians, and noble Glaykos, and naked Lykaon, and equal-handed Asteropaios, and Polydoros the rumbler, all the most righteous of heroes, thirsty for bloodshed and buzzing like shameless mosquitoes.

And now the heavens were filled with gods and heroes, and ablaze with arms; and the earth below rang with the noise of the feet of them, as they rushed together for the fray. For we, the Olympians, lilac ravening lions, were leaping out, fulfilling the will of loud-thundering Zeys ordaining a backward chase of the Latins. They, indeed, of necessity were compelled to give way; and many fair brands, dark-scabbarded and dark-hilted, fell to the earth, some from the hands and some with the severed hands of warriors, so that the black earth was splashed with a hail of the juices of heroes.

But, scattering, the Latins broke, and fled in confusion, driven in utter rout; and hero called after hero to engage in single combat, slaying each his own. And, wherever the king of gods and men saw them thickest in flight, thither did he guide his blooming chariot with resounding cries; and, under his axle trees, the Latins fell prone and were ground up, till not one remained in life: but they were pushed into the land of the shades.

And, even as tempests oppress the black earth in autumn, when Zeys pours forth rain most vehemently, being wrath against men who judge crooked judgments forcibly and drive justice out: so, mightily, then, we followed the blameless gods of the Romans; and they fled as men flee before lions and bloody unicorns. For Panic and Terror and terrible Fear bounded behind them yelling hideously: so that they fled, over the mountains of Macedonia, and woody Epiros, and the Ionian Sea, and also over Apulia, never staying, till (at length) they cowered above the Capitol of Rome, expecting the doom of the vanquished.

In this manner, was there war in the wide-rolling heavens.

The Thirty-First
Papyrus

*B*UT King Zeys called together the areiopagos of the immortals.

And, when the twelve great gods were standing round, in their well-carved lofty war-chariots, the Latin gods crouched, miserable, whimpering, chained, in the midst before them. And it was openly manifest that they, presumptuous ones, overweening in arrogance, had the audacity to shape themselves (as far as they were able) after the manner of the divine ones who inhabit olympian palaces: as the barbarians, Egyptians, or Sikels, or Thrakians, or Bithynians, whom the Argives take for slaves, mimic the manners of their masters, clumsily counterfeiting their aspect. Yet, as the Argives are mortal and so are the barbarians, being alike in that respect but not in anything else, in the same way both the Olympian and the Latin gods were immortal, agreeing in no other similitude. But all the company of heaven marveled exceedingly, and none knew the counsels of King Zeys.

But the Father and King of gods and men, whose joy is in the thunder, spoke, saying: "Hearken to me, O all gods and all ye blooming goddesses, hearing that which my mind within my breast commandeth me. And one thing let none assay, be it goddess or be it god, to thwart my opinion: but approve it, ye, unanimously, that I may quickly accomplish it. For ye know how far I am made the mightiest of all gods. Go to, now, ye gods, make trial that ye may know. Fasten ye a golden rope from heaven; and all ye gods lay hold thereof and all goddesses: yet could ye not drag me from heaven to earth, even Zeys, the counselor of The Supreme, not though ye toiled sorely. But, an I were minded to drag it, then I should draw you up, with the blooming earth and the sea withal: by so much more am I beyond gods, and beyond men, and all the rest of it."

Thus he spoke: but we all kept silence and were still, marveling at his saying, for he spoke very masterfully. But, at last, the bright-eyed goddess Pallas Athene said: "O our father Zeys, well we know (even we) that thy might is unyielding. Yet we have piety for these thy prisoners, fools, who now shall perish and fulfill an evil fate."

Then Zeys the Cloud-gatherer smiled at her, saying: "Be of good comfort, dear child: for I am not minded to be unkindly. But, hearken, O all gods and all ye goddesses; and see the justice of Zeys. For these cringing immortals (from what part of the heavens they come, I know not), having taken shapes similar to ours on some false pretenses, audacious ones, have not been content with the worship of their Romans, but, bursting with arrogance, they have presumed to claim also the worship of the rolling-eyed Argives. Long, indeed, have I been patient with them, with fair words and deeds: but they have ventured to bring war to lofty Olympos. Witless that they are, to be wrath in their folly against Zeys, who (sitting all by himself) careth not, nor taketh any thought about them: for I deem that I, among immortal gods, am manifestly pre-eminent in power and might etcetera. Wherefore, let them content themselves with whatsoever sorrows I shall send on each one of them."

But fierce impetuous Ares stood high in his war-chariot, whereto were yoked his horses Fear and Dread; and he slapped his strong thighs with his hands flatwise, saying: "O lord of the lightning and the dark cloud, smite them with the thunderbolts; and let them lie among the dead in dust and blood."

But, when they heard this awful word, the Latin gods leaped up to touch the beard and the knees of Zeys, crying aloud in a panic-terror as they bobbed up and down, saying: "We supplicate thee by thy beard, and by thy knees, and by thy parents, to take good store of gold and korinthic bronze (which is platinum and better than gold) as a ransom, and to let us go in peace."

But, unto them, the Father and King of gods and men, with grimmer gaze, responded, saying: "Dogs, dogs, supplicate me not by beard or knees or parents: for neither a tenfold nor a twentyfold ransom can make amends for rebellion. Nevertheless, seeing that ye be immortal, even as are also we others, white Death may not come anigh you. But let us hear much-contriving Odysseys, the Peer of Zeys in counsel: for perchance he hath some apt unwinged sentence of judgment in his wily mind."

Then, indeed, I stood up before all the blooming company of heaven, in my silver-shining chariot inlaid with crabs and moons in mother-of-pearl, but Love was my charioteer; and thus I said: "Immortality to immortals, and nothings to nothingness."

And all the gods and goddesses (bestowers of good things) stood in their own war-chariots; and inextinguishable laughter arose among the blessed gods, when they heard my wily words.

But great Zeys said: "It pleaseth us; and, so, of our own free will, we command that it shall be done."

And, immediately, all the gods and goddesses of Olympos leaped upon all the blameless gods and goddesses of Rome, Zeys upon Juppiter, and Hera upon Juno, Helios Hyperion upon Sol, and Selene upon Luna, Phoibos Apollon upon Apollo, and Artemis upon Diana, Ares upon Mars, and Iakkhos Dionysos upon Bacchus, Eros upon Cupid, and Aphrodite upon Venus, Hermes upon Mercury, and Pallas Athene upon Minerva, Demeter upon Ceres, and Hephaistos upon Vulcan, Hades upon Pluto, and Persephone upon Proserpina, Kastor and Polydeykes upon Castor and Pollux, Herakles upon Hercules, and Poseidon upon Neptune, and innumerable others upon others innumerable, pouncing upon them, like falcons biting the bloody brains of baser birds, buzzards, and such, sucking out their immortality.

And the forms of the Latin gods, like flies in the webs of assiduous spiders, lifeless, and very void, fell back, dropping from heaven to earth; and the speed of their falling ground them to powder, so that they became as red dust, and a most awful portent for their Romans on whom they fell. For, by chance, at this same time, the Romans were perturbed by a political crisis, connected with that Gajus Julius Caesar, a king of men and a shepherd of the people. For, when they saw fierce fiery warriors fighting on the clouds, in ranks and squadrons and right forms of war, which drizzled blood of heroes on the Capitol, and, when they heard the neighing of horses and the groans of ghosts of heroes, slain, shrieking, squealing, going to the land of shades, then, indeed, blind madness entered into them; and they slew their precious Caesar. Thus, the heavens themselves blaze forth the death of princes.$FThis I take for a somewhat Shakespearian reminiscence (or prevision) on the part of Mr. C. *Cf. Julius Cæsar,* Act II., Scene ii. – A.H.

But the immortal gods, more amply immortal than ever (if that were possible), returned to their dear motherland bearing the spoils of victory; and the divine ones inhabiting olympian palaces began to receive the worship of the Romans, as was due.

In this manner, was there peace in the wide-rolling heavens.

The Thirty-Second Papyrus

*B*UT King Zeys lavished rich rewards, dividing the Roman territories among gods and heroes, giving temples to some and altars to others, to say nothing of blank walls eligible for immortal effigies. But, because I was by no means anxious to have assigned to me the worship of mortal men (for, having been myself a man more than once, I know something about the value of men's worship; and I care as little for suitors who adulate as for enemies who feel bound to propitiate), then, the Father and King of gods and men deigned to give me a wish, confirming the same with his nod, which is the surest pledge among the immortals. And I said that I would treasure this wish in my heart, so that I might use it on occasion: for I desired, at that moment, nothing more than to live in peace and love with Golden Helen. And that, I did.

Living in peace and love, thus, we entertained ourselves with hunting bears, dragons, and urchins,* on the long slopes of lofty Olympos, or with delicate banquets in the halls of various gods. I, also, went frequently to and fro among mortal men, generally invisibly, amusing myself with their affairs. Also, I was wont to disport myself in my well-benched galley, a wonder to be seen, being drawn by Love over the grey-green sea at my will. For Hermes my grandsire, and bravely steadfast

---

* I do hope and trust, and (in fact) I believe, that he means "hedgehogs": though I confess that I myself never derived much real sport from the chase of those beasts. Perhaps "porpentines" would be a more exact rendering. — A.H.

Herakles, and my own cousin Perseys of the sea (the most renowned of heroes), used to accompany me in my jaunts; and, when these immortals saw my faithful slaves Neandros and Thalos, being cognizant of their fidelity and their fearlessness, and, also, having observed the ingenious mind and the stalwart form of Neandros and the luminous innocence of Thalos, then, indeed, they shewed them signal favors, putting into their minds a knowledge of many secrets which the gods and heroes find useful at times. Nor were the slaves afraid to have to do with these divine ones, having already braved the terrors of the netherworld with me, than which there is nothing more terrible, excepting a really horrid woman. But, because I (by magic art) had bound their lives to mine, and, because Great Zeys, in reward of my endurance and my wiles, had endued me with immortality, so Neandros and Thalos, being immortal as well (though they were neither gods nor heroes, but only the most comely and most faithful and most clever of slaves), became habituated to mingle themselves as conveniently with immortals as with mortals. Which is a wonderful and blessed thing.

But, after a few moons, when I from time to time returned to lofty Olympos, it seemed to me that Queen Helen was less cheerful than heretofore. And, when, one day, I found her sitting alone in her close chamber, weaving a white and silver shirt for me to wear at banquets, and the lids of her amber eyes were reddened as though with weeping, then, indeed, I required her to declare to her dear husband the cause of her grief. But she laid her head on my breast, letting fall a round tear: nor did she hide aught from me.

For, the long-smoldering jealousy of blameless Queen Aphrodite (the lady of the dog-star) had been breaking forth; and she was quite unable to remember good manners in the presence of Queen Helen. But it was plain to us all, that, as Queen Helen was far lovelier than she, Queen Aphrodite was no longer the goddess of beauty, though she still was the goddess of certain kinds of love. Yet, even on the last count, she complained, being shockingly jealous and upset. For she was aggrieved because ruddy young Love gave her little of his blooming company, having bound himself (with a silver chain) in service to me and to Queen Helen, flying here and

there through air and sky for our exclusive diversion, neglect-
ing her (his mamma) and other divine ones inhabiting olympian palaces. Which, indeed, was not altogether untrue:
though hitherto we had not given the matter a thought.

Furthermore, white-armed Queen Hera (the most righteous of goddesses), had been speaking unpleasant words. For
that prim matron, being jealous also, because King Zeys the
Swan had procreated Golden Helen and her Great Twin
Brothers out of matrimony, was wont to sneeze more or less
covertly, giggling, flinging the names of victorious Theseys
and sandy-haired impotent old Menelaos and woman-mad
Paris at my stainless wife, designing to shame her and to
deprive her mind of ease.

And all this was a very dreadful thing for a chaste and
loving wife to bear. For, though bright-eyed Pallas Athene,
and silvan Artemis (that wise athletic maiden), and fruitful
Demeter and powerful Persephone (those noble matrons),
and fair-ankled Hebe, and Iris of the rainbow, and all the
other lady goddesses, being well-bred as well as well-born,
behaved themselves to Queen Helen as to an equal, peerless
in beauty and admirable for her faithful love, nevertheless,
the unconcealed jealousy of the two flawed the fair apricock
of her perfect joy. And, moreover, it must not be denied that
the plague of Queen Aphrodite and the spleen of Queen Hera
(both quite blameless) was, or would be, a cause of wrath, and
secret stirring up of strife, and wordy bickering, and malice,
and hinted lies, and curious reservations, and careful slight-
ings, which would set all heaven by its blooming ears. And
that is what no honest goddess can endure with a calm and
holy mind.

Now, because of my unalloyed happiness, and because of
my light-hearted absences, I had been ignorant of all these
matters. But, when I understood them, having reproached
myself sufficiently on account of my selfishness, then, indeed,
divine Fury inflamed the mind in my noble breast with desire
of bloody head-cuttings and eye-diggings and revenges and
slaughters and maimings and stonings and spine-impalings.
But, first, I consoled Queen Helen properly.

Then I began to bethink me of most shocking things, to
wit, of certain cunning wiles whereby those two blameless

goddesses might be made laughingstocks, ridiculous among the divine ones who have never lost their faces. For I remembered that this would not be very difficult, for, once upon a time, Great Zeys himself had occasion to dangle white-armed Hera (the most righteous of goddesses) between heaven and earth for several months, having fastened anvils to her fat ankles, because she was excessively offensive. And even Hephaistos of the strong arm once caught blameless Aphrodite, his wife, diverting herself gaily with Ares; and he cast a magic web about them so that all the gods and goddesses might go and gibe at them at pleasure. And, indeed, it would not be difficult for anyone to make Queen Aphrodite look absurd: as most of the gods and heroes, and very many articulately-speaking men, well know.

But Queen Helen was averse from all unkindness, and, as aforetime, when persecuted, she begged me to take her away from the netherworld, and from Khalkis, and likewise from Rome, so now, indeed, she implored me to take her away from the height of Olympos, going (she said) peacefully, to seek some distant little kingdom on the wide-bosomed earth, where we (divine ones and immortal), having ourselves endured unmentioned and unthought-of pains, and possessing the secret wisdom of the gods, might live in peace and love with ourselves, doing good and kindly deeds among mortal men.

Now it happened, by chance, that (in my wanderings to and fro) I had never been altogether unmindful of the prediction of Belmarduk the god of Assyria, which he made to me when I dreamed in my barge in Egypt. And, once, when I was flying in my Love-drawn chariot, over the Aigaian Sea, and over Asia and Galatia and Kappadokia and Armenia, I espied the fair little realm of Moxoene, where mountains and pine and oak forests were set round and about the salt Thospitian Sea; and the folk of the place were singularly comely, and intelligent and brave, having also ingenious and reverend minds: but they seemed to be as sheep without a shepherd.

Wherefore, I determined that the time had come for obeying the decrees of The Supreme, fulfilling the prediction of Belmarduk the god, and the sixth prediction which Thalos my innocent slave read in the palm-mirror. Moreover, I remembered the wish which Great Zeys had confirmed to me.

For which causes, then, I gave a great and splendid banquet to the immortals; and, when we taken away the desire of eating and drinking (for I provided very exquisite odors of unmentioned and unthought-of fragrance), then, I stood up on my throne before them all; and my lordly spirit thus addressed Great Zeys, saying: "O Father and King of gods and men, let it not be imputed to me for an evil word when I ask that the drink-offering may be poured, and that I may go upon my way. For I am a little tired. For it seems that there is jealousy among the immortal goddesses because of the superior beauty of Golden Helen, to whom white-armed Hera and Aphrodite (lady of the dog-star) have spoken unwinged words. And they also complain because tameless Eros, the oldest and youngest of all gods, bath willingly tamed himself so far and for this occasion only to go before me and before Queen Helen in the way. For which cause, then, this is my wish, which thou already hast confirmed to me by thine irrevocable nod. I wish to go away at once, and in peace, from this blooming peak of Olympos, with Queen Helen my unsullied wife, and with my gear, that we may live once more among earth-trampling men, among whom we shall not be the least, seeing that we are immortal and have the secret wisdom of the gods. And I have found the kingdom of Moxoene by the Thospitian Sea, where I wish to dwell. Nosh then, send me on my way, giving me good fortune that I may take my noble wife to the beautiful home which I shall make for her. But ye, blessed gods, be pleased to abide here, all of you, making glad your own blooming wives and children, and enjoying all sorts of delicious delights."

Thus I spoke. And my heart and lordly mind were exultant in my breast. For immense confusion and hubbub arose among the immortal gods; and the two jealous queens (the most righteous of goddesses), thoroughly exasperated by the wily and audacious mildness of my contemptuous words, bridled and sniffed, tossing their heads and beating their fat knees, glancing this way and that, madly, and saying that so many rash things had never been said before for them to sit there and hear.

But wing-footed Hermes, my grandsire, said: "Let him go where he will, this much-enduring much-contriving Odysseys who is surely Peer of Zeys in counsel, and Queen Helen who is indubitably the loveliest of mortals or immortals: for my rede is that my child deserves to be satisfied. But I myself will never be very far away from him in Moxoene; and, when ye gods by chance shall want a messenger, take blooming Iris of the rainbow."

But bravely-steadfast Herakles said: "Let him go where he will, this hero Odysseys, and Queen Helen the most faithful of wives: for they ought to have some happiness after so much ill. But I myself will be at their call, whenever they ask for a champion."

But in like manner also spoke my own cousin Perseys of the sea, the most renowned of heroes. And all the important gods and goddesses signified approval in the customary manner.

But Eros leaped up, blindfolded, naked, like a young and ruddy flame; and he said: "Oh, let them go where they will. But thou, O Great Zeys, whom I not seldom have wounded, be ware that I will not desert such true lovers as these. And, if thou keepest me here, thou wilt keep no more of me than my body. But I will make me a nest in their hearts forever and ever. For I know where I am a welcome guest, and where I am unwelcome, and where I am treated simply as a blooming pastime with childish play, and where with due worship and honor."

Then, the Father and King of gods and men drew down his immortal eyebrows: for the matter was an extremely grave one; and he gave judgment, saying: "Let us by any means secure a quiet life. And, forasmuch as King Odysseys desireth to leave us peaceably, retiring to an earthly kingdom with his dear wife and his proper paraphernalia, let him go to Moxoene thus. And let them have all health and comfort in their going. It pleaseth us; and, so, of our own free will, we command that it shall be done."

Therefore, when Morning donned her saffron robes, and ascended from bathing in the streams of ocean, to give light to immortals and mortals, then, all the divine ones (save the two blameless queens), having loaded my chariot with sweet gifts, came gateward to speed us on our way. But Aphrodite the lady of the dog-star (the most righteous of goddesses) pettishly called for her son, holding him between her knees for once, and caressing his ruddy young neck, with malicious intent to prevent him from going with us.

But then, indeed, a marvelous portent was manifested.

For my gigantic silver-shining chariot, inlaid with crabs and moons in mother-of-pearl, stood in the gateway of lofty Olympos loaded with my gear. And, poised on the front of its rail, was the silver image of Love, larger than life, blind-folded, naked, most alluringly proportioned, with his well-winged arms spread abroad in the very act of taking flight; and his reins were girded with the silver chain, of which the taslets dangled behind down to the rail of the chariot. But, when Queen Helen saw that invidious hag detaining our charioteer out of jealousy, then, she looked at me sadly, letting fall a round tear, not knowing how we should go. To whom I spoke unwinged words, saying very firmly: "Mount, my child, nor be affrighted with any amazement whatever: for dreadful among mortals and immortals is the wrath of a suppliant. And we, indeed, are the suppliants of Love."

Thus I spoke: but we two mounted in turn; and Queen Helen pulled the chain, having confidence in the promise of the god. And, as she worked the magic enchantment, both our hearts glowed with undying fire. And we saw young and ruddy Eros, clasped between his wretched mother's knees, become suddenly white and rigid: but he himself came; and the silver image of Love lived, and was Love, bursting into ardent life, and flying away with us, leaving no more than the wraith of Love with Aphrodite (most righteous of goddesses) howling on lofty Olympos.

Thus, then, I left the abodes of the immortals, coming to rule my kingdom of Moxoene on the grain-giving earth.

The Thirty-Third Papyrus

*N*OW the deeds which I have done and the wiles which I have wrought, in my kingdom of Moxoene, are on this wise. And, seeing that they are both great and numerous, I will have them fairly written out by the hand of Empedokles son of Polypemon, my scribe, on one-and-twenty new rolls of fine papyrus, and sealed with my kingly sigil.

On the first roll, it shall be written of my coming with Queen Helen to Moxoene, flying out of the open heaven in my silver-shining chariot, having a glorious sheen like the moon. And, when, the people saw us, they received us with gladness and piety and exquisite sacrifices: for, though we scintillated with truly godly splendor, and appeared to be of very much more than mortal stature, yet we were benign of aspect and not terrible; and the tribes (also) of the country are not slavish or timid by nature, but brave and strong, and of an upright ingenious mind.

On the second roll, it shall be written of the stablishing of my kingdom. For, when the news of my coming went abroad, then, the chiefs of the fifteen tribes between the Great River* and River Araxes and Media Atropatene with Assyria and Mesopotamia came, of their own free will, to pay homage to me, swearing faithful allegiance. And these were the fifteen princes of the fifteen tribes of Akilisene and Derxene and Phasianene and Bagravandene and Dasranalene and Khorzianene and Balabitene and Astianene and Anzitene and

---

* Euphrates, of course. — A.H.

Sophene and Arzanene and Gordavanene and Arapakitene and Thositene and Moxoene.

On the third roll, it shall be written of the constitution of my kingdom as a limited theocracy: for I, the king, and Helen, the queen, accept the obedience and the worship of the nation, as god and goddess of Moxoene, for the present and in the absence of anything better. Here, also, it shall be written of the manner of the said obedience and worship: of the language of Moxoene: of my kingly name Balthazar, and the signification of the same.

On the fourth roll, it shall be written of the *Sacred Lavation and of The Spell of The Three Who are One,* a most efficacious mighty magic enchantment, which, in the very beginning, I wrought upon the persons of all and singular my subjects, in my Thospitian Sea, will-he nill-he: with the names and histories of the two of evil mind who repudiated it, whom a flying dragon ate that same afternoon.*

On the fifth roll, it shall be written of the mysteries, which I study and cause to be studied by the few who are worthy; and of the altar, of sunstone and moonstone, to Mithra, Unconquered Father of Fathers, which I set up in my palace for myself and my own, whereat I myself minister as mysteriarch among my sons.

On the sixth roll, it shall be written of the fair children borne to me by Queen Helen, my beloved wife and true: to wit, my darling Diyllos (superb and glancing-eyed like my friend Diokles) born under the Moon and the Crab, and my very dear son Nikolaos born under Hermes and The Virgin, and my twin-son Haliastos and my twin-daughter Halianthe born under Oyranos and The Waterman; and of the *Sacred Lavation* and *The Spell of The Three Who are One,* which I

---

* The word here is "pterodactyl." The largest known specimen of this abominable winged lizard measures about six meters from wing-tip to wing-tip. Its frightful crocodilish jaws seem to indicate a very voracious appetite. But I was unaware that the species persisted till so late a date. Perhaps I ought to add that the "pteranodon" was about the same size: but the wing-dimension of the "rhamphorhynkhos" was only a little over two meters. Both, however, seem to have been extremely nasty creatures. – A.H.

wrought upon them all at birth.

On the seventh roll, it shall be written of Queen Helen, my meet help and my heart's constant joy: of all the deeds which she (the divine one of goddesses) has done for the women and children of my kingdom, teaching them the arts of love, obedience, service, housewifery, comforting them in sorrow. Here, also, shall be written of my sweet daughter Silver Halianthe, my sea-flower, who (having been born in my galley on my Thospitian Sea, and having been bred by Queen Helen) has become her golden mother's second self.

On the eighth roll, it shall be written of my friend glancing-eyed Diokles, and of my own cousin Perseys of the sea (the most renowned of heroes), who came to my kingdom while my sons were young, to teach them all those things which the sons of heroes and of kings must know, and to shew them what the sons of heroes and of kings must be.

On the ninth roll, it shall be written of Hermes the Helper and of Eros the Great Enchanter, and of my two faithful slaves Neandros and Thalos. Here, shall be written of the mighty magic which Eros taught to ingenious Neandros my slave, and to my dear son Haliastos desiring it, so that they found out wells of fragrant oil wherein pitch beautifully floats, and also wells of limpid water, for the magic instruments which they make, wherewith they cut the air into compact blocks, storing the same in the secret parts of chariots (which, also, they make), so that the said chariots, fish-shaped, run on the earth, or fly in the air, or swim in and on the sea, more swiftly than a bird or a thought, having no sails nor oars nor even horses to draw them. And with these I win great victories over hairy barbarians, even over the Parthians with their blooming elephants. And here, also, shall be written of the wisdom unspeakable which Hermes taught to ingenious Thalos my slave, and to my strange and very dear son Nikolaos desiring it: so that I placed them over my royal college of mages seeking wisdom, which I stablished on the peak above my Thospitian Sea.

On the tenth roll, it shall be written of the death of my darling son Diyllos, in my war with the Kilikian pirates, in the moment of victory with his circle of dead about him as high as the well-folded tablets of his breast. Herakles lighted

his funeral-pyre, heaped with his chariots, his arms, his tro-
phies, and a few of his toys. I could not burn my own work,
the most beautiful body of my son. I preserve it, using the
best of all my magic art, so that it will be sweet and fresh for
me forever and ever. Here, also, shall be written of the fair
and kingly crypt, where I have hidden that vesture of my
darling son, with my private treasures; and of my daily visit
to look upon him.

On the eleventh roll, it shall be written of the embassador
who came from Caesar Augustus, demanding my submission,
requiring me to send my sons, with the sons of neighboring
kings, as hostages, to Rome. Here, also, shall be written of
the manner of my dealing with the said embassador, at high
noon, on a terrace of my palace builded of white jade and
alabaster and eye-chalcedonyx and silver, on the shore of my
Thospitian Sea: to whom I casually appeared, of immortal
stature, blazing like the serene and vivid moon, arrayed in
ermine and silver tissue sown all over with rose-crystals and
blue moonstones, flying through the air across the sea in my
silver-shining chariot inlaid with crabs and moons in mother-
of-pearl, having with me (in the chariot) Queen Helen, daughter of Zeys the Swan, robed in gold and amethyst tissue, with
her gold hair floating like a web of woven sunbeams, and
with immortal Hermes the Luck-bringer, wing-footed, golden-wanded, flying (as usual) above my head, and with immortal Love, my charioteer. Here, also, shall be written of the
splendid ceremonies which I caused to be observed at the
interment of the Roman embassador, after his intempestive
demise.

On the twelfth roll, it shall be written of the names of all
the mages of all kingdoms on the wide-bosomed earth, whom
I have brought into my kingdom, where they teach their
wisdom to me and to my mages, and learn ours, serving me
in both ways. Here also shall be written of the histories of
those mages, and of the magics which they have used as
masters.

On the thirteenth roll, it shall he written (in the hand of
Empedokles son of Polypemon, and in his own words) of
who he was and whence he came: but he shall write also (in
my words) of the reason why I brought him into my kingdom,

and of what he has done there.

On the fourteenth roll, it shall be written of the book of magic enchantments which I (of my wisdom) compiled for my royal college of mages seeking wisdom: of the parts of the said book, and also the secret* . . .

---

* Most unfortunately this Thirty-third Papyrus ends abruptly here. — A.H.

The Thirty-Fourth Papyrus

*N*OW I, Queen Helen, daughter of Zeys, an immortal, say these words to be written fairly by Empedokles son of Polypemon, scribe of my beloved lord and true husband King Balthazar of Moxoene, whom the immortals and the Argives call King Odysseys, but he calls himself Nikolaos the Crab, viceroy of Victory queen of the stalwart stately Anglicans.

And these are the words which I shall say for the scribe to write.

*Y*esterday, at dawn, our strange and very dear son Nikolaos Diadokhos came with the faithful Thalos from our royal college of mages.

They said to the king that they had seen a great new Star, suddenly shining in the southwestern heaven, far brighter than any other star ever seen, and moving southwestward.

My lord and husband the king, having straitly examined them, became filled with fear and gladness strangely commingled. I never have seen him thus.

My lord and husband the king enacted an act of regency, naming me, Queen Helen, as Regent of his kingdom of Moxoene.

My lord and husband the king arrayed himself in his silver-shining panoply, and he caused our strange and very dear son Nikolaos Diadokhos and the faithful Thalos to put on their garments of glory.

My lord and husband the king summoned his silver-shining chariot; and he caused our strange and very dear son Nikolaos Diadokhos and the faithful Thalos to mount to their places.

My lord and husband the king, with his own hands, took out of our treasury that casket of rock-crystal, three spans long and two spans deep and one span broad, which, during his leisure of these many years, he has carved with crabs and moons and inlaid with blue-moonstones, binding it with hasps and hinges and bands of silver, all with his own hands; and he filled it full with our royal quintessence of gum-olibanon, which he has sublimed, also with his own hands during his leisure of these many years.

My lord and husband the king kissed me in a manner which he never has used before, bidding me to be of good heart and ready to receive tidings of great joy.

Having done all these strange things, my lord and husband the king ascended his silver-shining chariot, with the two mages aforesaid, taking with him the rock-crystal casket of frankincense aforesaid; and, so, he very swiftly departed southwestward, at sunset, following the Star.

Now I, Queen Helen, daughter of Zeys, an immortal, having already endured manly evils, and being now perturbed in my mind, have caused these words to be written, that I may place them in a most secret holy crypt. And I will place them with that which is most dear, which is there, and with the secret silver urns which contain toys, and with the secret silver chest which contains writings, because these are the chief treasures of my lord the king.

And, when I have done this, I will see the secret holy crypt closed by Empedokles son of Polypemon and by the faithful Neandros. And I will seal the door with the royal sigil. And I will see the very door itself hidden by the faithful Neandros.

And I will do all these things, that my lord and husband the king may find his secrets safe, when he shall return to me. For I know not when he shall return to me.

EXPLICITUR

www.ingramcontent.com/pod-product-compliance
Lightning Source LLC
Chambersburg PA
CBHW022013010726
47494CB00003B/1017